Praise for Mab
Featuring Nancy C

"America's two greatest girl detective __ _____ _____ _____ __ ___ _____ __
pop culture be more irreverent?"

—NEW YORK NEWSDAY

"Maney, who evidently grew up bent in a straighter-than-thou environment, has
had a field day with our conventions. Wittily, subversively, she has exposed the
underbelly of America: it's softly rounded, and warm."

—TORONTO GLOBE AND MAIL

"In a gem of a book-length parody, the author faithfully hews to the narrative and
plotting style of juvenile series fiction, her remarkably straight face making the
goings on all the funnier. I loved this book..."

—ELLERY QUEEN MYSTERY MAGAZINE

"You'll laugh until your dress gets mussed...Maney knows '50s America like she
majored in Ozzie and Harriet."

—LAMBDA BOOK REPORT

"The sequel to THE CASE OF THE NOT-SO-NICE NURSE is another hoot, a lampooning of
girls' fiction of the past full of hapless, do-gooding detectives with 'keen
sleuthing abilities, up-to-the-minute fashion sense, and gracious finishing-
school manners.' With a honey like Cherry, who is always careful to keep an
ample supply of freshly starched, white linen handkerchiefs in her seasonally
appropriate handbag, we know Nancy can't miss."

—BOOKLIST

"Utter kitsch, done with class and distinction. Maney tools the pages like an
expert, in the process bringing up a lot of dialogue about the role of lesbianism in
the gay '90s, albeit subtly."

—YOUR FLESH MAGAZINE

A Ghost in the Closet

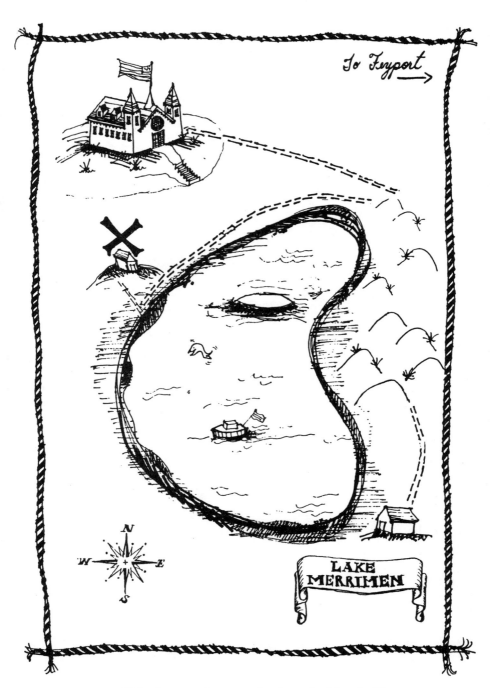

"It's the secret map we've been looking for!"

A Ghost in the Closet

A Hardly Boys Mystery

Second Edition

Mabel Maney

Published in the United States by Cleis Press Inc., P.O. Box 14684, San Francisco,

California 94114.

Printed in the United States.

Cover design: Scott Idleman / Blink

Logo art: Juana Alicia

Second Edition.

10 9 8 7 6 5 4 3 2 1

LIBRARY OF CONGRESS CATALOGING-IN-PUBLICATION DATA

Maney, Mabel, 1958–
        A ghost in the closet : a Hardly Boys mystery / by Mabel Maney
             p.   cm.
ISBN 1-57344-095-7 (paper) : $14.95
                1. Women detectives—United States—Fiction. 2. Youth—United States—
Fiction. 3. Gays—United States—Fiction.
I. Title
PS3563.A466C36
813'.54—dc20   94-29820
                                                            CIP

Contents

Dedicated to the memory of Billy Tipton
"He sang in a high voice."

and to Herbert S. Zim,
whose delightful and informative books
have provided many hours of pleasant reading

As always
for Miss Lily Bee
and
for Miss Coco,
who will be sadly missed

Special thanks to Leasa Burton
for her keen editing skills
and
buckets of gratitude
to my sweet boy chums
for their generosity, grace and wit
Tom Metz
Donald Smith
Chuck Stallard

Prologue

"I can hardly wait to get home and show Father all the exciting new French detective techniques we learned while on our vacation!" Joe Hardly said eagerly. The dark-haired, muscular lad, one half of the crime-fighting team known far and wide as the Hardly boys, leaned against the rail of the majestic Queen Mary and gazed at the wide expanse of blue water all around them. In two days, they would arrive in New York Harbor, catch a speedy train to their beloved hometown of Feyport, Illinois, and be reunited with their parents, world-famous detective Fennel P. Hardly and his wife, Mrs. Hardly. Although Joe had had a swell time on their six-week jaunt through Europe, the tousled-haired lad was eager to get back home and resume his exciting life as a famous boy detective.

"Are you as anxious as I am to get back to work?" Joe asked his older brother Frank as he took a stick of cherry gum from the pocket of his baby blue cardigan-style overshirt in washable rayon and popped it in his mouth.

"I'm fit and rested and ready to go," Frank replied with a smile as he ran a hand through his thick, close-cropped blond hair, then slipped a cable-knit tennis sweater over his head. His cruise-wear outfit of white cotton sunburst-print clamdigger trousers and matching top was just the ticket for a sun-drenched day aboard ship, but now that the sun was setting, the boy detective was getting mighty chilled!

"Oh, I do hope Father's got a good mystery brewing for us. After all that sightseeing, I sure am anxious for some real action!" Frank said wistfully.

"Father's probably embroiled in a new case this very minute," Joe cried. "Why, I bet as soon as we get home, we'll be pulled into an exciting adventure!"

CHAPTER 1

"Stop, Thief!"

"I'm sorry, son, you'll have to let me examine the contents of your pockets before I can let you in the auditorium," a man in a trim blue uniform ordered as he kept his eyes on the crowd and grabbed hold of Midge Fontaine's arm, preventing her from entering the Lake Merrimen Auditorium, a civic center in the heart of the bustling resort town that had been host to many an exciting event, from square dances to pie contests, but none so thrilling as the annual Dog Show.

Midge squirmed out of the man's grasp and resolutely crossed her arms over her strong chest. "No one goes through my pockets," she cried angrily, thinking to herself, "except for my girlfriend Velma!"

"If I don't search you, you can't go inside," the officer shot back as he studied Midge's trouser pockets suspiciously.

Girl detective Nancy Clue pushed past her chum. "Officer, what's the problem?" she asked politely.

"Well, if it isn't Miss Nancy Clue!" the man exclaimed as he recognized the famous girl sleuth known far and wide for her keen detective work and fashionable outfits. Today, Nancy was attired in a darling blue and white checkered raincoat and matching hat, and had navy blue rubber boots on her petite feet.

"Here on a case, eh, Miss Clue?" the man smiled knowingly.

"That's right, officer," Nancy played along. If truth be told, she and her chums, the newly-wed Midge Fontaine and Velma Pierce, and her own date, Cherry Aimless, Registered Nurse, were there for a frolicsome day amid canine competition and not hot on the trail of a new mystery.

"We're going to miss the beginning of the Obedience Trials," Midge groaned as she peeked inside and saw that, although it was still early on a rainy Saturday morning, the civic center was already teeming with dog lovers dressed in snappy sports outfits, anxious to partake of the festivities promised for that day. "If we don't hurry there's not going to be any place left to sit," she pointed out. The annual canine contest was one of the most eagerly anticipated affairs in the gay resort town, coming as it did in the middle of a typically quiet Illinois summer, and no one was as pleased to see the sights as Midge Fontaine, a dog lover through and through.

A shock of recognition crossed the officer's face as he got a closer look at Midge. She was a muscular girl with close-cropped blond hair and a strong jaw, which at that moment was set in a scowl. "Sorry, I didn't recognize you straight off, Frank," the man waved them through, adding, "Chief O'Malley sure will be glad to know his favorite boy detective is back in town."

"Thanks," Midge replied with a grin. Since she and her chums had arrived in the small Midwestern town of River Depths ten days ago to help girl detective Nancy Clue solve the baffling mystery of *The Case of the Good-For-Nothing Girlfriend*, the handsome girl had been mistaken over and over again for a boy. And not just any fellow, but the celebrated detective Frank Hardly, a clean-cut lad with a sensible nature and a keen eye whose daring exploits had made him as much a household name as his feminine counterpart, Nancy Clue. The two sleuths were in fact old chums who had solved many a mystery together.

On Midge's first day in River Depths, a townswoman had taken one look at her muscular build and masculine appearance and announced to all concerned that Frank Hardly, who had been vacationing in Europe with his brother Joe, was back in town. Midge had done nothing to correct the woman's mistaken impression, and had in fact enjoyed the little charade.

"Being Frank is fun," Midge thought as she and her group hastily strode past the guard and lost themselves in the crowd. "Why are they searching people at the door?" Midge wondered aloud. She had never been to a dog show with so much security!

"Myra Meeks is exhibiting her prize-winning poodle today," Nancy said with a chuckle, "and her husband, Judge Meeks, has probably called in the police to make sure her Precious isn't stolen."

At the mention of the town's meanest matron, Midge made a face. Since their arrival in Illinois, the girls had had many an unpleasant encounter with the worrisome woman. "I hope we don't run into her today," Midge groaned. She checked her watch. "Let's catch the end of the Obedience Trials," she suggested.

"I know you're in a hurry, Midge, but first I simply must powder my nose," Cherry insisted.

While her girlish chums ducked into the ladies' lounge, Midge waited nearby with her face buried in the dog show program.

Five minutes later Midge checked her watch and frowned. The Parade of Hounds would begin soon, followed by the Toy Dogs Procession in which miniature animals were wheeled around the center ring on specially built carts.

"Honey, we're going to miss the best parts," Midge pleaded through the cheery pink door of the lounge, but there was no reply. "They're probably doing their hair," she realized. She ran a hand through her own short, masculine hairstyle, which required little more than a quick combing and an application of hair preparation.

"Velma, let's go," she cried. Golly, they were missing the opening remarks from experts in the field. As a devoted dog lover, Midge knew there were one hundred and twenty breeds recognized by the American Kennel Club, and the stories of these dogs were filled with heroism and humor, delightful anecdotes and high adventure—and she didn't want to miss one little bit!

Midge felt a sudden tug at her elbow. "Pardon me, young man," a soft voice said politely. Midge whirled around to find a slender elderly woman dressed in an impeccably tailored lightweight navy blue suit with a prim lace collar and starched white cuffs standing behind her. Tucked under each arm was a miniature teacup poodle the exact color of her nicely coifed gray hair. The woman peered at Midge through horn-rimmed glasses, with a puzzled expression on her face.

"Er—I'm just waiting for my wife," Midge explained weakly. "She and her friends went in to fix their hair." Midge was telling the truth, for just last week in a touching ceremony sure to be remembered by all, she and her longtime love Velma had been united in marriage.

The woman smiled sympathetically, then nodded at the program in Midge's hand and said, "Would you be a dear and tell me where the petite poodles are being housed? I have a program in my purse," she went on, indicating the worn yet still good black clutch under one arm, "but my hands are too full to retrieve it. I do so want to win this year," she confided as Midge leafed through her program detailing the 1959 Lake Merrimen Dog Show. "If I can only keep Pierre and Patsy calm until show time, one of them is sure to win Best of Show in their breed!" The woman's friendly brown eyes lit up in delight as she dreamt of the shiny trophy awaiting the top pet poodle.

Midge thought that the handsome pets were sure to impress the judges, and told her so. The woman flushed with excitement at the kind words. "I'm Miss Penelope Parsnips, but everyone calls me Miss Pansy," she offered. "It's an old family nickname," she explained. "I'm the local librarian, and while you could say books are my business, poodles are my passion!"

"I'm—" Midge began, but the excited woman cut her off. "Oh, everyone knows who *you* are," Miss Pansy cried in delight. "I've heard about you and your brother and your expert detective work on many occasions, Frank Hardly. Your father, the world-famous detective Fennel P. Hardly, must be awfully proud that his sons are following in his footsteps to such great acclaim!"

Midge had to grin. These Hardly boys sure had a reputation!

After ascertaining the location of the event, Miss Pansy bade Midge a fond farewell. "I hope your wife comes out soon before you miss any more of today's excitement," she cried. "Be sure to come see us perform in the Pageant of Poodles."

Midge took the pencil she had tucked behind her ear and made a bold check next to the one o'clock show. In the margin, she wrote the names Pierre and Patsy. Midge's keen eye told her Miss Pansy's pet poodles were top notch.

"One sees more poodles in dog acts than all other breeds combined," Midge was fascinated to read as she browsed through her catalog. A feminine giggle interrupted her. It was her girlfriend, the vivacious Velma Pierce, and she had brushed her short, dark curly locks until they shone. Right behind her was Nancy, who had shed her raincoat to reveal a crisp shirtwaist cinched with a slender belt, in the prettiest blue that set off her shiny titian locks to their best advantage, and her date Cherry, similarly attired in a smart shirtwaist of the palest yellow and carrying a white patent-leather clutch purse.

Midge sighed with relief and jammed her program into the

back pocket of her rumpled men's trousers. She did her best to look annoyed.

"I'm sorry we took so long," Velma exclaimed as she gave her patient girlfriend a kiss. Midge's frown immediately turned into a big grin.

"I'm afraid it's all my fault," Cherry admitted. "While I was powdering my nose I noticed a girl wearing the cute cornflower blue uniform of a Veterinarian Nurse, and I just had to ask her a few pertinent questions about her exciting profession." If truth be told, the conversation had done Cherry a world of good. Although she was greatly enjoying her stay in this lovely Midwestern town, she had to admit she was a little lonesome for the hustle and bustle of the big city hospital that had, until three weeks ago, been her whole world.

Until her recent adventure brought her to Illinois, Nurse Cherry Aimless had been a happily overworked Ward Nurse specializing in women with nervous disorders at Seattle General Hospital. During a visit to San Francisco to see her Aunt Gertrude, she had been caught up in the exciting *Case of the Not-So-Nice Nurse,* where she had met her longtime idol, detective Nancy Clue, and Midge and Velma, too! That simple vacation had turned into the adventure of a lifetime, for not only had Cherry helped rescue a convent of kidnapped nuns, she had also fallen deeply and truly in love with her favorite girl detective!

Only days later, the chums had been swept up in their most recent mystery, the dramatic *Case of the Good-For-Nothing Girlfriend,* which had proven to be their scariest adventure ever! Helpful housekeeper Hannah Gruel, who had been like a mother to Nancy Clue since the death of her real mother many years ago, had been charged with killing Nancy's father, famous attorney Carson Clue!

"Thank goodness that's all over," Cherry sighed in relief. "Has it just been a week since Nancy faced a certain jail sentence by bravely admitting that it was *she* who had murdered her father, only to be exonerated at the very last minute when Carson Clue's true nature was finally revealed?" Cherry wondered to herself. Why, if public sentiment hadn't been behind her, Nancy could very well be in prison this minute, Cherry realized with alarm as she clutched her chum's slender, white cotton-gloved hand.

Who would have guessed that just days before, the charmingly outfitted girl at Cherry's side had been locked in a damp, drab jail cell? Luckily, once the truth about her father had been revealed and people could see that Nancy had had *no* choice but to shoot him, the good citizens of River Depths had demanded she be let go and that all charges be dropped.

Nancy smiled and gave Cherry's hand a little squeeze. "Lucky for us, everything's back to normal," that confident squeeze said.

Cherry felt a sudden stab of guilt. All week she had been trying to get her feelings straight about Nancy. When they first met in San Francisco, they fell instantly and truly in love. But after two glorious weeks, their romance had soured, and Cherry had been forced to take a good long look at her idol. Not liking all she saw, the gentle nurse had since demurred whenever the subject of love came up. Cherry knew that since Nancy's release from prison, she had done all she could to rekindle their earlier love, but there was just one thing standing in the way.

"A great, big good-looking girl with bulging biceps and the warmest smile I've ever seen," Cherry thought dreamily. San Francisco Detective Jackie Jones, a calm, capable girl with rich brown skin and large black eyes, had shown up at Nancy's door to help her chums solve their last case, and had stolen Cherry's heart in the process. "Maybe I was never really in love with Nancy to begin with," Cherry thought. "Could it be that I'm really, truly in love with Jackie, and my feelings for Nancy were merely a girl's first crush?" Still, Cherry felt a little tingle when she gazed at her attractive titian-haired chum, who had stooped to pet a frisky Scottish terrier, a plucky little breed whose independent spirit and reckless courage had long held it in good stead with the dog-loving public.

"Nancy *has* been awfully sweet to me since she was released from prison. And who could blame her for acting a little short-tempered during her murder trial?" Cherry asked herself. "After all, she was under an awful strain." The more Cherry pondered this, the more sense it made. Could it be her feelings for Jackie, a top notch detective with a steady gaze and a confident manner, were merely the admiration of one dedicated professional for another?

Cherry blushed. She always blushed when she thought of the strong, cocksure detective who had an uncanny habit of showing up just when Cherry needed her most. "Time will tell. Just be patient, and you'll see who's the right girl for you," Velma's sensible words rang in Cherry's ears. Since meeting the older, more sophisticated Velma Pierce, Cherry had, again and again, turned to her for guidance on matters of the heart, as well as for fashion and hairstyle tips.

"After ten years with Midge, Velma must know everything there is to know about romance," Cherry realized. She snuck a peek at her favorite couple, who were standing arm in arm whilst poring over the fascinating program. She was thrilled to see them happy and smiling again. Midge and Velma were true and devoted lovers, but a silly misunderstanding last week had almost pulled them asunder! Luckily, love had prevailed, and the two were wed in a lovely ceremony in Nancy's living room, attended by all of River Depth society.

Cherry puzzled her pretty brow. There was one thing she still didn't understand. If Midge was masquerading as Frank Hardly, and had married Velma while in disguise, was Velma Mrs. Midge Fontaine, or really Mrs. Frank Hardly? "Maybe now isn't the best time to bring that up," Cherry decided. "Since everyone's having such a swell time."

The chums had kept a low profile for days, waiting for the news to blow over that it had been Nancy who had murdered her father. "Not that it's been a dull period in the least," Cherry murmured to herself. Why, the house had been a whirlwind of activity!

Shortly after Nancy's release from jail, the president of the River Depths Bank had arrived with a briefcase stuffed with stocks and bonds and insurance policies for Nancy to peruse. There were numerous financial decisions for River Depth's newest heiress to mull over, for besides inheriting the comfortable three-story brick house and her father's considerable bank account, Nancy had come into a large trust left to her by her late mother, Rebecca Clue. Why, the interest alone would keep Nancy in fashionable frocks and necessary accessories for the rest of her days!

When Nancy had begged Cherry to be her date for the show, Jackie had suddenly announced that she had official work to do, strapped on her gun and left the house. Cherry was frankly relieved that she didn't have to choose between two escorts for that day!

"Although Jackie *is* missing all the fun," Cherry thought woefully as she followed the others through the crowd to the center arena where the Parade of Hounds was underway. Soon Cherry forgot all about her troubled romances as many delightful dogs, led by a handsome bloodhound, paraded about in a large circle.

"These can't all be hounds," Cherry exclaimed to Midge. "They look nothing alike." As she said this, she noticed a burly man clad in a tight-fitting shiny black suit prick up his ears and tilt his head so as to hear Midge's response. Cherry was glad she wasn't the only uninformed one in the crowd!

Midge quickly explained that all sorts of contrary-appearing dogs, from the merry beagle to the regal Afghan, were hounds. "There are two classifications of hounds: coursing hounds, which use their eyesight for tracking, and tracking hounds, which rely on their acute sense of smell," Midge explained earnestly, adding, "Dogs have a sense of smell three hundred times that of humans."

"Bloodhounds are often used by the police to solve crimes," Nancy interjected. "I had one with me when I cracked *The Case of the Fetid Footwear.*"

"Goodness!" Cherry exclaimed. Before she could hear any more about Nancy's exciting case, a roar went up from the crowd. It was the Cavalcade of Collies! The crowd applauded in approval as the majestic looking, thick-coated herding dogs rounded up sheep, jumped over barriers, and saved a small boy from a simulated swimming accident. Cherry was not at all surprised to learn that the plucky dogs had long been used to aid mankind during times of national emergency.

"Aren't they the cleverest dogs you've ever seen?" Cherry cried to Nancy as she jumped to her feet and smoothed out the wrinkles in her skirt in preparation for a trip to the cafeteria.

"And so loyal, too," Nancy exclaimed. "Why, they're practically famous for their dutiful obedience to their masters!" Nancy put one arm on Cherry's shoulder and looked her straight in the eye. "Loyalty has always been one of my favorite characteristics in a girlfriend," she confided. "Don't you think it's one of the most important virtues ever?"

Cherry gulped. "Goodness, I'm starved!" she cried. "Is anyone else hungry?"

As they consumed a yummy luncheon of ham salad sandwiches, cabbage slaw and fruit compote, Midge happily read aloud more interesting things about the delightful dogs. She had taken copious notes in her program during the trials and declared herself quite taken with the handsome beasts. Next the girls browsed at a nearby booth offering good bargains on necessary items. Nancy purchased a cute tartan collar for her terrier, Gogo, and Midge picked up a handsome braided red leather collar and leash set for her own dog, Eleanor, a black and white cocker spaniel left at home in Warm Springs, Oregon with close chums.

"Attention ladies and gentlemen!" a voice blared out over the loudspeaker. "The Wiener Dog Races will begin in four minutes' time in Exhibition Hall C, followed shortly thereafter by the Pageant of Poodles in Exhibition Hall D!"

"I met two poodles who are going to compete," Midge told her chums. "I promised their owner we'd be there to cheer them on."

Cherry had to smile. Tough, sarcastic Midge always became a puddle when it came to pooches! The happy group was eagerly making its way down the long corridor connecting the exhibition halls when suddenly a tall, thin man in a dark-colored trenchcoat with an upturned collar stepped right in their path.

"Hey!" Midge cried as the man took an umbrella from under his arm and thoughtlessly shook it out, spraying the hapless girls with rain water before disappearing into the sea of dog lovers. "What the—!" she added as she felt someone jostle her from behind. Midge turned around to find a burly man in a shiny, tight-fitting black sharkskin suit behind her.

"Sorry, sonny," he grumbled as he slipped something into his jacket pocket and walked briskly away. Midge checked her pocket and was relieved to find her wallet still there.

"How discourteous that trenchcoat-clad man is!" Cherry exclaimed, realizing that he had gotten water on her new ballerina flats. Not only that, he had left a puddle that could prove dangerous on the slick, tile flooring! Cherry opened her purse and whipped out a clean handkerchief so she could mop up the mess, but stopped when she spied the look of astonishment on Midge's face. By now, Midge had had time to check all her pockets, and had discovered a queer thing.

"That man in the black suit stole my program!" Midge gasped angrily.

CHAPTER 2

Dog Gone!

"At first I thought he had taken my money," Midge explained. "I've got my wallet, all right, but my program's missing. Why would he steal a five-cent program?" she cried, more bewildered than angry.

"I'll bet you just dropped it, Midge," Cherry piped up. "What possible reason could someone have for stealing your program?"

"You're right, Cherry, I probably left it in the cafeteria," Midge sighed after a quick look around. "And it's got all my notes about my favorite dogs in it!" Midge looked decidedly downcast.

"I'll get you another," Cherry cried as she fished a nickel from her coin purse, walked over to a vendor and purchased a crisp new program.

"Thanks, Cherry," Midge grinned. Then an expression of alarm crossed her face. She checked her watch. "We've got just seconds to go before the Pageant of Poodles starts, and I promised Miss Pansy we'd be there!" Quick as a wink, the girls took off for Exhibition Hall D, but as they got close to the room they heard a terrible cry, one that sent a chill through the gay little group.

"*Help! Help!*" someone cried. "*Someone's—kidnapped— the—miniature—poodles!*"

They raced to the Petite Poodle Room, which proved a pandemonious place indeed. People were milling about, talking excitedly. "That's the third dognapping this summer in Central Illinois!" they overheard one man exclaim.

"So that's why the police are here," Midge realized.

"They must have suspected something like this might happen," Nancy surmised.

Meanwhile, Cherry had begun fussing over Miss Pansy, who was lying flat on her back on the cold tile floor. Cherry noted

22

with approval that the Veterinarian Nurse she had met earlier in the ladies' lounge had loosened the woman's garments and had made a pillow for her out of a pile of small woolen dog sweaters. The color was coming back in the elderly woman's face and soon she was able to sit up and tell the girls the dreadful details of the tragic event.

"It's the most awful thing," Miss Pansy said in a shaky voice. Tears welled in her soft brown eyes. "I left Pierre and Patsy alone in their stalls for just a moment so I could purchase a cucumber sandwich and a cup of coffee. In the excitement of the day, I had forgotten to have any breakfast," she explained weakly.

Cherry kept a cheery expression on her face, but inwardly she frowned. Of all people, a librarian should know that breakfast provides the fuel that powers the human engine! Cherry sent a bystander off for a cup of tea and some dry toast. As soon as Miss Pansy had had some nourishment and regained her strength, Cherry would set her straight about the most important meal of the day!

Miss Pansy continued her story. "When I came through these doors and looked over and saw *this*, why, I must have fainted," she said in a tremulous tone. She gestured limply toward a row of tiny stalls, each outfitted with a plush pillow, rubber toy, colorful ribbons, and a gay sign bearing the occupant's name.

But Tiny, Stella, Precious, Bubbles, Patsy and Pierre were gone!

Tears welled in Cherry's eyes. She had never seen a sadder sight than those six, small empty beds.

"Oh, Frank, you've simply got to do something," Miss Pansy begged Midge. "Oh, and Nancy Clue, you're here, too," the woman sighed in relief as she spotted the well-known girl detective.

Setting aside her own desire to frolic on this gay day, Nancy got right on the case. "Miss Pansy, was there anyone in here when you came through the door? Did you see anyone suspicious milling around earlier?"

But Miss Pansy was too perturbed to pay attention. "Pierre and Patsy have never spent the night away from me," she cried. "Why, they'll be petrified!"

"Maybe they'll escape and find their way home," Cherry

said brightly. "Why just today at the Cavalcade of Collies I overheard a heartwarming story about a dog named—"

Nancy stepped in. "I must question Miss Pansy before she forgets important details that might crack this case," Nancy told Cherry. Cherry nodded. She made a mental note to tell Miss Pansy the rest of the inspirational story later, for surely she would find comfort in it!

"Miss Pansy, did you see or hear anything suspicious earlier today?"

Miss Pansy shook her head. "Nothing happened that indicated a crime of this nature was about to be committed here!" Miss Pansy shuttered. Lake Merrimen was a gay little town where people were friendly and nothing bad had ever happened. Until today!

"There must be some—" but before Nancy could continue, a familiar person interrupted her. It was Mrs. Milton Meeks, well-known society matron, president of the River Depths Women's Club, and a Wiener Race judge. She was clad in a stylish navy blue linen suit accessorized with an ornate diamond and sapphire starburst brooch and matching earrings, and reeked of the most odorous rose perfume. By the looks of it, Mrs. Meeks wasn't at all pleased to have been called away from her post.

"What's going on in here?" she huffed. "The Pageant of Poodles was scheduled to begin five minutes ago. We're all going to fall dangerously behind," she cried as she checked the small, diamond-encrusted watch on her wrist.

"At-ch-oo!" Miss Pansy gave a little sneeze. Quick as wink, Cherry handed her patient a fresh handkerchief. Could Miss Pansy be malnourished *and* catching a cold? In that case, she would need medical care—and quick!

Miss Pansy sneezed three more dainty little sneezes, then explained. "It's your perfume, Myra. I'm terribly allergic to roses."

Mrs. Meeks rudely ignored her. She just stood there in her blue and white spectator pumps and looked annoyed.

"Mrs. Meeks, all the poodles are missing!" Cherry cried. She stood by with her portable first-aid kit in hand in case Mrs. Meeks fainted from shock, for she knew from a recent feature in *The River Depths Defender* that Mrs. Meeks owned an apricot poodle the exact color of her new sectional sofa.

"My Precious is gone?" Mrs. Meeks gasped. "It can't be," she cried. She turned pale as a ghost. "Who's the fool who left these valuable dogs alone? Where's the Poodle Room Monitor? Why, I'll make sure that particular individual never darkens the door of the Dog Show again!"

Cherry put a comforting hand on her elbow. "There, there," she said. She knew Mrs. Meeks' angry words were just a cover-up for jangled nerves. "Surely your Precious will turn up, and in good health, besides," she said in a calm tone.

"You don't understand," Mrs. Meeks said in a huffy tone as she shook off Cherry's effort. "It's not only that someone's stolen my prize poodle, worth over one hundred dollars, but he was wearing a white leather collar my jeweler made special just for today, using diamonds from one of my tiaras! It's worth thousands, I tell you, thousands!" she moaned. "My husband, Judge Milton Meeks, has the authority to close down this show if my diamonds are not found," she declared angrily. "He'll do it, too," she promised. She then took a crisp bill from her handbag. "I'll give fifty dollars to whoever returns it to me," she declared.

As people raced out of the room in search of the kidnapped canines, Midge grew red with anger. Somewhere out there, six small, frightened dogs were being held against their will, and all Mrs. Meeks cared about were her diamonds!

"Mrs. Meeks, did you happen to mention to anyone else that your Precious was wearing real diamonds in his collar?" Nancy inquired.

Mrs. Meeks flushed angrily. "Surely you don't think I'm as naïve as that!" she snapped. "Why, no one but myself and that nice gentleman who helped me carry in Precious' stall knows his collar is studded with genuine diamonds."

"Mrs. Meeks, what did this man look like?" Nancy asked eagerly.

Mrs. Meeks sighed and rolled her eyes. "I don't see how it could make any difference, but he was wearing a dark trench-coat and carrying an umbrella."

The girls gasped. Why, it sounded like the same rude fellow who had splashed them not ten minutes ago!

Nancy's bright blue eyes glittered in excitement. Her keen mind was racing a mile a minute. Mrs. Meeks had given them a fine start to solving this dognapping!

A sly smile came over Nancy's face. "Mrs. Meeks, I do so adore your lovely perfume," she said in an admiring tone. "Would you be a dear and let me sample some?" The older woman, flattered by Nancy's interest, sprayed her arm liberally with the heavy floral scent. "And the other arm, too," Nancy urged. Mrs. Meeks complied, until Nancy smelled like a rose bush in bloom.

How odd, Cherry thought, for just that morning, Nancy had declared that she thought obvious fragrance on a girl gauche. Cherry had agreed, knowing that the clean smell of well-scrubbed skin was all the scent a young lady needed, unless it was a special dress-up occasion, of course.

Nancy gathered the girls around her. "Be on the lookout for the fellow in the trenchcoat," she said in an urgent tone whilst she waved her arms about until the perfume was dry. "It's our only lead. Let's go!" After leaving Miss Pansy in the capable hands of the Veterinarian Nurse, they raced out of the room and fanned out through the civic center, searching for the suspect.

"Be careful," Nancy warned them. "Dognappers are a particularly ruthless breed," she said, her eyes narrowing in anger. "They care little that the stolen goods they're transporting are living creatures. We must find those dogs soon, before any harm befalls them!"

CHAPTER 3

A Daring Rescue!

A quick search of the four main exhibition halls proved fruitless. "Have you seen a man in a dark trenchcoat carrying six poodles and an umbrella?" they queried everyone they met, but to their utter dismay, no one remembered any such fellow.

"What's that peculiar odor?" Cherry heard people cry when they smelled the aromatic sleuth. But Nancy didn't seem at all concerned by the commotion she was causing as she pushed through the crowd, craning her neck in search of their suspect and waving her arms about.

"Nancy's so brave," Cherry thought, her bosom swelling with pride at the sight of the flailing detective.

A shrill yip suddenly caught their attention. "Was that a poodle, Midge?" Nancy asked her chum.

Midge shook her head and pointed toward a small cage being wheeled by an elderly gentleman. Inside was a tan and white chihuahua perched on a purple velvet pillow fringed by gay green pom-poms. "A poodle's yap is higher and shriller," Midge explained.

Just then a coon hound threw back his head and started to howl. Soon all the dogs in the room were barking and howling, whining and whoofing. Nancy led her chums back to the hallway, and once there, explained her scheme.

"I deliberately sprayed myself with Mrs. Meeks' potent perfume hoping to gain the attention of her poodle Precious. Midge, didn't you say earlier that a dog's sense of smell is three hundred times stronger than that of a human's? I was so hoping that Precious would recognize this odor and bark."

Cherry gasped. Nancy's keen logic never ceased to amaze her!

"But in that din, we'll never recognize Precious' bark," Nancy continued. "I'm going back to the Poodle Room to search for clues. Midge, you search the Police Dog Room, Cherry, you check out the Saint Bernard Rescue Trials and Velma, search over there by the dancing terriers," she directed.

But before the girls could split up, Midge spied a tall, thin man wearing a dark trenchcoat, not ten feet from her. He was pulling a large black trunk with one hand and had an umbrella tucked under the other arm.

"There he is!" Midge cried to her friends. "Hey, you! Stop!" she yelled, taking off after him. At the sight of the girl, the man's face blanched in fright, and he took off down the long corridor; the heavy trunk rocked to and fro as he rudely pushed past people, striking some of them in the legs.

Cherry was thankful that she had had the foresight to include in her first-aid kit sterile bandages and germicidal ointment for the scraped shins of surprised spectators.

Midge leapt over an enormous Irish wolfhound in an effort to catch the suspect, who, despite his heavy burden, was slipping away. He would have disappeared around the next corner had he not become entangled in the leash of a miniature smooth-coated dachshund who had unwittingly blocked his path.

"Curses!" the man cried, dropping the black trunk as he struggled to free himself. Just as Midge was closing in on him, he glared at her with a fierce mocking gaze, opened his umbrella over his head and—poof! In the wink of an eye, the man disappeared in a cloud of pink smoke!

Cherry gaped at the spot where the man, just moments before, had stood. "Why, he's gone!" she shrieked. "The trunk is moving!" Cherry then cried. The trunk was indeed bumping about on the slick tile floor, seemingly of its own volition!

Midge, her wits still intact, raced over to the trunk but found it locked. Using Velma's nail file, she was soon able to break the lock and fling open the lid. Midge grinned with glee when six nervous poodles in various stages of disarray hopped out and covered her face with little wet kisses. The crowd gave a happy sigh of relief when they saw the missing pups. True, two poodles' topknots had been tangled beyond ready repair, and Mrs. Meeks' Precious would surely benefit from a good bath—and quick—but on the whole, the six missing dogs seemed to be in fine fettle.

"Frank Hardly's saved the dogs!" the crowd cried. "Hip, hip hooray!"

CHAPTER 4

Thwarted!

"Despite our queer encounter with that devious dognapper, all in all I'd say it's been a lovely day," Cherry exclaimed as she slipped off her ballerina flats and stretched out on the wide back seat of Nancy's snappy canary-yellow convertible. It was a soft summer night and the little group was as happy as could be. Nancy and Cherry were contentedly curled up in the back seat while Midge was behind the wheel, expertly steering the automobile down the country lane leading to River Depths. She had one arm around Velma, who was humming a gay tune.

The girls had made quite a day of it; first the Dog Show and the exciting rescue of the purloined poodles, then a leisurely supper at a quaint restaurant overlooking the lake, and to top it off, a romantic movie at the Royale followed by scrumptious chocolate sodas at an inexpensive but clean corner drugstore.

Midge grinned. She had a crisp new fifty-dollar bill in her wallet—her reward for returning Mrs. Meeks' diamond dog collar—and her girl by her side.

"It's been a great night, hasn't it?" Velma sighed contentedly as she snuggled closer to Midge.

"Sure has," Midge replied. That evening *had* been fun, but their earlier experience at the Dog Show had left her feeling uneasy. Who could relax knowing innocent dogs all over town were in danger of being snatched? "If only we could have caught that fellow," Midge thought to herself. "Nancy, do you think—" but she stopped when she realized no one in the back seat was listening. Cherry and Nancy appeared to be lost in their own world, one of summer evenings spent round a windswept lake.

"Lake Merrimen is certainly one of the loveliest bodies of

water I've ever seen," Cherry chirped happily, recalling the sight of the large, limpid lake ringed by giant paper birches, the best-loved tree in America. As dusk fell, the inky black water reflected the starry skies and the creamy white bark of the tall, elegant trees shimmered in the moonlight. Cherry made a mental note to write a letter that very night to her nurse chums back in Seattle describing the high white clouds, deep blue water, boats and passengers in bright summer clothing that dotted the calm surface of the crystal-clear lake.

Cherry, an Idaho girl, secretly wondered what it would be like to be a Lake Resort Nurse and spend her summers cautioning vacationers about the dangers of sunstroke, or to be a Prairie Nurse in a nifty tan uniform warning people about the hazards of grass allergies. Either job, Cherry knew, would be a challenge!

"Why, I could be happy being an Illinois Nurse," she suddenly realized. She snuck a peek at Nancy, who was leaning on the door of the car, her titian-haired mane blowing in the warm breeze. Her eyes were shut, but Cherry could tell by the contented expression on her face that she was having the very same thought!

"Golly," Cherry gulped. All day long, she had wished Jackie was with them, but now she couldn't get over how lovely Nancy looked in the warm glow of the midsummer moon. Suddenly the tender feelings she had once had for Nancy came flooding back.

Just then Nancy opened her eyes and gave Cherry a winsome smile. "Lake Merrimen is everything I said it would be, isn't it?" Nancy asked softly.

"It certainly is," Cherry enthused. "Imagine seeing for myself a Midwestern lake whose water is purported to cure chicken pox *and* halitosis," she cried.

"Next visit, we'll use my boat, the *Swift Sleuth*, and I'll take you to the spire of rock that juts up from the middle of the lake. It's called Treasure Island," Nancy promised with a twinkle in her eye.

"Now I know firsthand why they call this part of the country America's Playland," Cherry chirped. "Why, a girl could spend years exploring all its natural wonders!"

Nancy gave Cherry's hand a warm squeeze. "I was so hoping you'd say that," she sighed happily.

Golly, was Nancy asking her to stay in Illinois? To spend her life bringing comfort to sick Midwesterners? Cherry quickly fumbled about for a topic that would steer the conversation away from a future of which she was still so unsure.

"Although you explained it earlier, I still don't understand how that man managed to vanish in a puff of smoke," she began. "It simply isn't possible. Why, it defies all known laws of gravity and science!"

All he had left behind was the large black trunk now safely stowed in the trunk of Nancy's convertible, and a small pile of pink powder which Nancy had scooped up in her handkerchief and stowed in her purse for later analysis.

"While his disappearing act was certainly a clever trick, it's one any professional magician could replicate," Nancy reasoned, switching in a flash from a starry-eyed romantic to the level-headed detective known and loved by all. She added, "Why, when I was working on *The Case of the Ill-Timed Illusion,* I went to Professor Casmire Cardini, the world-famous magician, for help. He taught me one important lesson: things are seldom what they seem."

"But he disappeared in a cloud of smoke," Cherry insisted. "He opened his umbrella, smoke appeared and he was gone. I saw it with my own eyes!"

At this, Nancy chuckled. "That's what makes it *seem* like magic," she said. "He most likely used the smoking powder as a diversion so he could slip away, change his outfit and walk out of the arena disguised as your average dog lover. It's an old illusionist's trick. In fact, I've seen stage shows where master magicians have made elephants, lions and even whole houses seemingly disappear!

"Why, Professor Cardini once demonstrated an illusion in which a woman was transformed into a man!"

"Goodness," Cherry cried. As a trained nurse, that was something she'd certainly like to see!

"Many is the time I've found a mystery to be nothing but an illusion hiding the truth. This is frequently true of cases involving ghostly hauntings," Nancy told Cherry in a modest tone.

Cherry shivered. She was by nature logical and clear-thinking, but still, the thought of ghosts sent a little shiver down her spine. She pulled her thin summer cardigan around her shoulders. Nancy, seeing her distress, put her arms around her chum and held her close. She began stroking Cherry's neck with a slow, gentle motion that made Cherry quiver in the queerest way.

Just then Midge swerved into the circular drive in front of the stately Clue residence. Cherry flew right out of Nancy's arms.

"Sorry," Midge grinned. "I almost missed the driveway. Oh, look, Jackie's home," she cried enthusiastically upon spying a light from Jackie's second-floor bedroom in the charming three-story brick house. "Hey, Jack, we're back," she hollered.

"Honey, you'll wake the neighbors," Velma cautioned.

Midge nipped her girlfriend gently on the ear. "*I'll* wake the neighbors? Who's the noisy one in *this* family?" she teased. Even in the moonlight, Cherry could see Velma turn bright red. The flushed girl hopped out of the car and headed inside the house, Midge hot on her heels.

"I simply must get out of this dusty dress," Nancy murmured in Cherry's ear. "Shall we go to my room and find something cool to slip into? I've got two pairs of shantung silk lounging pajamas—one creamy white, and the other, the palest of pink. They would be divine on a warm night like tonight."

Cherry had to admit she *was* feeling decidedly wrinkled. "I'll take the ice cream to the freezer first," she volunteered. Housekeeper Hannah Gruel, who was tucked in bed recovering from the heart attack she had suffered while in prison falsely accused of the murder of Nancy's father, would turn seventy-two in just two days, and the girls were planning a quiet celebration to honor the woman who had been like a mother to Nancy since the death of her real mother twenty-two years ago.

"Swell," Nancy breathed excitedly. "I'll meet you in my room."

While Nancy raced upstairs, Cherry deposited the fresh-churned frozen concoction in the deep freeze of the cheerful modernized yellow and white kitchen. "This is the very room in which Carson Clue was shot," she shivered, staring at the linoleum in front of the Frigidaire where the well-known attorney had lain. She had to admit she was still a little shaken up by all the talk of ghosts. Just then Cherry felt something brush her calf. "Eek!" she cried, spinning around to find, much to her relief, that it was only Nancy's little terrier, Gogo, playfully nipping at her ankles.

"Phew," Cherry breathed with relief. She reached for the box of crunchy dog biscuits at the back of the counter and accidentally knocked a tea cake off the platter piled high with treats that Velma had baked especially for Hannah's birthday party. Gogo immediately pounced on the sweet, and quick as a bunny, pushed open the screen door and fled. Cherry raced after her.

"I hope she doesn't make herself sick," Cherry thought worriedly as she searched the fragrant garden for the small dog. She had stomach-ache potion in her first-aid kit, but she had no clue how much to give a terrier. It didn't matter—Gogo was long gone.

Cherry sighed. From where she stood, she could see Nancy's bedroom window, her light ablaze. "I'd better get upstairs before Nancy starts to fret about me," Cherry thought. But she couldn't bring herself to go inside just yet. Somehow, she just didn't feel ready to face Nancy—or those shantung silk lounging pajamas!

CHAPTER 5

A Difficult Decision

 "I'll sit for a moment first and enjoy these lovely flowers," she told herself, plopping down on the wrought-iron bench overlooking Hannah's award-winning begonias.

"Just last week, I sat on this bench with Jackie," Cherry remembered. "She held my hand and looked into my eyes and—" She blushed when she recalled the day Jackie had asked her to return with her to San Francisco. Detective Jackie Jones had already spent a week in River Depths, and her vacation time was running out fast. Cherry knew she was waiting around for an answer—but what answer would she give her? Would Cherry travel west with the dashing police detective or would she choose to stay in this Midwestern fairyland in an attempt to recapture her lost love?

"Oh, Cherry Aimless, Registered Nurse, you're such a silly goose," Cherry cried aloud, as she was wont to do when faced with a particularly puzzling predicament. As a nurse, Cherry had made many a tough decision and always reacted with lightning-quick action and a cool head, earning her the respect of nurses everywhere. But in matters of the heart, never before had she been so unsure of her feelings.

"Well, just that once, when I had a mad crush on Miss Peebles, the School Nurse, and mother explained to me that when a girl likes an older girl, it's not a crush in the romantic sense, but rather it's that she admires the way the older girl carries herself: her poise, charm and attractive, modern way of dress," she mused.

Cherry chastised herself loudly. "You're acting like a lovesick schoolgirl!" She shook her head and resolutely jumped up off the bench. "A cool bath and a fresh outfit might be just what I need," she reasoned. She headed for the house, but as she mounted the back stairs she got a sudden surprise.

Jackie was lounging on the wide porch swing, gazing at the sparkling night sky.

Cherry turned bright red. "Oh, hi," she smiled weakly, wondering if Jackie had been witness to her tortured murmuring. She turned redder still, after she got a good look at Jackie, who had recently stepped out of a refreshing bath. Her jet-black hair was slicked close to her head, and she was clad in a pair of old, soft-looking dungaree trousers and a snug white tee-shirt that showed off her bulging biceps to their best advantage.

Jackie returned her stare, then smiled warmly. "I've been sitting here enjoying the meteor showers," she explained. "They say when you wish on a falling star, your wish comes true," she continued in a soft tone. "Know what I wished for?"

Cherry turned scarlet. "I got you something at the dog show," she cried, fishing around in her patent-leather clutch for the brown paper bag that contained Jackie's souvenir.

Jackie gave a bemused grin when she opened the bag and held up a handsome braided red leather collar and matching leash.

Cherry blushed. "Oh, that's Midge's," she cried. "This is yours," Cherry said, handing Jackie a small brown bag. Inside, wrapped in layers of protective tissue, was a handsome porcelain figurine of a collie, its head cocked to one side. "The eyes and the ears were painted by hand," Cherry explained. The figure had cost a pretty penny, but the look of delight in Jackie's eyes told Cherry that it was six dollars and fifty-nine cents well spent.

"It looks just like the dog I had as a kid," Jackie grinned with pleasure.

Cherry's heart started to pound uncontrollably. "I got my mother cute plastic coasters in the shape of Scotty dogs," Cherry babbled nervously. "And I got Lauren a book about dogs who have rescued people from peril."

Jackie smiled at the mention of the youngest member of their little gang, sixteen-year-old Lauren Rooney. The troublesome teen had accompanied the gang east from San Francisco, and although she was often underfoot and was too fond of unhealthy snacks, she had proven herself an invaluable aid in times of danger.

"I hope Lauren's having some good clean fun at camp,"

Cherry continued. "Wasn't it nice of Bess and George to secure her a scholarship so she could spend a week out-of-doors learning necessary craft skills?" Nancy's oldest chums, Bess Marvel, a giggly girl with a pleasingly plump figure and a sunny disposition, and George Fey, a girl with a boy's name, had left a few days before for their annual stint as counselors at nearby Camp Hathaway, an exclusive girls' camp situated on nearby Clear Lake.

"The house sure is quiet without her," Jackie admitted.

"Even Midge seems a little lonely since she's been gone," Cherry marvelled. "I had no idea she could be so maternal."

Jackie laughed heartily at this notion. "Speaking of maternal, I believe that letter is for you," she said, pointing to a small cream-colored envelope lying on a nearby wrought-iron glass-topped circular table.

Cherry gasped in delight when she spied the familiar neat handwriting. It was a letter from her mother, Mrs. Doris Aimless of Pleasantville, Idaho! Cherry eagerly ripped open the envelope. Ever since she had spoken with her twin brother Charley, a successful interior decorator in New York City, and received the shocking news that both their parents had had complete and utter nervous breakdowns, Cherry had been on pins and needles awaiting word of their progress. Perhaps this would be it! She eagerly read the missive aloud.

27 July 1959

Dear Cherry,

You'll never believe it, but your father and I have gone and done the most unexpected thing! We've checked into the lovely Tamarack Lodge, "Where Friendly People Go To Frolic!," a delightful resort with comfortable accommodations, inspiring scenery and the best cuisine.

We've met the most congenial people, and we are participating in all sorts of fun activities. Don't be surprised if you get a darling set of pot-holders for your birthday!

I hope you are having a relaxing holiday as well. Your brother Charley says you're visiting a new

girlfriend in Illinois. That's nice, dear. My friend
Mavis Minot once visited her cousin Marjorie in Ohio
for the Snow Carnival. Are you anywhere near there?
How long can you be away from the hospital?
Remember, August comes sooner than you think.
Shouldn't you be getting your fall wardrobe together?
I heard Kloppman's is having a sale on woolen
nurses' capes, and if I remember correctly, you're due
for a new one.
Well, I could go on and on about the fun we're
having, but it's time for luncheon. Today it's oxtail
soup, boiled fish, jellied vegetable ring and orange
sherbet. Your father says to say hello.

Love,
Mother

P.S. If you're wondering whether to stop in Pleasant-
ville on your way back to Seattle, you needn't bother.
Mrs. Henry next door is watering my zinnias and Miss
Lily Bee from the bridge club is watching Snowpuff.

Cherry looked mighty puzzled. "Charley told me Mother
and Father had been taken to a nearby, thoroughly modern
sanitarium staffed by the finest doctors using the most up-to-
date equipment available to treat nervous disorders, and here
they are, already returned to normal and on vacation," she
cried out. She knitted her pretty brow. "Perhaps I'm not as
up-to-date on nervous disorders as I imagined. I had no idea
they were so curable!"

This was a worrisome thought, indeed.

Jackie checked the return address on the envelope Cherry
had dropped on the ground. "This envelope's been stamped
Pleasantville Sanitarium," she pointed out.

Cherry gasped. "I know Mother is suffering from a case of
hysteria, or in layman's terms, an unconscious attempt to
escape from some unpleasant reality. Could it be she's suffering from delusions, too? Oh, no," she cried, throwing up her
arms up in alarm. "I must get in touch with Doctor Joe and
let him know!"

Jackie tried to comfort the nervous nurse. "I'll bet your mother's just pretending to be on vacation so she doesn't spoil yours," she guessed.

Cherry considered this. Jackie had a point. "It would be just like Mother to keep a stiff upper lip," Cherry agreed. She paused a moment in quiet contemplation. The words from her nursing school manual came back to her: *Faith is a real remedy, good cheer is a powerful medicine, and confidence is part of the cure for every nervous patient who gets well.*

"So if Mother chooses to pretend she's at a resort, perhaps it's a good thing after all," Cherry decided aloud. Suddenly she had a grand thought. "I'll write back to Mother pretending I believe her little ruse. I'll ask her to describe the colorful people she has met and the nature hikes and other entertainments. That way, she'll write me cheery, therapeutic letters which will speed up her recovery. Then she'll regain her confidence and, in no time at all, be back to her normal contented self."

"What about what your mother mentioned at the end of her letter?" Jackie blurted out. Would Cherry decide to go back to Seattle and resume her place on the Women's Psychiatric Ward, or worse, would she choose to settle in River Depths and play nurse to Nancy's detective? Jackie's heart was pounding with anticipation. What would Cherry do?

"Oh, I think my woolen nurse's cape can stand another season's wear," Cherry assured her.

"No, I mean about going back to Seattle," Jackie blushingly stammered.

"When I arrived in River Depths, I wrote the hospital asking for a short leave of absence, at no pay of course," Cherry informed her. "I've got plenty of time."

"But I don't," Jackie was tempted to cry out, forgetting for a moment Midge's helpful advice. *Let Cherry come to you. She's stuck on you for sure, but she needs to get over Nancy first. Just give it time.*

"My vacation's up soon, and I'll have to return to San Francisco," Jackie explained in a calm voice that masked her thudding heart. If she left Cherry behind, she'd surely lose her to Nancy!

Cherry looked at the downcast expression on Jackie's handsome face and suddenly realized the longer the good-looking detective stayed in Illinois, the longer she was kept away from her vitally important police work. Cherry knew only too well that crime, like illness, accidents and disease, never took a holiday!

"If only I could make up my mind," Cherry chided herself silently. "I know I have feelings for Jackie that lead me to suspect I'm in love with her, but what about Nancy and the night of passion we shared? I can't just turn my back on that without first thinking things through long and hard. Plus, Nancy really needs me now. Why, she's got so much to do, what with inheriting this house and selecting her fall wardrobe!"

Cherry had realized just how much work it was to *be* Nancy when two days earlier, a dressmaker had wheeled in racks of the latest fall fashions. Nancy had spent the entire day running about the house in various stages of undress while she selected the outfits she would need for the coming year: pretty daytime frocks, sleek going-to-town suits, modest bathing costumes, vibrant ski togs, sophisticated evening sheaths and fancy off-the-shoulder gowns just right for a country club dance. The next day, Velma, Cherry and an exhausted Nancy had lain about the living room sipping refreshing iced tea and pouring over fashion magazines, selecting shoes and handbags, scarves and gloves to round out Nancy's new wardrobe.

"I could be a real help to her here," Cherry told herself. "After all, I did take a vow to go wherever I'm needed most!"

Jackie clutched her porcelain figure in her large, strong hands. She felt she couldn't wait one more minute to find out if Cherry shared her feelings! "Cherry, I've got to know. Will you—" Just then Nancy swept onto the porch carrying a tray loaded with all sorts of goodies, and wearing a black felt poodle skirt with white and pink appliqués that showed off her trim waistline. Her pert bosom was covered with a snug white topper and on her petite feet were black patent leather slip-ons.

"You look charming!" Cherry cried as Nancy set down the tray and spun about to unfurl the circumference of the fetching skirt. Nancy stopped twirling, however, when she got a look at the dog statue in Jackie's hands. A peevish look crossed her pretty face.

"It's a swell gift, isn't it?" Jackie boasted, fingering the hand-painted figurine proudly. It would look fine sitting on the mantle in her small but cozy apartment. "*Our* apartment," she thought dreamily as she gazed at Cherry.

Nancy gulped. She had assumed Cherry was purchasing the statue for a nurse chum. Her wide blue eyes narrowed in anger. "There's another skirt just like this one in cherry red lying on someone's bed," Nancy cried out in a forced cheery tone. She was talking to Cherry but glaring at Jackie.

"A poodle skirt for *me?*" Cherry flushed excitedly. "Oh, Nancy, you shouldn't have! Why, they're so expensive!" She kicked up her heels and raced upstairs, secretly relieved that her conversation with Jackie had come to an end, at least for now. Cherry had the feeling that Jackie was about to ask her a very important question, the kind of question a girl dreamt of, only Cherry wasn't sure what her answer would be!

"When will you be sure?" she leaned in close to the mirror and asked the girl in the darling new outfit peering back at her. All Cherry knew was that each time Jackie looked at her, she lost her ability to think clearly. "But is it true love?" Cherry wondered, "or merely a hormonal surge coursing through my body, and impairing my ability to think straight? And when, oh, when will I know for sure?"

CHAPTER 6

Thwarted Again!

"You're looking mighty chipper this morning!" Cherry announced as Nancy came into the kitchen clad in a darling sports outfit consisting of lightweight cotton plaid pedal pushers and a crisp white blouse with a Peter Pan collar. Her trademark titian hair had been brushed until it shone and the charms on her gold bracelet, one for each mystery she had solved, jangled cheerfully on her wrist. In one hand was a picnic hamper and in the other a soft blanket. "Are you going on a picnic?" Cherry wondered.

"*We're* going on a picnic," Nancy grinned. "We're going back to Lake Merrimen!"

Cherry smiled. Only moments before, she had been sitting alone and confused at the kitchen table. Why, a trip to the lake and a yummy outdoor meal was exactly what she needed! "I'll make sure everyone's up and dressed in casual clothes in no time at all," she promised. Before she could see the enraged look on Nancy's face, Cherry had raced out of the kitchen and up the stairs.

"Darn and double darn!" Nancy cried as she hurled her picnic hamper across the linoleum floor. She slammed out the door, saw the morning edition of *The River Depths Defender* on the porch and gave it a good kick. She flopped on the porch swing, and only then did she notice that the front page was carrying a familiar story.

"Hmmn," Nancy thought as she bent to pick up the paper.

POODLES SAVED FROM PERIL!

River Depths, Illinois—A fiendish dognapper struck yesterday at the Lake Merrimen Dog Show, but was thwarted when well-known detectives and Illinois residents Frank Hardly and Nancy Clue moved quickly and saved the day. The culprit, however, escaped and may continue to plague the Central Illinois area as he has for the past two months.

Nancy gave a little start, then remembered her own Gogo was upstairs asleep on the foot of her bed.

"It's a horrible crime," Nancy sighed as she threw the paper down next to her. Normally, the inquisitive girl would have jumped on the case, but at the moment, she had little patience for sleuthing; the police would have to tackle this one without her. She had her own precarious predicament to resolve.

Meanwhile, clad in crisp summer lightweight frocks, Velma and Cherry were in the kitchen, preparing delicious food meant to be eaten out-of-doors and chatting happily about the fun day ahead. "Twenty sandwiches should be enough for the five of us, don't you think?" Cherry asked as she placed the last cold meat sandwich in the hamper next to the celery sticks, deviled eggs and molasses cookies.

"I think four is Midge's limit," Velma grinned. "Speaking of my husband, where is she?"

"I imagine she and Jackie snuck out for a smoke," Cherry tattled, surveying their fare. "Now all we need is fruit and we've got a well-rounded meal."

"I'll get some cling peaches from the pantry," Velma offered. When she opened the door to the walk-in closet at the far end of the kitchen, she was surprised to find Midge and Jackie inside with their heads together.

"What are you two scheming about?" Velma teased.

The girls jumped apart. "We're talking about the poodle-napping incident that happened yesterday," Midge said innocently.

"Sure," Velma twitched her lips. "More likely, you're talking about the poodle *skirt* incident of yesterday," she countered.

Midge gave Jackie a little wink; Jackie grinned and left the pantry.

"Midge, do you remember what you promised me?" Velma warned in a low tone as she searched the shelves for peaches.

"To love, honor and obey?" Midge answered slyly.

Velma frowned. She put her hands on her curvy hips and mustered her best glare. "You promised not to interfere with other people's love lives," she reminded her.

Midge arched one brow and leaned against a shelf. "Don't get *that* tone of voice with me, Miss Velma Pierce," she grumbled. They had all been up late socializing, and Midge was in no mood for a fight, let alone a picnic! All Midge was doing was helping out a buddy, and if Velma didn't see how truly made for each other Jackie and Cherry were, well—

"Exactly what tone is *that*?" Velma demanded to know, her green eyes ablaze with anger.

"That I'm-right-and-you-know-it tone!" Midge snapped back.

Velma stood on tiptoe, put her arms around Midge's neck and pulled her close. "Let's not fight, honey," she whispered as she planted little kisses on her girlfriend's neck. Midge moaned and snuggled close.

"You spend entirely too much time thinking about Cherry and Nancy and Jackie," Velma chided her, adding, with a smile, "when you could be thinking about me."

"I'm glad we're an old married couple," Midge smiled. She gave Velma a soft, slow kiss and ran her hands up and down her curvy figure.

Midge unzipped Velma's summer frock and caressed her smooth back. Velma blushed as Midge pulled down the top of her dress to reveal her soft shoulders and bountiful bosom. "What if someone comes in here?" Velma moaned as she let her frock slide to the floor, standing unclothed except for a nylon half slip and a cream-colored lacy bra.

Midge kicked the door shut. The latch clicked into place. She dropped to her knees, pushed up Velma's slip and began mouthing the soft flesh of Velma's inner thighs. "I think of you all the time, Velma," she sighed. "Some days it's all I can do to walk and talk in your presence," she laughed ruefully as she slowly pulled down Velma's panties. A minute later Velma forgot all about their angry exchange.

There was a timid knock at the door.

"Velma, Midge, are you in there? We're ready to leave." It was Cherry and she was sounding frankly frazzled.

"Woyhl ae hrfg ix a mutnim," Midge cried, her voice all muffled.

"What?" Cherry cried. "Midge, I can't understand a thing you're saying."

"We'll be out in a minute," Midge repeated. She waited for the sound of receding footsteps, but none came.

"Why don't you go ahead and we'll catch up," Velma suggested.

"But you don't know where we're going," Cherry was quick to point out.

"Leave us a map!" Midge moaned.

"Oh, if you only knew what was going on out here!" Cherry cried, sounding on the edge of hysteria. "George's jalopy won't start and Jackie says she's not riding in Nancy's car with just the three of us, so if you don't go, Jackie won't go, and I'm not sure I really want to be alone with Nancy, and if you don't go and Jackie doesn't go and I don't go, Nancy will have to go alone and she'll be awfully disappointed and besides, we've got a whole hamper of food that will spoil! I know you two are busy smooching in there but could you please come out *right now!*" she pleaded with all her might.

Midge groaned. "The next time I stick my nose in other people's romances will you please remind me of this moment?" she begged her girlfriend as she wiped her mouth on her sleeve and got to her feet.

Velma slipped into her panties. There was nothing she needed to say. This time, Midge had learned her lesson for sure!

CHAPTER 7

A Surefire Scheme

 Big rain drops splashed down on the girls as they motored ahead in Nancy's shiny craft, the *Swift Sleuth*, through the white-capped waters of Lake Merrimen toward the rocky spire jutting out of the middle of the deep lake. The small island was only twenty feet in diameter, but afforded visitors a clear panorama of the full splendor of the lake. Nancy was eager to show Cherry every bit of the lovely landscape, knowing how the girl adored nature and all its breathtaking views.

"Drat!" Nancy cried aloud. "I can't believe we've hit bad weather. Just an hour ago, the sky was clear and the clouds were big and white and puffy. Why, there wasn't a nimbostratus for miles!" They had missed their chance to boat in calm waters all because they couldn't agree on the seating arrangement in the car!

"How disappointing," Nancy wailed. "This day is not turning out at all the way I had planned!"

Cherry covered her hairdo with a portable rain bonnet, and Midge constructed a hasty umbrella for Velma from that day's newspaper. "Shouldn't we turn back?" Jackie wondered when she realized Cherry was beginning to shiver.

"We're almost there," Nancy insisted as she tied her chiffon scarf tighter around her hair, and put on some speed. She handed her binoculars to Cherry and said, "Take a look. Isn't it a charming little island?"

Cherry peered at the rocky mound. "Nancy, now that we're closer, I can see that those buoys surrounding Treasure Island are covered with signs," Cherry noticed. "*Keep Out By Order of Judge Meeks,*" she read. Just then, the boat was hit with a rush of cold air—a sure sign that a thunderstorm was not far off!

"We really should go back," Cherry urged. "Storms are the most dangerous of all weather phenomena, and a small boat in choppy water is no place for five girls in lightweight summer clothes!"

After a flash of lightning to the west, Nancy began counting. "One-thousand-and-one, one-thousand-and-two, one-thousand-and—" but before she could go any further, they heard a clap of thunder. "Light travels at about one hundred eighty-six thousand miles per second and sound at about one thousand one hundred feet per second," Nancy figured aloud. "So if I'm calculating correctly, this storm is less than a mile away!" She quickly turned the craft around and sped for shore.

Nancy kept the boat on an even keel and they made it to the dock just as mighty bolts of lightning began striking down on the lake.

"To the car," Cherry cried, knowing that the metal body would shield them from danger. They hopped inside Nancy's convertible and put up the top just as it began to rain in earnest.

"I can't believe this is happening," Nancy grumbled as she used her hankie to dry her new cotton navy dotted-swiss culottes, which showed off her blue eyes to their best advantage. In her white straw purse was her yellow polished cotton swimsuit with its built-in panty and bra, but it would see no wear today. "Another chance for romance ruined; another outfit mussed beyond repair!" she thought in distress.

Nancy had to blink fast to keep hot tears from spilling down her cheeks. Luckily she was wearing her new smart Caribbean-style sunglasses with dark green lenses that hid her teary eyes.

Nancy started the car and headed for home. That afternoon had been a disaster, romantically speaking, but the day wasn't over! She schemed as she steered the car over the damp streets, occasionally glancing in the rear view mirror, which gave her an excellent view of the back seat. Somehow, in their mad scramble to get to safety, Jackie and Cherry had ended up alone in the back seat! Nancy almost ran off the road when she saw Jackie lean over and whisper something in Cherry's ear.

"Oops!" Nancy cried as she hurriedly straightened the wheel. "I must have hit a wet patch," she explained. She gripped the wheel and made herself concentrate on the road ahead. "As soon as I get Cherry alone, I'll ask her to spend the evening with me. I just know if I can get her away from Jackie long enough, I can make her fall for me again!"

CHAPTER 8

A Romantic Rendezvous

"—then we'll be served the most delicious meal consisting of pioneer stew, soup, green salad with special dressing, home-made hot rolls and boysenberry jam, sherbet appetizer, green vegetable and coffee, baked or French fried potatoes," Nancy told Cherry excitedly. "And after supper, we'll gather round the camp fire and sing old pioneer songs with Bud and his guitar or sit in covered wagons and listen to tales of long ago as told by old-timers!" Nancy's eyes sparkled in excitement as she described the delightful evening ahead. She knew, too, exactly what she would wear—a bewitching new rayon crepe paisley print pouf skirt paired with an off-the-shoulder blouse and sophisticated flats. A velvet ribbon in her pert ponytail would complete the picture.

"It sounds like a magical evening," Cherry admitted, then added ruefully, "but I'm afraid I'm all booked up for tonight."

Nancy was stunned, but before she could say anything the doorbell rang. "Flowers for a Miss Cherry Aimless," the lad said as Nancy flung open the front door.

"I'm a Miss Cherry Aimless; they must be for me!" Cherry exclaimed. "Golly, no one's ever sent me flowers before," she cried as she raced to the door to accept the square white box. She was so excited she almost forgot to tip the delivery fellow!

Cherry put the box on the coffee table and, with shaky hands, opened the lid. Inside was one perfect white gardenia and a little card.

To the greatest girl ever. See you at seven. J.

"This is my first corsage!" Cherry cried aloud, but she was talking to herself for Nancy had fled the room. Cherry was too starry-eyed to notice. Why, when Jackie had asked her to accompany her out this evening, Cherry had assumed she would merely throw a sweater over her day frock and stroll to a nearby diner for a hamburger and a thick shake, perhaps to be followed by a picture show. Now she knew why Jackie had spent the supper hour tinkering with George's old jalopy—they were going on a car date!

Cherry took the delicate bloom from the box and held it to her bosom. "I'll need something nicer than this rumpled cotton dress to pin this lovely corsage to!" she realized. "And I'll have to bathe and fix my hair and polish my nails and find fresh stockings to don and—oh!" she cried when she checked her sturdy nurse's watch. "It's already after six!"

Cherry ran to the kitchen and put her corsage on the second shelf of the Frigidaire, next to a yummy-looking gelatin mold, then raced upstairs. "Velma will advise me, and maybe even let me borrow her sophisticated black chiffon siren sheath, too," Cherry hoped. If she was to be ready in time—and be the kind of girl deserving of that gardenia—she'd need an expert's help!

She took the stairs two at a time, raced down the hall and burst into Midge and Velma's room, forgetting in her haste that unannounced entrances into other's bedchambers can be startling affairs indeed! Midge was so surprised she flung herself off Velma and went crashing to the floor.

"You're not hurt, are you Midge?" Cherry asked.

"I'm fine," Midge gasped.

"Good," Cherry said. This was no time to have an accident! "Velma, I need your help, and quick! I'm going on a *real* date tonight, and I haven't a thing to wear that Jackie hasn't already seen me in! May I borrow your best frock?" she begged. "I promise I won't get anything on it!" Cherry plopped down on the bed, threw up her arms in alarm and confessed, "I don't know how to act or what to expect. I've never been alone with Jackie before—what if I can't think of anything to say? Oh, why didn't I listen when my mother gave me her fifty-three tips for successful dating?"

Velma smiled and smoothed her skirt down over her thighs. "I can help you in the outfit department and do something a little more dramatic with your hair if you like," she promised. "As for advice, mine is just to be yourself. Jackie is already crazy about you; anything you do will be the right thing." She turned to her mate lying on the floor. "Midge, do you have any dating tips for Cherry?"

Midge got up off the floor, smoothed her hair and took a cigarette from the pack on the night stand. "Always remember to lock the door," she grumbled.

CHAPTER 9

A Lovelorn Nurse

"The rain makes a pleasant sound on the convertible roof," Cherry thought as she stared out the car window at the festive lights of downtown Lake Merrimen. Ever since Jackie had opened the passenger door of George's jalopy and Cherry had hopped in, taking care not to let her snug sheath ride up over her thighs, she had been unable to think of even one clever, lighthearted comment to get the conversation rolling.

"Say *something*," Cherry scolded herself. She knew it was Jackie's duty to provide transportation and make recreational decisions, and hers to keep the conversation light and playful. Trouble was, every time she *did* think of something clever or amusing to say, one look at the big handsome girl sitting beside her and all thoughts flew out of her head.

"The...er...rain is...uh...nice," Cherry remarked shyly.

"Yes, it is," Jackie said.

Cherry dropped her gaze and became absorbed in admiring the gardenia on her bosom.

"It looks nice with your dress," Jackie said.

"What? Oh!" Cherry colored. "Yes. My dress. It's Velma's you know." She smoothed out the wrinkles in her lap. While the dress was indeed a sophisticated number, its plunging neckline worried Cherry. "I hope I don't catch a chest cold!" she murmured.

"What was that?" Jackie wondered.

Cherry jumped. "I—I—didn't say anything," she stammered.

"Oh, I thought you did," Jackie explained. She checked her rugged detective's watch. They had reservations at a fancy supper club somewhere on this block and Jackie was having trouble finding the place. If truth be told, she was having a hard time keeping her mind on anything at that moment—anything, that is, but the gorgeous girl in the clingy dress sitting on the edge of her seat.

Cherry clutched her small beaded bag, just big enough to hold hankie, lipstick, compact and emergency thermometer, to her breast. It was on loan from Velma, along with the impossibly high heels on her feet, the jangling bracelets over her black elbow-length gloves, glamorous make-up, luscious perfume, and even her black lacy push-up bra. Midge had been sad to see that item go out the door!

"Well, it looks nice on you," Jackie told her.

Cherry turned pink. Did Jackie mean her brassiere? Cherry peered down her dress and was relieved to see her undergarments were safely out of sight. Good thing, because droopy slip straps were a sure-fire recipe for fashion disaster!

"Your dress. It looks nice on you," Jackie repeated.

"I don't normally wear outfits this snug," Cherry admitted. "I'm much more accustomed to wearing a blousy uniform gathered at the waist with a simple belt, sensible, low-heeled rubber-soled shoes, my crisp cap and in the winter, my cunning midnight blue cape." The minute the words were out of her mouth she could have kicked herself. Some date she was turning out to be! She had broken the second of her mother's fifty-three rules for successful dating. "Never talk about yourself!"

"That dress certainly suits you," Jackie said as she pulled the car into a spot outside the gay-looking supper club. "But then again, I've never seen you in anything that didn't," she admitted as she cut the engine, slid her arm behind Cherry and flicked up the lock on the door.

A funny feeling stirred in Cherry as she breathed in deeply, reveling in Jackie's scent, a combination of soap and Aqua Velva. Cherry had never seen Jackie so handsome as she was tonight in her dapper dark lightweight wool suit with its boxy jacket that draped her strong frame beautifully, and its pleated, cuffed trousers pressed to perfection. "I could cut my finger on that sharp crease of her trousers," Cherry thought. She blushed when she realized she was staring at Jackie's thigh.

"Are you ready?" Jackie murmured softly. She gave Cherry's gloved hand a little squeeze. Cherry couldn't help but blush again as she felt Jackie's eyes sweep over her curvy figure, starting with her creamy white shoulders and working down to her womanly hips.

"Ready for what?" Cherry cried in alarm.

Jackie grinned. "Dinner," she said.

Although Cherry had doubted she could consume even one morsel while wearing that snug dress, twenty minutes later she had managed to drink two glasses of sparkling champagne and nibble on some scrumptious canapés. While Jackie ordered a delectable meal, Cherry looked with wide-eyed wonder around the Macambo Room, exclaiming over the soft sapphire blue walls, blue and white draperies and white marble dance floor. "This place is heaven!" she exclaimed as she watched happy couples glide across the room to the gay tunes of the Phil Bolero Orchestra. "And I love these white leather settees; they're so neighborly!" she cried as she boldly scooted closer to Jackie, who smiled and ordered another bottle of champagne.

"Oh, two's my limit!" Cherry protested when the bottle was brought to the table. "Well, maybe three," she giggled. She patted her ruby red lips with her napkin before taking a sip of her champagne to prevent an unaesthetic smudge on the fine glassware. She paused when she realized Jackie was staring at her every move.

"You're such a girl," Jackie admired her happily.

Cherry blushed. "I have my mother to thank for that," she acknowledged.

"I'll send her a thank-you note in the morning," Jackie grinned as she refilled their glasses. Cherry smiled. Not only was Jackie the handsomest girl she had ever seen, she was so mannerly! Cherry began to relax, and soon the girls were talking and laughing like old friends.

Their scrumptious supper was served, but neither girl had much of an appetite. Cherry forced herself to taste the yummy food, but found it difficult to swallow. Her mouth was dry, there were butterflies in her stomach, and her knees were shaking so badly it took all her concentration to walk to the ladies' lounge when she felt the urge to powder her nose. It was the most wonderful feeling in the world!

"I could stay here forever," Cherry sighed when she rejoined her date. As she slipped into the settee, she slid even closer. Before she knew it, Jackie had put her arm around her, and Cherry let it stay there.

"Let's come here every night," Cherry said in a gay tone, knowing all too well that their days together might be numbered. Would Jackie run out of vacation time before Cherry made up her mind?

"I'll reserve this very table," Jackie played along.

"And we'll have champagne with every meal," Cherry cried as she downed her drink. It was her fifth glass of champagne, but she didn't care. For tonight, she was more than simply level-headed Cherry Aimless, Registered Nurse. She was Cherry Aimless, Registered Nurse, headed for love!

———— CHAPTER 10 ————

Girl Trouble!

"Ninety-eight, ninety-nine, one hundred." Nancy had brushed her trademark titian mane until it shone, but it did no good. She threw the silver-backed brush across her dressing table, knocking over some expensive perfume in the process, but Nancy didn't care. The only thing she did care about—an attractive dark-haired nurse with a bubbly nature and a ready smile—had been gone now for five hours, and might never be coming back!

"I musn't dwell on those two," Nancy told herself as she slipped into her luscious pale pink shantung silk pajamas and tied a pert bow around her hair. "It's already midnight, and I've simply got to get some sleep so I will look my best tomorrow." She knew she'd have to act fast to regain the advantage in the contest for Cherry's hand.

"But what shall I do, Gogo?" she asked the little terrier who was curled up in her usual place. Nancy felt a stab of pity as she remembered the terrified expressions on the faces of the kidnapped poodles when they popped out of the trunk. "I should really call Chief O'Malley at the Lake Merrimen Police Department and offer my services, seeing as how I'm so good at solving cases like these," Nancy thought guiltily. "But going off on a case will mean leaving Cherry and Jackie alone, and I can't afford to do that!" she quickly reminded herself.

Nancy sighed as she threw back her snowy white chenille bedspread, slipped under the covers and turned off the small bedside lamp. Midge and Velma had gone to bed the second supper was over, so Nancy had spent the evening helping Hannah sew side darts in some new cotton blouses. As the hours dragged by, Nancy knew Cherry and Jackie's dinner date must have turned into something more!

Tortured by the thought of those two together, she tossed

and turned, finally falling into a uneasy sleep. She awoke to the unmistakable sound of George's old jalopy pulling into the drive. Nancy slipped out of bed and raced over to the window. Golly, Jackie and Cherry had finally returned!

She watched with bated breath as Jackie helped Cherry from the car and escorted her to the front porch. She could hear hushed giggles as the two girls crept in the house. Nancy waited for the sound of footsteps on the landing, and when none came she threw on her quilted housecoat and fuzzy slippers and snuck down the stairs. "Where could they be?" she wondered as she peeked over the banister into the empty living room. She pulled her robe tight and crept into the kitchen.

The squeak of the porch swing and more laugher reached her ears. Nancy checked the kitchen clock and was surprised to find it was three in the morning! "Why, it's positively *indecent* to stay up this late," she thought as she blinked back tears. She crept closer to the back door, taking care to keep in the shadows. Although she couldn't make out what they were saying, the way Cherry was sitting, practically in Jackie's lap with her face turned up in rapt adoration, told Nancy that she'd better do something fast!

Nancy raced to the study and shut the door, then picked up the telephone and spoke urgently into the receiver. "Operator, please connect me with the Hardly estate in nearby Feyport—and fast!"

Her chums Joe and Frank Hardly had just returned from their European vacation. "I was going to give them a few days to shake the wrinkles from their travel clothes and get their land legs back, but this is a genuine emergency!" Nancy thought.

She tapped her fingers nervously on the mahogany desk while she waited for her connection to be put through. "I'll ask Frank and Joe to luncheon tomorrow to meet the gang," she schemed. "I'll serve Joe's favorite cheese-and-egg pie and wilted leaf lettuce salad, then I'll ask Frank to step outside to the garden, and once there, ask him what to do about this romantic dilemma. I'll wear my new sunflower yellow pique sunsheath—Frank's sure to appreciate the careful detailing, especially the embroidered collar—"

"Hello?" a sleepy lad's voice queried at the other end of the line. Nancy took a deep breath and tried to steady her voice, but once she heard the masculine tone of her close chum Frank, her words came tumbling out all willy-nilly. "Oh, Frank," she sobbed. "I need your help. I've got trouble—*girl trouble*—of the most terrible kind!"

——— CHAPTER 11 ———

The Mystery of Love

"Get the paper, Gogo," Midge commanded cheerfully. The perky terrier, who had taken up her post at Midge's feet, hoping to catch a stray toast crumb, raced out the dog door and returned seconds later with *The River Depths Defender* in her mouth and laid it at Midge's slipper-clad feet. "See how much she's learned since we've been here?" Midge grinned at Jackie as she unfurled the paper and glanced at the front page. "Next I'm teaching her how to make the beds," she joked, but her expression turned serious when she saw the news item at the bottom of the page. "Someone tried to snatch a teacup poodle from an elderly woman in nearby Battle Creek," she gasped.

But Jackie was too busy moping to notice. Too busy, really, thinking about Cherry and last night.

Midge tried to push the distressing news out of her mind. She put down the paper and got her chum a hot cup of coffee.

"Ugh!" Jackie cried after she took a gulp of the strong brew.

"Good, huh?" Midge asked as she poured herself another cup and popped a piece of bread in the toaster.

"Like rocket fuel," Jackie grimaced. "Where's Velma?" she wondered. "She makes great coffee."

"Out with Cherry," Midge told her. "Cherry was desperate for some girl talk so they went downtown to window shop," Midge paused and added dramatically, "The big news is that the latest fall fashions are in!"

"Goodness," Jackie replied. "And you didn't wake me? I simply *must* order my fall tee-shirts!" she grinned. Then she groaned. She wasn't in the mood to clown around this morning, not after two bottles of champagne and three hours' sleep—alone! "Did Cherry mention what she needed to talk about so urgently?" Jackie pumped her chum.

Midge shook her head. "I don't know anything that goes

on around here," she admitted. "But I do know someone stayed up pretty late last night," she teased, adding hastily, "not that I was eavesdropping or anything. It's just that when I got up in the middle of the night to get Velma a glass of water I heard voices coming from the porch. Frankly, it sounded like an astronomy lecture out there—" Midge stopped kidding when she saw the glum expression on her friend's face. "Didn't the date go well?" Midge asked.

"It was the best time I've ever had!" Jackie exclaimed, adding, "That is, until we got home. I don't know what happened! We dined and danced and talked for hours—long enough to make me certain that Cherry's the girl for me! When I brought her back here, we sat on the swing for an eternity, but each time I got up the nerve to kiss her, she'd start pointing out constellations," Jackie lamented, adding, "Although last night wasn't a total waste. I *did* learn everything a girl could ever want to know about the Big Dipper."

She put her head in her hands and groaned. "Now I want her more than ever," Jackie admitted. She was beginning to think she would never get to Cherry, at least not while they were under Nancy's roof.

"You mean you two were together practically the whole night and you still haven't even *kissed* her?" Midge cried in alarm.

Jackie nodded gloomily. "Pathetic, isn't it? How long were you alone with Velma before—you know—"

"Ten minutes," Midge grinned.

Jackie's jaw dropped open. "You kissed Velma after just ten minutes?" she cried.

"She kissed me," Midge set the record straight.

"And you let her?" Jackie gasped.

Midge coolly lit a cigarette. Then a big grin lit up her face. "I could tell the minute I met Velma that she wasn't just any girl. As far as I was concerned, she could do whatever she wanted."

"Cherry's not just any girl, either," Jackie cried. "Why, you could safely say, when it comes to Cherry, there's no one else like her!"

CHAPTER 12

A Torrid Tale

That very moment at the Hardly estate, a distraught girl clad in fetching but rumpled pajamas was echoing those very same words. "There's no one like Cherry, I tell you! She's the girl for me! And I've lost her—forever!" Nancy's torrent of tears spilled into her cup of cocoa.

Frank Hardly, a fair-haired fellow with a thoughtful demeanor and a lean yet muscular build, shot his younger-by-one-year brother Joe, a handsome fellow with basset-hound brown eyes and a friendly face that was now etched with concern for his fretful friend, a worried look. "Get more handkerchiefs," he mouthed. Joe raced to the little laundry room off the kitchen, and was relieved to find a stack of clean, starched hankies on the ironing table. Quick as a wink, he snatched some up and raced back to the kitchen just as Nancy was threatening to use the sleeve of her shantung silk pajamas to mop her face.

"Good thing!" Frank whistled in relief. Shantung silk was almost impossible to get clean—lipstick especially stained it so!

"Now take a deep breath and start from the beginning," he urged. He had never seen his friend in such distress! When Frank had opened the door in the middle of the night to his pajama-clad chum, Nancy had gasped out an astonishing story about having murdered her father, traveled to faraway San Francisco and brought home "the nicest nurse you'll ever want to meet" before flinging off her trenchcoat, collapsing in a heap on the davenport and falling into a fretful sleep. Now it was early morning and the boys were sitting in the sunny, modern Hardly kitchen, wearing lightweight plaid cotton robes thrown over striped pajamas and consuming fresh biscuits and warm beverages while trying to make sense of the dramatic events that had befallen Nancy while they were abroad.

"It all started one day last month when I shot Father to death in the kitchen," Nancy began.

Joe gasped in alarm and dropped his buttered biscuit, which tumbled under the table. He dove to get it, bumping his head in the process. He grimaced and rubbed the sore spot. "You shot your father?" he yelped. "Golly!"

Frank gave his younger brother a glare which cautioned him against further exciting their already perturbed chum.

Nancy told them of the horrific circumstances that had compelled her to take up arms against her father, sparing no details. "When I was a child—he forced me to do things—in my bedroom—late at night," she explained in a whisper.

"And when I finally told Hannah of his terrible misdeeds, she threatened to hand Father over to the proper authorities. That's when he attacked her! So I ran to the den, picked up his rifle, raced back to the kitchen and shot him."

"Oh," Joe gulped. He reached for a fresh hankie. "That's the sweetest thing I've ever heard. You and Hannah were trying to protect each other!"

Nancy nodded and wiped a tear from her eye. "It was at Hannah's insistence that I threw some outfits in a bag and fled to San Francisco, leaving her behind to confess to the murder. I tried to start a new life—oh, I met some new chums and fell in love and we saved a convent of kidnapped nuns from the clutches of an evil priest—" She took a big breath, and continued, "—but try as I might, I couldn't forget about Hannah languishing in her jail cell, so my friends and I came back here and I confessed to the killing. Lucky for me, when I revealed in court the heretofore unknown diabolical aspects of Father's personality, I was exonerated of all charges in his death."

"Phew!" Joe gasped in relief.

"But not before we accidentally ran over Police Chief Chumley, who turned out not to be my friend *at all!* Why, he not only stole my letters proving Father's true nature, he tried to frame Hannah with false evidence!"

"Golly!" Joe cried.

"What a horrible shock it must be when someone you admire and trust turns out to a be totally different person," Frank cried.

"People aren't always what you think," Nancy sighed. "I have to admit, it's been a rather frightful month. But now everything's back to normal. Hannah's out of jail, I've inherited the Clue estate and have had a chance to start selecting my fall wardrobe before the season begins. But there's still one thing—" she struggled to continue as tears welled up in her eyes.

"I've lost my one and only true love," she sobbed, "which has *never* happened to *me* before!"

Joe sniffed loudly. Could things get any worse for their plucky pal?

"You mean that nice nurse you mentioned last night, don't you?" Frank said softly.

"Yes," Nancy sobbed. "Nurse Cherry Aimless, the sweetest, kindest, prettiest girl in uniform I've ever met. And she was all mine, until I made a series of stupid blunders that broke her heart.

"But I was under an awful strain, what with the murder trial and being in jail and all that," she added quickly. "If I could have just one more chance with her, I know I could prove I can be the best girlfriend ever—" she broke into heartfelt sobs. With trembling hands, she reached inside her pocketbook and took out a packet of thin, yellowed envelopes. She drew a letter from one of them and recited:

> *To see her is to love her,*
> *And Love but her for ever—*

"My deceased mother, Rebecca Clue, sent these lines to her lover Helen right before Mother's tragic death in a fiery car crash twenty-two years ago," she tearfully explained. "When I found these letters I knew that this was the kind of love I wanted to have with Cherry. But just like Mother, I've lost my chance for happiness."

Joe blew his nose in his hankie. Stories of tragic love, whether in real life or in the movies, always made him weep!

"Go to her and tell her all this," Frank urged wisely. "If she's a nurse, she must possess a sensible nature. Surely she'll forgive you, and in time, see that you've mended your ways." Frank was a practical fellow whose sound suggestions had averted many a catastrophe.

"I can't seem to get her alone long enough to tell her," Nancy sniffed. "The other day at the Dog Show when I was tracking some kidnapped poodles I could tell she was watching me in admiration, like the old days—"

"Well, then—" Frank started.

"There's more," Nancy cried abruptly. "I was such a fickle girlfriend, I practically pushed Cherry into the arms of a handsome police detective from San Francisco who's been staying at my house. They went on a dress-up date last night, and when I left the house at three, they were sitting on the back porch taking in the stars!"

"You must ask this girl to leave immediately," Frank urged.

"I can't," Nancy cried. "She helped secure my release from prison. Besides, I don't blame her for falling for Cherry—any girl in her right mind would! She's so, oh, I don't know. She's just so Cherry!"

Frank and Joe exchanged sad looks. Had Nancy finally fallen truly in love only to find herself jilted?

"Oh my," Frank fluttered, "dear me." He and his brother were clearly out of their realm of expertise. Girls' love lives always seemed so very complicated, especially to two fresh-faced lads whose devotion to their family—not to mention their exciting careers as famous detectives known far and wide for their keen sleuthing abilities—left them little time for romance!

Joe fetched Nancy another cup of cocoa and an apple turnover, fresh from the oven.

"I'm in quite a jam! What ever am I going to do?" Nancy exclaimed, after first taking a bite of the flaky fruit pastry. An interval of tense silence followed as the boys pondered their chum's predicament.

"I saw a movie once with a love triangle between Rock Hudson, Doris Day and this other fellow, and the way they solved it—"

"Joe—" Frank groaned, warning that this was no time for movie memories. This was real life and they had a real-life problem to solve!

"Well, do you have a better suggestion?" Joe asked, pursing his lips.

Frank's tanned, clean-cut face bore a thoughtful expression. In times of trouble, he always turned to his parents, Mr. and Mrs. Fennel P. Hardly, for their sage advice, but they would be out until late that evening, and by the sound of it, Nancy needed to make her move soon! Suddenly Frank uttered a low exclamation. "I've got it," he cried. "We'll call Uncle Nelly! He knows practically all there is to know about love stuff," he reassured Nancy.

Joe gave a whoop of delight. "Better yet, let's just go see him!" He was eager to show his favorite uncle all the keen fashions they had picked up in Paris, especially his new snug slim-legged slacks.

"You mean your uncle, Nelson P. Hardly, the world-renowned antiques dealer currently residing in New York City?" Nancy queried. "Why, I can't possibly travel to New York dressed like this!" she cried as she looked ruefully at her rumpled lounging outfit. Nancy pushed her tangled titian hair out of her face and wiped the tears from her eyes. "I'll simply have to run home and slip into a suitable travel costume— perhaps my new City Black rayon crepe frock," she mused. "It's awfully sophisticated but not too fussy; just the ticket for a humid afternoon in the city."

"Although I agree that your new frock sounds divine for a hot city day, especially if paired with those cute black and tan broadcloth silky sheen pumps of yours, there's no need," Frank enthused, "as Uncle Nelly and his chum Willy are spending the summer at our family cottage on nearby Lake Merrimen."

"Besides," Joe spoke up. "We could go through Mother's closet and find a simple summer frock suitable for a trip to the lake. Mother's a tad taller, but seeing as this is an emergency, I don't think anyone will hold an unfashionable skirt length against you."

"Where are your parents?" Nancy wondered.

"On our return, we found this note," Frank told her.

Welcome home, boys! Mrs. Hardly and I have gone fishing. I've got a feeling we'll be bringing home quite a catch! There's a tuna-noodle casserole in the fridge. Will return late Monday.

Love, Father

When Nancy wrinkled her pretty nose, Frank chuckled. "Don't worry," he said. "That's just Father's way of telling us he's off on a new case."

"I hope he's working on a mystery that will require our help," Joe cried with all the boyish eagerness of an excitable lad. He was always ready to tackle something new!

Fennel P. Hardly, one of the best detectives the world has ever known, was frequently called away at the drop of a hat to chase a cunning criminal or track a vital clue. Mrs. Hardly, a soft-spoken woman whose serene temperament was the perfect counterpart to her husband's more spirited nature, often accompanied Mr. Hardly on these adventures. The devoted couple was inseparable, and despite their long union, often acted like newlyweds.

"Calm down, Joe," Frank teased. "We've already got *The Case of the Ruined Romance* to solve!"

Ten minutes later, the three chums, freshly bathed, combed and attired in sporty summer clothes, were headed toward the city of Lake Merrimen, twenty miles west of Feyport. Little did the three chums realize the queer adventure that lay ahead!

───── CHAPTER 13 ─────

A Knotty Affair

"Turn left at Old Main Road, then drive seven miles until you see an old green cabana; turn there and go down the dirt road about a half-mile," Joe had directed Nancy in case she lost sight of their jalopy. Nancy, an expert driver, easily kept up with Joe's speed, and soon both cars were at the turnoff for Lake Merrimen.

"Boy, is Uncle going to be pleased to see us," Joe grinned as they got closer to the charming cottage.

"And these turnovers, too," Frank inhaled deeply. In his lap was a basket of warm apple pastries. "The food in Europe was delicious," he admitted, "but there's nothing like these famous Hardly apple turnovers to satisfy a hearty fellow's appetite!"

Soon they were in front of the small but sweet cottage that had been in the Hardly family for generations, but had fallen into disrepair as the lads grew older and became involved in interests of their own. Uncle Nelly, the artistic one in the family, had spent the summer redecorating the once-shabby getaway. The now-attractive home housed a good portion of his collection of fine furnishings.

"It has all the charm of an old English cottage," Nancy exclaimed as she parked the car under a gnarled dogwood tree and hopped out. The wide, low-slung house, set on a hill directly overlooking lovely Lake Merrimen, had been painted a brilliant white, and the ample wood-slated porch that ringed the domicile bore a fresh coat of forest green paint. White wicker chairs sporting comfy-looking chintz pillows were scattered about the porch. A small calico cat lay sleeping on a pillow, and cheerful chickadees chirped overhead.

"Uncle Nelly," Joe sang out. "Rise and shine. Your two favorite nephews are here!"

"Hush, Joe," a cautious Frank warned. "They might be sleeping. See—the chintz curtains are still drawn."

"Bosh," swore Joe. "On a beautiful summer morning like this?" He bounded onto the porch, eager to see his uncle after six weeks abroad. He peeked through the picture window past a part in the curtain and spied his uncle lying flat on his back on a blue velvet-covered Queen Anne daybed. "That must be new," Joe mused, not recalling having seen the attractive antique in his uncle's New York showroom. Joe was just about to tap on the window when suddenly he had a shocking realization. Uncle Nelly wasn't lounging on the daybed—he was *tied* to it with a silk cord that left him unable to move an inch! Furthermore, a red kerchief used as a gag prevented him from calling out for help!

Joe threw up his hands in alarm. "Frank! Uncle Nelly's been robbed!"

Frank leapt to the window and peered inside. After witnessing the shocking scene for himself, he manfully burst through the door and raced inside to free Uncle Nelly, who was fully conscious and terribly excited. Frank yanked the kerchief from his uncle's mouth.

"Boys, what are you doing here? And Nancy, too?" Uncle Nelly blurted out as Frank untied his bonds. Uncle Nelly quickly snatched his crimson silk lounging robe from the foot of the daybed and slipped it over his white silk summer pajamas. On his feet were slippers of the softest leather. "Your visit is most unexpected," Uncle Nelly cried. His face was peculiarly flushed. "You so rarely drop in unannounced!"

"Lucky for you we did!" Joe retorted, looking his favorite uncle up and down for injuries. Their handsome, youthful uncle seemed none the worse for wear.

"What happened?" Nancy cried out.

"Uncle, were you robbed?" Frank added excitedly. Then he dropped his voice. Perhaps the hoodlum who had tied up Uncle Nelly was still here! He raced to the staircase with a determined look in his eyes, "If anyone's up there," he shouted sternly, "come out now!" He clenched his fists, ready to give the man a good thrashing!

Uncle Nelly chuckled and rubbed his wrists. "There's nothing to get excited about, kids," he declared. "My chum and I were just playing a game." He went to the stairs. "Dear, we've got company," he called in a sheepish, sing-song voice.

A few moments later, a handsome, virile-looking man wearing a casual slacks outfit and a resigned grin came downstairs. It was Uncle Nelly's favorite chum Willy! "So you want to thrash me, do you?" the man chuckled as he playfully gave Frank a punch to the chest. Frank grinned and gave Uncle Nelly's chum a hearty handshake.

Joe felt a surge of relief flood his body as he spied the muscular fellow, clad in snug black trousers and a striped tee-shirt stretched to the breaking over round, swelling muscles.

"We weren't expecting you today," Willy admitted as he threw an arm around the younger Hardly lad and gave him a manly squeeze. "But it sure is good to see you boys! And this must be the famous Nancy Clue," he said as he let go of Joe and gave Nancy a sturdy handshake.

"It's wonderful to see you, too!" Joe blurted out as he suddenly plopped down on the love seat, grabbed a petit point pillow and pulled it onto his lap. A look of intense concentration crossed Joe's face. "You've done wonders with this place while we were gone," he exclaimed, staring with keen interest at a still-life of fruit hanging on the opposite wall.

"It's like something out of a fairy tale," Nancy agreed.

"It's been the gayest summer ever," Uncle Nelly told them. "So many people have dropped by to look at our goodies, especially since someone started the rumor that this place is haunted!"

"Haunted!" Joe and Frank hooted with laughter. How could anyone think their family hideaway was haunted?

"It's been the best thing for business yet! We've been overrun with moneyed matrons eager to get a look at a haunted house, and once inside they always buy," Willy crowed.

Joe had to smile as he remembered other wild rumors that had spread through the little vacation spot. "Remember the story old Miss Witherspoon used to tell about the secret underground caverns of bygone days?" he chuckled.

"Poor Miss Witherspoon," Frank shook his head. The colorful town oldster had spent her last days at nearby River Depths Sanitarium after her wild tales of an underground city began scaring away tourists.

"Anyone for a famous Hardly apple turnover?" Nancy asked gaily as she handed Uncle Nelly the wicker basket of fresh pastries Frank had dropped. Despite her own troubles she had no wish to put a damper on this touching reunion.

"Let's have breakfast," Willy announced, shepherding the gang into his pleasant kitchen. Nancy relaxed for the first time in days as she watched Willy bustle about the cozy room, painted in soothing peach tones and decorated with starched white tie-back flounced curtains. Above the sink was a saucy shelf edged with ruffled gingham and holding a collection of dainty porcelain egg cups. She sipped her coffee as Willy tied an apron over his slacks outfit, took a bowl of farm fresh eggs from the Frigidaire and expertly cracked a dozen into a cast-iron skillet, next to a pan cradling a sizzling slab of bacon.

A few minutes later he plopped a plate of just-right eggs, yummy-smelling bacon and crunchy toast in front of her. "You'll feel better once you've had a bite to eat," he smiled. Nancy blinked back tears. He had seen right through her brave charade!

"Now what brings you three here so early?" Uncle Nelly wondered as he unfolded a linen napkin in his lap and took a sip of coffee.

"I've got a problem," Nancy admitted.

Uncle Nelly nodded. "I could see that right away. Get my sewing kit, Will," he cried. "I'll have that frock of yours fitted in no time," he promised Nancy.

Nancy cringed.

"It's not *that*, Uncle," Joe blurted out. "Nancy's lost the love of her life and is desperate to get her back!"

"You poor sweet child," Uncle Nelly murmured. "Tell me what's wrong."

Frank and Joe exchanged happy grins. Uncle Nelly would know exactly what to do to mend Nancy's shattered romance!

Willy got her a fresh cup of coffee and urged her to tell all. Nancy repeated her sad story, ending disconsolately, "It's no use! I'll never get her back. Never!"

"Don't say that," Uncle Nelly begged. "Surely there's a way to win back this nurse."

"I'm afraid not," Nancy said sadly. "I've probably already lost her to Jackie. And we were so perfect together," she sighed. "Why, with all the scrapes I get into, a nurse at home would be mighty handy. Plus, we have the same taste in frocks, and—" She blushed hotly, "—there's the way she makes me feel all warm and curvy inside."

Frank and Joe exchanged puzzled glances. Whatever did Nancy mean? "It must be something that happens to girls, like that *other* thing," a wide-eyed Joe whispered. Frank nodded.

"We'll put our heads together and come up with a plan!" Uncle Nelly and Willy chorused. But a whole pot of coffee later, they were no closer to a solution. Joe found his mind wandering to the luscious-looking strawberry chiffon pie on the sideboard. Willy grinned, got up and cut generous slices for all. "Uncle Nelly always said you were a good cook, but this pie really takes the cake," Joe crowed in appreciation.

"As my dear mother always said, 'The way to a man's heart is through his stomach,' " Willy joked, adding, "Why, when we were first courting, I used to—" He abruptly stopped as he was seized with a sudden inspiration. "Do you remember that terrible fight we had right before our first-year anniversary, Nelson?" Willy asked his chum.

Uncle Nelly nodded. How could he forget the worst day of his life?

"Your uncle and I had a terrible row over some silly little thing," Willy explained. "We didn't speak for one whole day, and I was frantic with worry that our romance had ended. Know what I did?"

"What, Willy?" the boys cried eagerly. Golly, they loved hearing stories about when their favorite uncle was a lad.

"I marched downtown and got a stylish haircut, selected a nice new suit, gave my shoes a lick and a promise and strolled up and down in front of Nelson's shop with a sailor chum of mine, pretending to be engrossed in the lad's conversation. Of course my heart was beating a mile a minute with eager anticipation. And I don't remember a word my young friend said, for I was too busy sneaking looks inside the shop to see if Nelson noticed I was out with someone new."

Uncle Nelly laughed as he remembered that long-ago day. "And I was busy peeking at them from between the slats of a lovely Queen Anne headboard, heartsick that I may have lost my Willy forever!"

"What happened next?" the boys gasped excitedly.

"Why, I raced out and begged Willy's forgiveness, and when he admitted it was all a set-up, I was so relieved that I instantly forgot what it was we had quarreled about," Uncle Nelly cried. "And the rest is history!"

"Since then we've only quarreled over the little domestic matters all couples bicker over," he added.

"And then rarely, if ever," Willy interjected. "For we've learned that a couple must compromise in order to sail the seas of happy matrimony. For example," he explained earnestly, "Nelson wanted to make the front rooms into a showcase for his fine collection of Queen Anne furniture, but I'm more of a Rococo Revival man myself. So we compromised and used pieces from both collections."

"I *thought* the daybed Uncle Nelly was tied to was a Queen Anne," Joe hooted triumphantly. *The Case of the Neoclassic Nightstand* had trained Joe's already-sharp eye for the widely-flared Spanish feet typical of that period.

"I appreciate the suggestion, but if Cherry finds me with another girl it will only convince her I've fallen back on my old ways," Nancy lamented. "That will toll the death knell to our romance for sure! I'm afraid it's no use, fellows. I've lost her for good." Nancy buried her head in her hands and let out a girlish wail. "This has never happened to me before! Whatever shall I do?" she cried.

"You could become a nun," Joe said helpfully. "Girls with broken hearts are always finding solace in convents." Joe stopped talking when he realized his brother was staring at him in the queerest manner. "Well, it happens in the movies all the time," he explained.

Frank had to chuckle. His brother Joe was the dreamer of the two; always whiling away his Saturday afternoons at the cinema. He liked musical romances best of all!

"I don't think I could join a convent," Nancy admitted, "as it means wearing the same outfit day after day."

She sighed. "For a minute there at the Dog Show, I thought Cherry might had fallen for me all over again."

"You mean you were there when the poodles were kidnapped?" Uncle Nelly shivered.

"I helped rescue them," Nancy admitted. "During the search I could tell Cherry was drawn to me again, as I was behaving like the sober, sane, sensible Nancy Clue she had loved from afar."

"That's it!" Willy cried. He looked at the three young chums. "Who is Cherry, really?" he quizzed them.

The three sleuths looked puzzled.

"A nurse?" Joe guessed tentatively.

"A nice nurse," Frank corrected him.

"The nicest nurse you'll ever meet?" Nancy offered.

"No," Willy crowed. "She's Nancy's number one fan!"

"She *was* until she got a good look at the *real* Nancy Clue," Nancy corrected him. "It's hopeless," she sighed dejectedly.

Willy took her tear-stained face in his large rough hands and gave her a good, hard look. "That's not the Nancy Clue I know so well, from magazine articles, newspaper accounts and word on the street. Nancy, we all make mistakes. You've got to forget about your past and move ahead."

"Gaily forward!" Uncle Nelly shouted.

"Batten down the hatches!" Frank urged.

"Man the torpedoes!" Joe cried in delight.

Nancy smiled tentatively. "Do you *really* think I could rekindle Cherry's infatuation with Nancy Clue, the detective, and eventually make her fall in love with Nancy Clue, the girl?"

"Absolutely!" the fellows cried.

"Oh, it's a grand idea," Uncle Nelly hooted. "A much better idea, Nancy, than buying a new frock, restyling your hair and making Cherry jealous. Although," he mused, "the new short, soft waves they're showing in the city would be fetching on you."

For the first time since she had arrived at the merry little cottage, Nancy looked truly hopeful. She took her compact from her purse, powdered her pert, but shiny nose and ran a quick comb through her tangled titian hair. "I must find a mystery to solve—and fast," she declared as she leapt up from the table and headed for the door. She threw her trenchcoat over her ill-fitting frock. "Quick!" she cried impatiently. "Can anyone point me toward the nearest haunted house? Do you know of anyone with any missing heirloom jewelry? How about a stolen clock?"

"But Nancy, you already have a mystery to solve," Willy pointed out. "According to news reports, the six missing poodles may have been found safe and sound and reunited with their tearful owners, but the fiend who snatched them is still at-large. You must bring this man to justice!"

"That's it!" Nancy cried. "I've been too befuddled to realize I had the answer right in front of me all along! Oh, thank you Willy! Thank you, Uncle Nelly!"

"Go home, take a bath, put your hair up, slip into your nicest lightweight summer sleuthing outfit, and find that poodlenapper," Uncle Nelly instructed. "I guarantee that before you know it, you'll have that man behind bars and have become the apple of Cherry's eye!"

Nancy pulled her detective's notebook from her purse, but before she could begin listing possible clues, she scrunched up her face in frustration. "Oh, no, I just remembered we're having a birthday party this afternoon for Hannah. I can't start on a case now!"

Uncle Nelly refused to give up. "Then have your little party. Willy and I will stop by later and announce that another poodle has been kidnapped. That way, the mystery will start on a dramatic note."

Nancy quickly agreed to the scheme. She hopped in her car and raced home to change into her prettiest party outfit. "Jackie may be a big handsome girl with a warm smile and a magnificent physique, but I'll bet I can show her a thing or two when it comes to detective work!" Nancy smiled confidently as she drove off.

CHAPTER 14

Captured!

Uncle Nelly's eyes twinkled with delight, "So halfway through the festivities, Willy and I will arrive and announce that a standard black poodle was just snatched from the corner of Main and Vine. Nancy will jump on the case, and eventually reclaim her rightful place as River Depth's greatest sleuth—"

"—and Cherry's favorite date," Willy excitedly cut in.

"What if Jackie realizes Willy and Uncle Nelly are lying?" Joe then asked worriedly. "Jackie's the law, and if she discovers they've reported a false crime, Nancy will look bad and lose Cherry for sure. Plus, we could get into big trouble." Stalwart Joe Hardly wasn't so concerned about putting himself in danger, but he was worried about the Hardly boys losing their reputation as straight-shooters.

"We've got to try," the others chorused.

Frank checked his radium glow-in-the-dark wristwatch, and gasped when he saw the time. "We've less than two hours until the party starts, and we've still got to bathe and change into festive outfits." Luckily the boys had had the foresight to throw a suitcase with their new sharply-tailored, wrinkle-free French slacks and short-sleeved Dynel shirts in cool summery colors in the trunk of their jalopy.

"There are clean fluffy towels and a finely honed razor in the washroom when you're ready," Willy told the boys as they raced to their car to get their luggage.

"Why don't we gather some flowers for Hannah while we're outside?" Frank suggested to his brother. Joe eagerly agreed.

"How exciting to be in the middle of an adventure!" Uncle Nelly was all atitter as he helped Willy clear the table and rinse the good china. Then a worrisome look crossed his face. "Whatever will we wear?" he cried.

Uncle Nelly went to the bedroom to select just the right

outfits for their roles as dognapping witnesses and party guests while Willy hopped in the tub. But before Nelly could decide between light, carefree summer suits or more somber blue slacks outfits, there came a knock at the door. He went downstairs and opened the door to two rather gruff-looking strangers; one a tall, thin man wearing a dark-colored trenchcoat and the other a burly fellow clad in an ill-fitting shiny black sharkskin suit.

"I'm sorry gentlemen, you'll have to come back tomorrow," Uncle Nelly demurred. But the men insisted that they were anxious to purchase antiques, so Uncle Nelly, never one to lose a sale, let them in.

"Who is it?" Willy called from upstairs.

"We've got customers," Uncle Nelly answered. "My partner is in the tub," Uncle Nelly grinned, "so I'll be your hostess today. Now what can I show you gentlemen? A lovely Queen Anne settee with scrolled legs and shell-carved knees? An elegant nineteenth-century Turkish frame chair upholstered in a luscious shade of cerise?" But all he drew were blank stares. Why, it was as if the men had no idea what he was talking about! Uncle Nelly concluded that he had two novices on his hands. "Is there anything in particular you're looking for?" he asked.

"Yeah, something really old," the burly man quickly replied. "Maybe something that's been stuck away in a closet. Got any closets here?" he asked as he looked around the lovely living room.

"Only the shallowest clothes closet," Uncle Nelly admitted ruefully. "And let me tell you, it's been quite vexing not to have sufficient storage. All our summer outfits are stuffed into a Japanese-inspired wardrobe with inlay flowers of yellow that once belonged to the actress Lillian Russell. But that's not for sale," he added hastily. "My nephew Joe simply adores it and I've promised not to let it leave the family. Now if it's a bureau you're after, we've got an excellent example of Early American craftmanship in our shop in New York City. I could have it shipped here."

"We'll need something today," the man insisted.

"We're getting ready to go to a party," Uncle Nelly confided. "I'm afraid it's not a good time to browse."

"Say, how long will you be gone?" the thin man in the

trenchcoat piped up. "Maybe we'll just come back after your party."

Just then Willy came downstairs with a yellow terry cloth robe wrapped around his strong frame and a rubber shower cap on his head. He had overheard Nelly's exchange with his two rather stubborn customers.

"My friend asked you to leave," Willy said sternly. "You can come back tomorrow."

"We'll get what we've come for *now*," the tall thin man jeered at Willy.

Willy grew red-faced with anger. "You get your nasty old selves out of our house," he ordered. "We haven't time, besides which, you are tracking mud all over my good rug. Now get out!"

The burly man in the ill-fitting suit shot Willy a sinister stare, reached in his pocket and took out a gun. He pointed the death-dealing .45 caliber pistol right at Willy!

"Hold it right there, buddy," he sneered. "One more move and it will be your last!"

Within minutes, the two thugs had tied Uncle Nelly and Willy back-to-back on two cane-bottom straightback chairs, and had used kerchiefs to gag the shaken chums. Willy fumed under his warm rubber shower cap and tried to struggle free, but it was no use. These men knew their knots!

CHAPTER 15

A Dramatic Entrance

"The calla lilies are in bloom and the ascending Aurora English roses are ripe for the picking," Joe announced as he stepped through the cottage door with his arms full of delicate white lilies and beauteous roses atop prickly stems. At the sound of Joe's voice, the gunman whirled around.

"No, not Joe!" Willy thought in anguish. The powerful man struggled to his feet, and staggering under the weight of his chum and the two cane-bottom straightback chairs, swung around and knocked the dark-suited gunman off balance, causing him to drop his weapon.

"What the—" the thin man yelled as he dove for his cohort's gun. Joe moved quickly, smacking him across the cheek with the thorny stems, leaving long bloody lines across his ferret-like face. The man shrieked in pain, pushed past Joe and took off down the porch. Joe gave chase, but before he could catch him, the man hopped in a dark sedan and sped away. The license plate of the vehicle was covered with mud, rendering it wholly unidentifiable. What's more, the front right tires of both Joe's jalopy and Uncle Nelly's trim coupe had been slashed!

When Joe raced inside, he found the remaining thug bound to a chair.

"Nice work, lad," Willy said, giving Joe a hearty slap on the back.

"That was a remarkable feat of strength," Joe shot back in awe.

Uncle Nelly swelled with pride. My, his chum Willy was strong!

Frank returned holding a nice arrangement of bellflowers and spring beauties, only to see the other fellows grinning widely whilst gazing at the trussed-up man. He smiled and rolled his eyes. "We really don't have time for more games," Frank chuckled as he lay his summery floral bouquet on the tea table. "We've got a party to go to!"

"This man was going to shoot Willy," Joe hurriedly explained. "And his accomplice got away, and slashed our tires so I couldn't follow!"

"I should have known right off that they were criminals up to no good," Uncle Nelly gasped. "Under normal circumstances, I'd hardly think ignorance of antiques a crime, but in this case—!"

An angry cloud covered Frank's face. "Who are you?" he demanded of the man.

"I'm not afraid of you, Frank Hardly," the man spat out angrily.

Willy grabbed the rude man by his poorly-constructed lapels and shook him soundly. "Answer the boy," he instructed, his face red with anger.

"Don't hurt me!" the man pleaded with the powerful Willy. "I'll tell you what you want to know. We're working for M— M—," was all the man managed to stammer out before fainting from fright.

"He must mean Mad Dog MacDougal, the notorious furniture thief!" the young sleuths chorused. "He must have escaped while serving his sentence at the state pen for that davenport heist in Chicago," Joe said knowingly.

"I'd better check his pockets and make sure we've relieved him of all his weapons," a cautious Frank declared. The eagle-eyed lad had spotted a suspicious bulge in the burly man's trousers! Joe's pulse quickened as he watched Frank frisk the fellow. Soon a satisfied smile spread over Frank's fair face, and he uttered a low exclamation.

"What is it?" Joe cried eagerly.

"It's long and hard and—why, it's a tube containing architectural plans of our charming cottage," Frank gasped, open-mouthed.

"They were planning to probe every nook and cranny of this place for our most private treasures," Uncle Nelly realized. He shivered at the idea of the two men handling their things.

"We've got to call Police Chief Mike O'Malley and report this immediately," the boys chorused. A fast five minutes later, the boys were falling all over themselves, telling the story to the handsome young officer in the trim-fitting blue uniform who was perched on their love seat, a thoughtful expression on his rugged face and a dainty teacup balanced on his muscular right thigh.

The chief furrowed his handsome brow as Frank explained his theory about Mad Dog MacDougal. "You're probably right, Frank," the chief praised the lad. "The architectural plans fit Mad Dog's modus operandi to a tee." The chief proclaimed that as soon as he got back to the station house he'd run a check on Mad Dog's whereabouts. "Another Hardly success story," he praised them. "Boys, you're going to put me out of business."

Frank beamed. That was high praise indeed coming from Lake Merrimen's beloved Chief of Police!

The chief shook his head. "What a summer! First, someone sees a ghost in your cottage, then a family from Oshkosh says there's a sea monster with fiery red eyes swimming in the lake; there's an attempted poodlesnatching from the Dog Show and now antique thievery! And Lake Merrimen used to be such a quiet little municipality!"

"A sea monster!" Joe cried eagerly. "Tell us more!"

"Joe, there's no such thing as sea monsters," Frank admonished his gullible brother.

"Just another case of sunstroke, I imagine," Chief O'Malley said with a good-humored sigh.

"Another piece of cake?" Uncle Nelly proffered a tray stacked with delicious delicacies.

The chief threw up his hands in protest. "I've got to keep in fighting trim so I can chase after criminals," he grinned, slapping his washboard-flat stomach with one strong hand.

"And *sea monsters!*" Frank laughed. "Right, Joe?"

Joe said nothing. He was too busy picturing the handsome young officer wrestling a muscular man to the ground; his biceps bulging as he pinned the fellow's wrists, sweat breaking out on his strong brow as he used his beefy thighs to grip the squirming fellow around the hips and hold him tight. Joe suddenly gave a low moan and threw down his plate. "Too much chocolate cake!" he hurriedly explained as he hunched over and made a hasty exit from the room.

Frank chuckled. He and the chief exchanged a knowing smile. Would Joe ever grow up?

CHAPTER 16

Party Games

Just as Joe was racing out of the room, Cherry and Velma were arriving at the Clue residence in River Depths to find a meat delivery truck parked in the driveway. "I've got a double order of fresh frankfurters for a Miss Clue," the amiable driver proclaimed. The girls gasped in delight as trays of luscious-looking sausages were dropped in their laps, along with fresh-baked rolls and a box of assorted condiments.

"What's happened to Hannah's simple birthday tea?" Cherry wondered when they got to the kitchen and saw the feast laid out before them—cauliflower flowerets with mayonnaise, stuffed celery, pickled onions in bacon, fried chicken, sweet potato croquettes, pear salad, lemon bread pudding and a double-fudge cake decorated with gay sugar roses. "All this and wieners, too?" Cherry cried. Good thing she had packed plenty of stomach-ache potion in her first-aid kit!

"We're having a patio party," Nancy announced grandly when she came in and saw Cherry staring wide-eyed at the food. She tied a frilly apron over her adorable casual outfit of a yellow and white checkered flared skirt and sunny yellow lightweight shell top. Her shiny titian hair had been brushed until it gleamed, and was tied back in a perky ponytail, topped by a black velvet ribbon. On her dainty feet were rubber-soled embroidered gold slippers, the perfect footwear to take her from kitchen to patio.

"We're having a combination Happy Birthday Hannah and Welcome Home Frank and Joe Hardly Party," Nancy explained. "They've just arrived and are awfully anxious to meet all of you. Especially you, Cherry," she added with a sly smile.

That must be why Nancy looks so gay, Cherry realized. "Then Frank must not mind that Midge has been posing as him all this time," she said in relief, "and has married."

Nancy looked momentarily dumbfounded. Golly, in all the excitement, she had forgotten to inform Frank of that one small detail! "As soon as I solve the mystery, I'll explain everything to Frank," she decided. "But first things first. I must make this a frolicsome party and not show any sign that I know I'll soon be on a case!"

"Velma, would you run out to the garage and find Midge and Jackie? Ask Midge to set up the twenty-four inch motorized grill with automatic built-in fire lighter and rotisserie. It's in the garage behind the speed boat and in front of my skis, if I remember correctly," Nancy recalled. "And ask Jackie to set up the croquet wickets on the grounds just west of the house. She'll find it in the cellar in a leather case propped up against the far left wall, next to the badminton racquets and my fencing mask." Nancy bustled about like a whirlwind in her pretty summer outfit.

"Cherry, would you take these smart, seven-inch tall teardrop glass-encased candles that provide over one hundred or more hours of windproof burning, colored an attractive sunset red, and place them on the occasional tables I've scattered around the patio?

"And when you come back from the garage, Velma, I'd like you to wrap Hannah's presents," Nancy directed. "They're piled on my bed along with sheets of wrapping paper printed with gay forget-me-nots. I'm going to run to the store for some lemons." She tied a chiffon scarf over her coiffure. "Be right back," she gave a happy wave.

"Nancy is certainly in a chipper mood," Cherry sighed with relief. "And to think I was afraid she'd be angry with me for staying out half the night with Jackie!"

For the next fifteen minutes, the happy house practically hummed with activity. Cherry put the finishing touches on the festive decorations, raced inside for a quick bath, then slipped into her nylon bouffant petticoat and, over that, her new elegantly simple toast and white dotted summer silk dress. Just for fun she added her charm bracelet with its tiny nurse's cap, shoes, thermometer and bandage scissors, and a dab of lavender cologne behind each ear.

"It's been a long time since you've worn your whites, Nurse Aimless," she scolded herself as she twirled in front of the full-length mirror while checking her hemline. For a moment, her thoughts turned to her friends at faraway Seattle General Hospital. As she was primping in preparation for a patio party, they were busy saving countless lives, comforting the truly sick and polishing their scuffed rubber-soled shoes!

"You've earned a vacation," Cherry told the attractive girl in the stylish dress reflected in the mirror. She wondered, though, how long she could wait before she would once again don the proud uniform of a Registered Nurse. Cherry knew if she said yes to Jackie's offer to accompany her to San Francisco, she would be back in uniform in a matter of days. "Thankfully, there are sick people everywhere," Cherry sighed in relief. She did miss nursing so!

She went to her suitcase, took out a small box and opened it. Inside, wrapped in white tissue, was her starched Stencer Nursing School graduation cap, its black velvet stripe symbolizing her lifetime of commitment. The day that cap was pinned to her curls had been the happiest day of her life, with the night she had kissed Nancy Clue with all her might a close second!

With shaky hands she placed the stiff, spotless cap on her short, dark curls and pinned it securely. "I'm ready to nurse again," she realized, her heart soaring with happiness. "But where am I to hang my cap? In San Francisco or in Illinois?

Why couldn't Cherry decide which path to take? "I must be true to my heart, and my heart yearns for Jackie. But how can I leave Nancy after all we've been through? How can I leave her just when she's starting to rebuild her crumbled life? But what if I miss my one chance for true love and a contented life with Jackie? I know she wants me to be her girl—I can just tell!" Cherry wanted to weep. "How am I to know what to do?"

Why, oh why, hadn't her mother covered this topic in any of her many useful lectures?

Suddenly Cherry could take it no longer. She *must* see Velma and finish the talk they had begun that morning. She ran out of the room, took the stairs two at a time and skipped out to the kitchen.

Cherry spotted Midge on the patio, arranging the platters of food in a decorative display on tables covered in gay cloths. Distraught as she was, she still laughed at the sight of Midge wearing a full-length frilly apron over her simple dark slacks and short-sleeved summer shirt and puzzling over the placement of pickles and pimentos.

"Nancy's not back from the store yet, is she?" Cherry quizzed her chum.

"Velma says Nancy will be back soon with plenty of lemons," came the reply. "I hope she gets grapefruit, too. After all, we can't have a patio party without lots of fresh-squeezed pink lemonade, now can we? What do you think? Would the radishes be more appealing carved like roses or carnations?"

Cherry looked puzzled. What could explain Midge's sudden interest in the fascinating world of decorative food presentation? Perhaps Midge has been out in the sun too long, she thought as she tried to recall the remedy for sunstroke. "Why on earth are you wearing an apron?" Cherry wondered aloud.

"To protect my outfit, of course," was the puzzled reply.

"Something *must* be terribly wrong," Cherry thought. The Midge she knew wouldn't be caught dead wearing an apron or cutting vegetables into pleasing shapes. Although, Cherry had to admit the cucumbers *did* look mighty tempting as canoes.

"Why don't you lie down inside, out of the sun," Cherry said in a soothing tone. "You could smoke a cigarette and rest."

Cherry's suggestion was greeted with terrible consternation.

"Lips that touch cigarettes shall never touch mine!"

Cherry gasped. How many times had she tried to get Midge to quit smoking? Although the tobacco companies had assured them cigarettes posed no danger whatsoever to one's health, and doctors recommended them as a sure-fire way to reduce tension, Cherry still thought the habit discourteous. Smokers were always flinging ashes everywhere, damaging fine dress fabrics and burning holes in expensive, delicate stockings.

"I'm going upstairs to get my first-aid kit and then I'm going to take your temperature!" Cherry said tersely. She headed upstairs, and along the way, bumped into Velma carrying a pile of gaily-wrapped gifts. Cherry's earlier concern for her own affairs had vanished. She knew a good nurse put her own needs aside, no matter the trouble.

"Velma, I have news for you," Cherry said in a level tone, trying not to alarm her chum. "Midge is acting queer!"

"What else is new?" Velma grinned.

"No, Velma," Cherry insisted. "Midge is acting *very* queer. Not at all like herself. Velma, she's out there on the patio wearing an apron *and* cutting vegetables into party shapes!"

Velma laughed and shook her head. "No, Cherry, that's not Midge."

Cherry was relieved that Velma fully understood the gravity of the situation. "That's right," she said. "That's just the shell of Midge—the real Midge has, for some inexplicable reason, become submerged somewhere deep within her own mind. But don't worry," she hastened to add. "I've plenty of experience with amnesia patients. I'll set Midge right in no time!"

Velma laughed until she wept. Cherry had seen this reaction before in people. "What the mind cannot handle—" she told herself. Now was her chance to practice the coolness and presence of mind for which her training had prepared her. Good thing River Depths had a fine sanitarium on the outskirts of town headed by the world-renowned Dr. Fraud.

"I think a trip to the patio will clear this up," Velma chuckled.

"Eek!" Cherry cried when they reached the courtyard, for now there were *two* Midges, only one was bent over the barbecue, full of dirt and grease, her shirt-tail hanging out of her pants, and the other was busy weaving necklaces of fresh flowers.

"Cherry, I'd like you to meet Frank Hardly," Velma said, waving her hand in the direction of the tidy Midge. Cherry blushed to the roots of her curly black hair.

"Hello Frank," was all she managed to squeak out.

"It's swell to finally be properly introduced," Frank bowed in his best continental manner. He offered her a selection of festive flower garlands to wear around her neck. "I've made one for every guest," he told the girls. "Although, Cherry, you might have to take off your nurse's cap first in order to get it over your head," Frank worried.

Cherry turned even redder when she realized she was still wearing her cap! Thank goodness Hannah picked that very moment to join the party, thus shifting the attention away from the sheepish nurse. Dressed in an elegantly simple lavender frock and low-heeled pumps, the attractive older woman slowly made her way out to the patio, relying on a cane. Gogo was at her heels, a festive ribbon tied around her neck. "Francis P. Hardly, welcome home!" Hannah cried with delight as she spied Frank. "It's been awfully quiet around here without you boys running in and out for Nancy's advice and some of my gooseberry pie," she teased. "Where's Joseph? At a matinee, I'll wager."

Frank grinned. "He's in the pantry with Nancy. They're looking for sugar for the lemonade," he explained. "And putting their heads together so Nancy can get a jump on this mystery and impress Cherry," he thought to himself with a secret smile.

CHAPTER 17

Puzzling Behavior

"And then Willy jumped up and swung Uncle Nelly around and knocked the man to the floor!" Joe said excitedly. He had just finished telling Jackie and Midge about the robbery attempt at the Hardly cottage.

"Willy must be exceptionally strong," Jackie said in awe.

"He's the biggest," Joe crowed. "Why, Willy's practically a real-live Hercules! You'll meet him later when he and Uncle Nelly drop by for cake," he added. "I happened to walk in the house just as the gunman was pointing his weapon at Willy and was able to divert his attention so Willy could act," he bragged.

Frank walked in the room and shot him a sharp warning glance. "Ix nay, Joe," that look said. "Bragging is a sport unbecoming to a Hardly boy!"

Joe excused himself. "I think I need another wiener," he murmured as he left the kitchen and headed for the patio where the party was in full swing.

Frank busied himself squeezing lemons for another refreshing pitcher of pink lemonade.

"Do you want me to run a check on those men?" Jackie offered.

"That won't be necessary," Frank told her as he poured cool water and plenty of sugar into the glass pitcher. "One's already in jail and Chief O'Malley's sure to locate the other any minute now. Besides, we're pretty certain they're thugs hired by the notorious furniture thief Mad Dog MacDougal." He didn't want Jackie to think the case was ripe for investigation. Why, she might take it upon herself to solve it!

"Not *the* Mad Dog MacDougal who swiped the chandeliers from the Des Moines Opera House during a performance of *My Fair Lady*?" Jackie wondered.

Frank nodded.

"Say, you Hardly boys are as fast as everyone says," Jackie said in frank admiration.

Frank shrugged modestly, but deep down he was pleased. This was high praise indeed coming from a San Francisco detective! Forgetting for a moment that Jackie was Nancy's romantic archenemy, he fell into easy conversation with the dashing detective. "I knew the minute I spied that fellow he wasn't an antique lover," Frank shared as he stirred the lemonade, "but Uncle Nelly's so unsuspecting he lets everyone in the door. Why, I took one look at that fellow's ill-fitting sharkskin suit and I knew he was in the wrong place!"

"*What* was he wearing?" Midge asked eagerly. Until now, she had been too busy gulping down delicious deviled eggs to pay much attention to all the cops-and-robbers talk, but Frank's description of the man had piqued her interest.

"The man we caught was clad in a too-tight black suit of a cheap fabric, the kind that wears badly and makes you realize you're better off paying the price for a well-made garment," Frank told Midge, confident that his own lightweight summer slacks were exacting in quality and workmanship. "I didn't see the guy who got away, but Joe described him to me as a tall slender man in a dark-colored trenchcoat with a long thin face and nervous, darting eyes."

Midge gasped. "The guy in the trenchcoat is the one who tried to kidnap the poodles at the Dog Show the other day," she told him, "and his friend is the one who stole my program!"

"So Mad Dog's moved into the dognapping business!" Frank swore angrily. "I'll call the chief right away and tell him to add kidnapping to the charges!"

He strode to Nancy's den and put in a quick call to his chum the chief, but was surprised to find that Chief O'Malley had been called away on official business and had left strict orders that no one was allowed to speak to the prisoner, *even* the Hardly boys!

"It's for your own good, Frank," the sergeant said. "That's all I can say. Good-bye."

When a puzzled Frank returned to the kitchen, he found Midge and Jackie mulling over the mystery of the disappearing dogs.

"We've got the dognapper's trunk in Nancy's car," Midge remembered. "And she's got a bit of his disappearing powder in her purse."

"But why were they at your cottage today?" Jackie wondered. "Let's go interrogate that fellow," she exclaimed.

"But the chief left orders that no one's allowed to go near the prisoner," Frank blurted out. Although the chief's strange orders puzzled him, at least they prevented Jackie from becoming officially involved in the case. "He must be working an angle," Frank hastily added.

"Let's see if we can trace the magic powder on our own, then," Jackie suggested.

Frank was about to say, "Good idea," but quickly stopped himself. His job was to keep Jackie from becoming involved in the mystery.

"But we can't leave now," Frank cried out. "We've haven't cut the cake!" Golly, was Nancy's one shot at happiness with the nurse of her dreams going to be ruined by his one divulgence?

Jackie and Midge exchanged queer glances. They couldn't believe the famous boy detective was choosing chocolate cake over a baffling mystery!

Jackie began to suspect something was afoot. She shot Midge a little wink. "Perhaps you're right, Frank," Jackie said. "I'll bet the Lake Merrimen police don't need us nosing around. And that cake does look awfully good."

Midge quickly caught on. "Yeah, I've been in enough mysteries for one summer," she sighed. "Hey, Jack, let's go outside for a smoke, shall we?"

"Phew!" Frank thought as he set the pitcher of lemonade on a doily-covered tray and carried it outdoors, little realizing the ruckus he had stirred up.

"Midge, something's up," Jackie whispered to her chum once they were out of earshot. "Did you see how quickly Frank backed off such an exciting development?"

"Yeah," Midge replied. "And have you noticed how jumpy Joe is? And earlier when we were roasting wienies, did you notice how Frank and Nancy kept shooting each other knowing glances?"

"Somehow I don't think that little smile of anticipation on Nancy's face is because she's waiting eagerly for the party games to begin. I've got the feeling those three have a secret," Jackie exclaimed.

Midge smiled, for she had a secret of her own. The minute she managed to maneuver a way to bring Jackie and Cherry together, Midge and Velma were going to slip away for an afternoon of *their* favorite game.

"Keep your eyes open and your ears to the ground, Midge," Jackie said as she snatched up her empty lemonade glass and prepared to rejoin the festivities. "I think Nancy and the Hardly boys are scheming a way to win Cherry back!"

"But it's not going to happen!" she vowed to herself.

CHAPTER 18

Cosmic Yearnings

"Oh, and a lovely fountain pen engraved with my initials!" Hannah Gruel exclaimed as she opened another gift. "H. H. G.— Housekeeper Hannah Gruel."

"It writes in regular *and* invisible ink," Joe pointed out. "So you can leave Nancy secret messages."

"Never have I received more thoughtful presents," Hannah sighed as she surveyed the pile of presents on the glass-topped wrought iron table in front of her. "*Sing Along with Mitch Miller*, a lacy bed jacket, *The Joy of Cooking*, this pen and my very own official Red Cross blood-pressure kit. Why, you kids are going to spoil me!"

"There's one more parcel to open," Cherry said, pointing to a smallish box wrapped in gay pink tissue and tied with a silver bow. Hannah opened the box and pulled out a clear bottle filled with rose-colored water. Taped to the neck of the bottle was a note. Hannah took her reading glasses from her pocket and read it aloud. "*Birthday wishes from Mrs. Milton Meeks.*

"Oh, dear," Hannah cried worriedly. "Just as I suspected. A whole bottle of Myra's homemade perfume. She sends a bottle to all the River Depths housekeepers on their birthdays. Now I'll have to wear it to church come Sunday," she fretted.

Everyone laughed.

"A toast to my dear friend Hannah who's been like a mother to me since the death of my real mother twenty-two years ago," Nancy proposed, holding her pink lemonade aloft.

"Here's to Hannah!" everyone cried as they raised their glasses high. Hannah beamed happily.

Cherry searched her brain for something clever to say. Her father, who loved a good party, always had at his fingertips a generous store of time-tested toasts on a wide variety of subjects. If only she could remember one of them!

"A porter on the *Queen Mary* taught me a grand toast," Joe recalled.

> *"Here's to the bachelor,*
> *a bright poppin' jay!*
> *How come he's so dapper?*
> *He's just born that way!"*

"Here's to chums, old and new," Frank exclaimed. "Especially my twin brother Midge."

Cherry giggled. Although she was embarrassed to have given a false diagnosis of amnesia, she had to admit that she was relieved to find it had been Frank Hardly behind that apron all along. "That explains a lot of things," she sighed aloud. "Now that you're together, I can tell you apart, but it isn't easy," Cherry admitted. "You do look shockingly alike. Frank," she teased, "there's not a Hardly girl in your family, is there?"

Frank shook his head. "There's been nothing but boys for generations," he said.

"Even I was fooled for a moment when I first met Frank," Velma laughed. It *had* been a little jarring to see someone who looked so much like her girlfriend standing at a buffet table making melon balls.

"I'd have to be suffering from amnesia before I'd put on an apron," Midge assured her girlfriend. "Not that it looked at all bad on you, Frank," she hastily added.

"You'll find, Midge, that an apron really does keep one's clothes tidy as pie," he teased. "You'll notice my shirt is as clean as a whistle!"

Everyone had a good chuckle when they looked at Midge's outfit, which was in its usual rumpled state. Her dark trousers were smudged with ashes from her ever-present cigarette and a smudge of grease ran up the sleeve of her Orlon short-sleeved summer shirt.

Velma picked at the front of Midge's shirt. "What's this?" she asked with a big smile. "Shrimp sauce?" Everyone could tell by the starry expression in her eyes that Velma wouldn't trade Midge or her funny habits for anything in the world.

"Any minute now, I'll fix it so we can sneak off," Midge whispered in Velma's ear.

"Frank's Mr. Tidy," Joe teased his older brother. "Why, Frank here is the only fellow I know who can chase a cunning criminal, rescue a marooned fighter pilot or wrestle a burly thug, all without losing the crease in his slacks. He's just like Father."

"Speaking of your famous father, I read that article in *Spy Journal* about those stolen rocket ship plans he managed to retrieve just as Russian agents were preparing to smuggle them out of the country," Jackie piped up. "That was good work."

At the mention of that case, Frank blanched. It had been his father's most dangerous mission, and for four fearful days, the Hardly family had held its breath waiting for word that Fennel was fine. Since that dreadful day, Fennel P. Hardly had, at the insistence of his family, forsworn dangerous cases of espionage.

Frank pushed his plate of cake aside and jumped up. He jammed his hands in the pockets of his handsome slacks and started to pace around the patio. He peered at the brilliant moon high in the Illinois sky; that same moon was now a trophy in a cosmic race between two giants—a race Frank feared they would lose!

"Why they wanted *our* rocket ship plans when they've already proven their superiority in space is beyond me," Frank said grimly. October fourth, nineteen hundred and fifty-seven had been a sad day for a boy detective with space dust in his eyes, for on that day the Russian satellite Sputnik I, the first-ever satellite in space, had flown overhead.

"Even Father couldn't stop their dominance of outer space," Joe sighed. Then he smiled brightly. "Here's hoping we reach the moon first," he toasted. "We will, too," he bragged, "because we've got the best scientists in the world and a government eager to spend untold millions for such an important endeavor."

Frank tipped his glass skyward. His eyes glowed. "So enchanting, so mysterious, but so far away that only in his dreams could man touch her barren beauty. This is our moon," he said dreamily.

"But why do you want to go to the moon?" Cherry wondered. "It doesn't seem like a very nice place to visit. There's nowhere to stay up there."

Frank and Joe were almost speechless with astonishment.

"Space flight will free man from the chains of gravity that tie him to this planet!" they cried.

"Plus in space, we can harvest new materials and create new products that will enrich all our lives," Frank pointed out. "New things for the home, schools, industry, and even hospitals."

"Dad says it could be a whole new world up there," Joe enthused.

"It will be, too," Frank asserted solemnly, "for peace in space means peace on earth."

"Think of it, Cherry," Joe added excitedly. "If we can develop our space arsenal, we can eventually ring the free world with such formidable weapons that an invader would think a long, long time before risking a war. Anyway, that's what Dad says, and he knows best. Why, he taught us everything we know about tracking crooks, cracking codes and the surveillance of dangerous characters," he bragged. "And not once has he failed in his endeavor to right a wrong or bring a criminal to justice.

"In fact, I think he's digging up clues for a new case right now," Joe said with an excited twinkle in his eye.

Frank smiled, caught up in his brother's enthusiasm. "I do so hope there's a good mystery for us to solve this summer," Frank cut in. "I'm eager to plunge into something new."

Frank's comment surprised Jackie. Why, the way the boy sleuth had acted earlier, a mystery seemed to be the last thing on his mind!

"A mystery sure would be fun right now," Cherry sighed. "Only not too soon," she added, "since I've just eaten."

Frank and Joe looked at each other slyly. Little did Cherry realize that *soon* she would get her wish!

Jackie looked up just in time to catch their exchange. "That does it," she thought. "Something queer is going on. Why are these two eager-beaver boy detectives content to while away the afternoon at a patio party while a thug who wrecked havoc at the Dog Show and then broke into their family cottage is loose and his partner is sitting in jail right now yet to be interrogated? What are they waiting for?" she asked herself.

"Frank, I suspect that—" Jackie began, but before she could go any further, Nancy jumped up, clapped her hands excitedly and squealed, "It's time for a game! Who wants to play?"

"How about a round of Powers of Observation?" Joe suggested.

"What's that?" Cherry wondered. "Is it difficult to play?"

"We blindfold a volunteer and have her describe a person in this room," Joe explained. "We play it all the time at parties in order to hone our detective skills."

"It sounds like fun," Cherry squealed.

A sly grin came over Frank's face. "We'll start with you, Cherry," he announced as he took a red-checkered cloth napkin from the buffet table and used it to blindfold her. Cherry allowed Frank to twirl her around three times, and when he let go, she began walking unsteadily around the patio with her arms outstretched. Nancy was just within her grasp when suddenly, startled by a cough from Midge, Cherry turned to her left, reached out and grabbed onto a muscular arm.

"Oh, it must be you Midge," she laughed as she ran her small, soft hand over a bulging bicep. She gave the massive muscle a playful squeeze.

"No, it's me," Jackie said in a low tone.

Cherry blushed, snatched her hand away and put it primly in her pocket.

"Now you have to describe Jackie," Joe cried. "That's the rule."

"Drat," Frank thought. He had hoped Cherry would choose Nancy, who looked especially fetching in her crisp summer outfit, but his plans had been foiled when Midge had suddenly choked on a stuffed olive.

"I wouldn't know where to begin," Cherry cried, all flustered.

"You can apply the Hardly Boys Identification System and work from the head down," Joe suggested helpfully. "For example, what's Jackie's hair color and style?" Joe prompted.

Cherry thought a moment and then stammered, "She's got shiny black hair fashioned in a flattering close-crop hairdo that shows off her strong features to their best advantage."

"Excellent," Joe said. "Now, can you describe her eye and complexion color?"

"Deep black eyes with just a hint of brown that makes them warm and inviting. I've seen them sparkle with intelligence and good humor, then flash with anger," Cherry sighed. Golly, this game was easier than she had imagined. Maybe she could be a detective! It was a queer sensation, wearing a blindfold. Why, it made her feel as if she and Jackie were alone in the room.

"And skin?" Joe prodded.

"Warm brown skin, the color of strong coffee with just a hint of cream."

Joe nodded. "Now for build and notable physical characteristics."

Cherry blushed deeply and threw off her lightweight cardigan sweater. Was it her imagination, or had the summer night suddenly turned much warmer? "Well, she's tall and has wide, strong shoulders just made for someone to cry on," she gulped.

A sharp knock at the front door brought the little game to an abrupt end. "Thank goodness," Frank and Nancy sighed with relief.

Midge grabbed Velma by the hand and pulled her into the garden. Frank went to answer the door.

"Why, it's Uncle Nelly and his chum Willy," Frank exclaimed. "And none too soon," he thought with relief. "Where have you fellows been?" he said under his breath as he let the men in. "You're here just in the nick of time!"

CHAPTER 19

The Telltale Slippers

 "Look who's here!" Joe cried. "It's our Uncle Nelly and his chum Willy! My, you two look rather excited! Uncle, has something happened?"

Uncle Nelly stumbled inside. "Boys, something awful *has* happened—the queerest thing—ooh!" He dropped into a nearby comfortable upholstered wing back chair, took the peach-colored silk kerchief from around his neck and began fanning his face, which was bright pink from excitement. Why, it looked as if he had been weeping!

Joe grinned. Trust Uncle Nelly to put on a show!

"Take a deep breath, Nelson," Willy said, clutching his friend's hand. "Frank, Joe, your uncle has something very grievous to tell you," he said in a grave tone. Frank noticed that even the unflappable Willy seemed shaken. He and Joe exchanged a delighted grin. This was going to be good!

"I almost can't say it," Uncle Nelly gasped. Joe brought him a glass of cool lemonade to steady his nerves. "No—" Uncle Nelly waved the glass away. "Not at a time like this!" Uncle Nelly moaned as he wrung his neck kerchief between his soft pale hands. "Oh, boys," he cried dramatically, "you won't believe the terrible turn of events!"

Frank was mighty impressed by his uncle's flawless performance. "Why, if we didn't know this was a set-up, I'd swear Uncle Nelly was really worried about something," he thought to himself.

"Uncle, are you trying to say that you've witnessed something that you think could be related to the recent Dog Show incident, and you're here to beg Nancy to take the case?" Joe urged him on.

Cherry gasped. My, Joe *was* good!

Jackie rolled her eyes. She smelled a rat!

Uncle Nelly appeared too overcome to speak. He buried his head in his hands and started to weep. Willy stepped in, and what he said made the partygoers gasp in horror.

"Boys, your parents, well-known detective Fennel P. Hardly and his attractive wife Mrs. Hardly, have been *kidnapped!*"

"Kidnapped!" Frank and Joe chorused. Golly, the fellows had gone and changed the mystery on them! Joe looked at Nancy and shrugged. Nancy looked momentarily puzzled, but the cool-headed sleuth quickly regained her composure.

Jackie ran to the closet for her detective's notebook and pencil stowed in her jacket pocket, but Nancy was ready. She hid a little smile as she reached for the notebook she had stowed earlier in the front patch pocket of her flared skirt. And she just happened to have a little pencil tucked behind one ear!

Nancy speedily quizzed Uncle Nelly.

"Did you see the kidnapping? Who do you think snatched them? Are you aware of anyone who bears a grudge against Mr. and Mrs. Hardly? What happened in the minutes leading up to this shocking incident?"

While Cherry thrilled to the sight of the comely girl taking charge of an important investigation, Jackie crossed her muscular arms over her strong chest and smoldered in the corner. "I'll get my first-aid kit, just in case someone needs a nurse," Cherry told Nancy.

Joe grinned. "Golly, Mother and Father have joined in on our little scheme," he whispered to his brother.

"For a minute there, I thought something really *had* happened to them," Frank admitted. "Why, Uncle Nelly ought to win an Oscar for his performance."

Joe agreed. "What *really* impresses me is that Uncle Nelly came all the way over here in his old carpet slippers. It certainly lends credence to his performance as the distraught relative."

Frank looked at his brother queerly. "Why, Uncle Nelly would *never* leave the house without the right shoes—"

"—unless something as terrible as a kidnapping *had* occurred!" Joe finished his thought, all wide-eyed.

"Something terrible has happened to Mother and Father!" the boys chorused in horror.

"That's what we've been trying to tell you," Uncle Nelly cried. "Frank—Joe—someone has stolen into your home and made off with your parents!" A long horrible moment of silence followed. Frank clenched his fists. His pleasant face grew stormy with rage.

"These perpetrators shall be brought to justice," the boy vowed, "or my name isn't Francis P. Hardly!"

CHAPTER 20

"Hold It Right There!"

"—and I was just about to hang up the telephone when suddenly I heard a loud, brutish-sounding man call out, *'Hold it right there, Fennel. You're coming with me! You too, Mrs. Hardly!'* Then what sounded like a scuffle ensued. Why, I could hear the unmistakable sound of good furniture breaking," Uncle Nelly cried.

"Not the beautiful Federal writing table you gave them for their last anniversary?" Joe cried in alarm.

Uncle Nelly nodded solemnly. He and Willy had raced to the Hardly house only to behold a terrible sight. "I'm afraid so, son."

The Hardly boys grew silent at the grim news. They were riding in Nancy's snappy convertible, with their uncle and his chum Willy in the back seat, trying to get the story straight while Nancy steered her large automobile swiftly, yet cautiously, through heavy evening traffic, anxious to get to the scene of the crime.

Frank could scarcely believe what was happening. Just minutes ago, he had been part of a gay scheme involving a simple dognapping and a love life gone awry; now he was leading an investigation in which his own parents were the victims!

Cherry sat in the front seat next to Nancy, her heart pounding in excitement and her cap sitting a little askew. "Golly, I've never been a Kidnap Nurse before," Cherry thought with a mixture of excitement and worry. Good thing she always made it a point to carry plenty of rope-burn salve wherever she went!

"Perhaps one of the many scalawags he's put behind bars has finally made good on his threat to pay him back," Joe offered.

"Does your father have many enemies?" Cherry asked

innocently. Who *wouldn't* like a swell guy like Fennel P. Hardly—crackerjack detective, loving father and doting husband to Mrs. Hardly?

Frank fixed a level gaze on Cherry. "I don't mean to alarm you, Nurse, but my father's work brings him in contact with many a nefarious character. Who knows where the kidnapper's trail will lead us."

Cherry clutched her first-aid kit to her bosom. "It's my job to go wherever I'm needed, and if the search for patients leads me to dangerous or scary places, well, I agreed to that the day I swore to nurse the sick and comfort the disturbed while keeping my uniform clean and starched."

Frank nodded solemnly. "I thought as much. Why, when I saw you on the patio wearing that attractive summer frock *and* your nurse's cap, I thought, 'There is one committed girl.' "

Cherry blushed with pride.

Joe tried to ready himself by taking inventory of the Hardly Boys Official Detective Kit. He ticked off the contents.

"Magnifying glass, portable microscope, calipers for measuring lengths of things, rubber gloves for messy inspections, one magnet, a pocket-size Geiger counter, chalk for outlining objects, collapsible telescope, walkie-talkies, file and bobby pins for picking locks, handcuffs, a handy rope, a can of grease for getting out of tight jams, and some dried prunes and graham crackers in case we have to hole up somewhere."

"No one touch anything when we get there," Frank warned Cherry, Uncle Nelly and Willy.

"Unless we find your parents bleeding from a gash in the head," Cherry corrected him.

"Right," Frank said. "Other than that, no one's to touch a thing until we dust for fingerprints. And don't walk on the grass. You might destroy valuable evidence, like suspicious shoe prints or tire marks."

"Oh, dear," Uncle Nelly confessed. "Boys, we may have accidentally touched a few things when we were there earlier, and I'm pretty sure I remember running haphazardly across your lawn."

"That's okay, Uncle," Joe told him. "We'll fingerprint you and Willy and use the results to eliminate your prints, plus your carpet slipper prints and those from Willy's boots should be easy to spot."

He explained to Cherry the value of shoe prints when tracking criminals. "Often a criminal can be tracked down with just a shoe or tire print. The Federal Bureau of Investigation, or the FBI as we call it, has on hand photographs of thousands of different kinds of shoe plates. After we make a plaster cast of the shoe print using The Hardly Boys Mold Making Kit, I'll photograph it, make a quick print in the fully-equipped photographic lab in our basement and send it over our teletype to Bureau headquarters in Washington, DC. By morning, we'll know what size shoe the kidnapper was wearing, its make and model, and perhaps the very store where he made his purchase."

"Goodness," Cherry cried. "And I thought nursing was scientific!"

"Although our methods have improved vastly in the last fifteen years, it's still often the simplest thing that helps us get our man," Frank was forced to admit. "While crime detection has always been shrouded in deeps veils of mystery, the truth is that many an escaped criminal is brought to justice on as slim a clue as a single fingerprint."

"Jeepers!" Cherry cried. "But what if the kidnappers wore gloves? What then?"

"Yes, Nancy, what then?" Frank asked. Nancy shot him a thankful grin in the rearview mirror.

"Often even the most hardened criminal will slip up and take off a glove for a second, which is just enough time for him to leave his calling card," she explained, remembering how, in *The Case of the Pilfered Pocketbook,* the purse snatcher had left just one pinkie print on the patent leather handle—but it was enough!

"You see, Cherry, each of us has one thing that is ours alone, and that's our fingerprints. Although many attempts have been made to alter the telltale marks, they always grow back the exact same way," she explained.

"John Dillinger tried to change his fingerprint patterns by burning them with acid," Joe added. "But it didn't work!"

"How dreadful," Cherry shuddered.

"Since so many people were fingerprinted during the war as a national precaution to protect against invasion from within, a large number of people are on file at the FBI Identification Division," Frank interjected. "Over seventy million in fact. Just one fingerprint would be enough to identify the kidnappers and point us in their direction."

Cherry shivered. She was a little nervous about what they would find once they reached the Hardly residence. She glanced at the car behind them. Jackie was at the wheel of the Hardly jalopy. Cherry gave her a little wave, and was rewarded with a big grin from Jackie, who was keeping her eyes glued on the car ahead, and especially the attractive nurse in the front seat!

Somehow Cherry always felt better when Jackie was near. Was it her big, strong biceps or her quiet, confident manner that made Cherry go a little weak at the knees? Cherry blushed to the roots of her unruly curls. "Get ahold of yourself, Nurse Aimless," she scolded herself. "You're on a case—perhaps the most dangerous of your career. Now is not the time to swoon over some girl—not even one as handsome, good-hearted, sweet-natured and downright sensible as Police Detective Jackie Jones!"

CHAPTER 21

Torn Asunder!

"Oh, no!" Joe shrieked as they raced into the informal cozy living room of the Hardly home. "The overstuffed flower-patterned chintz chairs which blend happily with the ice-green walls have been turned over and their cushions tossed about in a disorderly fashion!"

"Look—our worn but still good wool area rug in a subtle shade of the deepest cerulean has mud prints all over it!" Frank gasped in alarm.

"And the honey-colored wood shelves stuffed with well-thumbed books and the modern hi-fi cabinet stocked with contemporary favorites have been plundered and their contents scattered about!" they chorused unhappily.

"What a colorful, cheerful room designed for contemporary living," Cherry exclaimed as she brought up the rear, first-aid kit in hand. She wiped her feet on the scatter rug just inside the door before remembering Joe's warning not to disturb anything at the scene. "Oops!" she blushed. Then she gasped when she got a good look at the room. "Oh, no!" she cried. "This modern house of today had been torn asunder!"

Uncle Nelly and Willy jumped out of the way and let the detectives do their work. They stood in the foyer in wide-eyed wonder as the sleuths bustled about searching for clues. They felt, as antique dealers, there was little they could do to aid in the investigation. The men knew their job would come later, finding replacements for the damaged furniture.

"The shoe prints on the rug are crisp and clear," Nancy was quick to point out. "They're our first clue!"

But before Nancy could make her move, Jackie got to her knees and closely examined the muddy imprints. "They're men's shoes with a snub-toe. Because of the way the fibers of the carpet have been mashed down and judging by the length of the imprint, I'd say we're looking for a man between six feet and six feet, two inches tall, weighing one hundred and sixty to one hundred and sixty-seven pounds," she cried.

Cherry gasped. "Jackie, you're *really* something!" she said admiringly.

Nancy scowled.

Jackie grinned, then her smile faded. This was a kidnapping case, not a contest, she told herself. She must keep her head, something that was hard to do when Cherry was around!

"I'll dust," Nancy declared in an icy tone as she took her hankie from her pocket.

"No!" Cherry cried. "Remember what Frank said? We're not supposed to touch a thing!"

Nancy used the hankie to wipe her brow. "I meant *dust* for *fingerprints*," she informed Cherry tersely. She opened the Hardly Boys Fingerprint Collecting Kit and took out a jar of fine white powder. Using a soft brush, she began laying the powder on surfaces in the room. Her pretty face tensed as she concentrated on the task at hand.

"In here!" Joe cried excitedly from the den. Heeding the warning not to touch anything, Uncle Nelly and Willy could only look sadly at the damaged Federal writing table whose delicate legs were smashed beyond repair. Bullet holes riddled the top of the desk.

"The good news is that there's no sign of blood, which means no one was hit," Frank said grimly as he flung open the Hardly Boys Evidence Retrieval Kit. "The bad news is that this fellow meant business!"

Jackie used tweezers to pick up a slug from the floor. "This is from a .38," she announced.

Nancy took her gold-rimmed magnifying glass with its ivory handle from her pocket and made a careful inspection of the discharged bullet. "It looks foreign-made to me," she said with a smug little smile, making sure Cherry overheard. "See the unusual mark on the side?" she asked pointedly.

"But it's still a .38," Jackie said just as firmly. The two detectives glared at one another.

Frank and Joe exchanged nervous looks. Was there going to be a fight?

"Nancy, why don't you check the front lawn for shoe prints

and the driveway for tire tracks while Jackie, Joe and I finish dusting for fingerprints," Frank suggested.

Nancy raced outside. The eagle-eyed detective had spotted a set of distinctive prints below the dining room window and was eager to use her expertise to advance the case.

"I'll lift the prints in the living room while you boys dust the den," Jackie suggested. She quickly but thoroughly examined every visible print on the furniture and door jams, but soon realized her efforts were all for naught. She compared every mark she uncovered to a fingerprint roster from the Hardly Boys Detective Kit—they all belonged to members of the Hardly family.

Just then Nancy burst into the room, a big smile lighting up her pretty face. "I've got good news," she reported triumphantly. "I've found shoe prints that are sure to provide the first big break in this case. I'm making molds of them now; they should be ready shortly."

"That's a fine clue you've uncovered, Nancy," Frank cried. "You see, Cherry, criminals often slip up just like this. While this fellow was careful enough to wear gloves, he forgot about his shoes and left impressions that an average detective might have overlooked. But not Nancy. Why, it's hard to put anything past her!"

"I'll go see if my shoe print molds are dry," Nancy grinned as she raced out of the room.

"Wait a minute!" Jackie crowed with excitement a moment later. "I found something! There's a clear set of right-hand prints on the cover of this copy of *Inside Russia Today*, and they don't match any known Hardly prints. They're large, so they fit my earlier guess that the kidnapper was a tall fellow," Jackie pointed out.

"Fabulous," Joe enthused. He popped a close-up lens on his patented Hardly Boys Special Evidence Camera and expertly photographed the imprint. "I'll race downstairs to our scientific darkroom and put this film in quick developer, then make a print on fast paper and send it over our teletype to FBI headquarters to see if they have a match on file," he announced.

"Perhaps we can help you with your photographic work," Uncle Nelly offered. He was quite an accomplished amateur photographer, and although his work was typically confined to shots of antiques and some interesting natural studies of Willy, he certainly knew his way around a darkroom.

"Swell," Joe declared. "Frank, I'm leaving you in charge of the investigation."

Frank grinned and shot his younger brother a snappy salute. Joe, Willy and Uncle Nelly went to the basement laboratory where the Hardly detectives tested many of their own theories.

"Let's check out the den for more clues," Frank suggested.

Cherry and Jackie followed him to the back of the house and into an enchanting room sure to provide a pleasant atmosphere for many pleasurable hours of fun. Although the room was windowless, it was cheery nonetheless, what with its knotty ponderosa pine paneling, big comfortable easy chairs covered in sturdy blue and white Bouclé, Oriental rug in subtle shades of indigo and salmon, and built-in shelves crammed with crime novels and historical fiction. One wall was decorated with nicely framed certificates of appreciation, awards and merit badges attesting to the popularity and expertise of the Hardly family.

While Jackie bent over an oak table, piled high with books, to dust for more prints, Cherry put her hands in her pockets so she wouldn't be tempted to touch anything. "Goodness, your parents, Mr. and Mrs. Hardly, certainly are a comely couple," Cherry cried as she looked at a silver-framed photograph on the fireplace mantle. "Although, Frank, neither you nor Joe really resemble them or your Uncle Nelly, for that matter. Still, as a nurse I know that certain physical characteristics can skip a generation. You must take after your grandparents.

"That's not to say you aren't a handsome lad," she added hastily.

Frank grinned. "Oh, Joe's the beauty queen in our family," he joshed as he continued inspecting the carpet with his magnifying glass, looking for fibers and dust particles that could provide valuable leads.

"Now, Frank," Cherry scolded lightly. "You know that's not at all true. Why, either one of you could be a queen. You should have seen the way people swooned over Midge at the Dog Show the other day, thinking she was you. Luckily, Midge is true blue when it comes to matters of the heart."

"Just like Father," Frank enthused. Although the handsome and charming Mr. Hardly could have his pick of any partner at the Feyport Country Club dances, he only had eyes for Mrs. Hardly.

Cherry took a closer look at the snapshot. Mr. Hardly, a fine-boned man with a trim build, had sharply chiseled features and well-groomed, slicked-back hair. His broad shoulders provided an elegant frame for his dashing tuxedo. Mrs. Hardly had soft curly dark hair worn loosely around her shoulders, wide, light-colored eyes, a button nose and a perfect rosebud mouth. She was clad in an elegant evening dress of shimmering sea-foam chiffon.

"By the look on her face you'd think she was floating on air; she's so happy," Cherry murmured. "I wonder if I'll ever again gaze at anyone with that look of devotion—besides my patients, that is?" She snuck a peek at Jackie. She could imagine gazing into her eyes that way, Cherry realized as she blushed hotly.

"That picture was taken at the Midwest Detective's Ball a few years ago," Frank explained. "Father was honored for his role in cracking *The Case of the Corn-Fed Felon*. He was awarded that bronze trophy, shaped like an ear of corn, on the mantle."

"Your family has been honored many times," Cherry said as she examined the various trophies and statuettes bearing the good name of Hardly. "And what a lovely candelabra," she cried as she admired an ornate silver candle holder at one end of the mantle. "Although, I hope your mother trims these extra-long wicks before lighting these candles. This is a perfect example of the kind of careless thing that causes houses to go up in flames," Cherry told Frank.

"I'll remind her," Frank promised, throwing a little grin Cherry's way. His grin faded, though, when he saw what Cherry was talking about. He jumped up, snatched one of the thick red candles and examined it. A queer expression came over his face.

Jackie gasped when she saw what Frank had in his hand.

"That's dynamite!" the two detectives chorused.

"The thug who kidnapped Mother and Father must have been planning to blow this house sky-high, but was thwarted in his efforts!" Frank quickly deduced.

Just then Joe raced in with a wet photograph in his hands; Nelly and Willy were hot on his heels. Before Frank could say a thing about his own find, Joe waved the image in Frank's face and cried triumphantly,

"We've happened upon a most important clue! These fingerprints, when blown up four hundred times their original size, reveal a distinct pattern I'm sure I've seen before," Joe announced with glee. "But where could it have been?"

Frank peered over Joe's shoulder at the telling exposure. "Joe," he said a moment later in a tremulous tone. "I think it's time to break out The Hardly Boys *Spy Book*, for I fear the foes we're fighting are foreign!"

The boys exchanged a swift, anxious glance. "Father's working for *them* again!" that look said.

Joe wordlessly went over to the hi-fi, removed a record and returned it to its protective sleeve. He then unscrewed the turntable to reveal a secret compartment. Inside was a thick leather-bound book.

"These are prints of every known foreign agent currently operating in the United States. A select number of respected and trusted detectives are issued this book each year. They're asked, as professionals and patriots, to keep an eye on suspicious activity. Father checks each fingerprint he stumbles across in his cases against this book," Frank explained.

Jackie nodded. They had a similar book under lock and key at police headquarters in San Francisco.

Frank took a magnifying glass from his pocket and flipped through the pages. Suddenly, he got all excited. "See for yourself, Detective Jones," he cried as he handed his magnifying glass to Jackie. When Jackie finished with her examination, she declared Frank's evaluation top-notch. What she said next almost shook Cherry out of her sling-back shoes.

"Boys, what on earth do the Russians want with your parents?"

CHAPTER 22

Foreign Foe?

"Russians?" Uncle Nelly cried. "Oh, dear!" He swooned into Willy's arms. Just then Nancy raced into the room, a plaster mold in her hands. "You'll never guess what I've found!" she cried excitedly. She took a deep breath, then exclaimed, *"Russian agents are responsible for this terrible crime!"*

Nancy was a bit surprised when her dramatic announcement drew no reaction from her chums. "They must not believe me," the young sleuth realized.

"I'll prove it," she said aloud. "I found prints from United States government-issue shoes outside the house," she announced. "When I was working on *The Case of the Sensible Shoes,* I became somewhat of an expert in identifying different kinds of sturdy footwear," she explained modestly, "especially shoes worn by police officers, G-men and secret agents. While this snub-nosed, heavy-heeled, thick-soled shoe would lead some to think that it was an American law enforcement agent assigned to serve and protect us peeking through the Hardly window earlier today, I know better!"

Nancy pointed to a tiny moon-shaped impression on the heel of the print. "If you look closely, you'll see a telltale sign. See what it says? *Made in America.*"

Still no one said anything.

"Don't you see?" Nancy queried them. "The owner of these shoes made one mistake. Instead of taking his shoes to a government-sanctioned repair shop, as any United States agent knows to do, he took them to the same kind of ordinary shoe shop John Q. Public frequents, the result being the shoemaker used heel plates bearing the proud words we see on so many of our fine goods, from precision engineered hi-fi stereos to the safe automobiles that give us Americans the freedom to travel our vast land in style. It could only be the work of the Russians, given their love of sensible shoes."

Nancy gave them a smug smile. Why, everyone had been stunned into silence by her keen detective work! That weekend seminar covering Special Agent Shoes had really paid off, she realized.

"We already know the Russians did it," Joe informed her. "Jackie found some fingerprints that matched those of a notorious Russian spy."

Nancy bit her bottom lip to keep it from trembling. "I must go wash this plaster dust from my hands," she gulped as she fled the room.

"But why would the Russians want your parents?" Cherry cried aloud. "Your father's not a secret agent!"

"There's only one answer to that question," Frank feared. "Father's working on another top-secret mission for the United States Government!"

"What a relief," Cherry exclaimed. "Then the Federal Bureau of Investigation is sure to find your parents in no time at all. I bet they've already been found and are on their way back here this very minute. I'll tell you what," she suggested cheerfully. "I'll tidy up while you boys call the Bureau headquarters."

"I'm afraid there's one problem with that plan," Frank informed her. "We can't call the FBI."

"Why not?" Cherry wanted to know. "Isn't it their job to lend a helping hand to citizens in times such as these? Surely the FBI will want to know if your father has been kidnapped, seeing as he's working for them."

"He's not working for the FBI, Cherry," Frank corrected her. After first extracting a pledge from his chums to never reveal what they were about to learn, Frank blurted out, "He's working for a government agency so secret that no one, not even the FBI, knows it exists, and even the people who work for it don't know what it's called!"

CHAPTER 23

Chili con Carne and Baked Alaska

Frank and Joe exchanged an anxious glance. "We'll have to tell them everything," that glance said, "for if we're going to rescue Mother and Father we'll need all the help we can get!"

"I'm going to show you something no one outside our nuclear family has ever seen," Frank told his chums. He reached deep into his trouser pocket and took out a small brass key. He crossed the room and unlocked the door to a shallow closet just large enough for a rack of trenchcoats. He pushed aside the clothes and disclosed an electronic panel with blinking red lights. He quickly punched a series of buttons, then stepped back as the wall slid open to reveal a dark, windowless room the size of a walk-in wardrobe closet. A tinny-sounding beep-beep-beep emanated from somewhere in the room.

"Nancy has a little room like this off her bedroom," Cherry gasped in recognition. "It's lined with cedar and stuffed with evening gowns and sweaters, ski togs and angora sets, little hats and fancy gloves and the most adorable handbags."

Frank threw on a switch and soft overhead lights blinked on. As the little group walked into the secret room, Cherry gazed about in wonder. It *was* like Nancy's walk-in wardrobe closet, but it wasn't, for where Nancy had specially built narrow shelves for her hats and shoes, the Hardlys had a map of the world. And where Nancy had a built-in jewelry chest, the Hardlys had a giant ham radio with speakers and microphones and a complicated looking antennae. "Golly," Cherry breathed as she looked at the blinking mechanical contraptions and buzzing gizmos.

"This is the Hardly Family Command Center," Frank told them. "You're the first outsiders to know our secret. Why, even Father's government contact doesn't know this room exists."

"Terrible things could happen if certain people knew of the location of Father's command post. Why, they could plant listening devices in this room and learn all sorts of top-secret things!" Joe blurted out.

Cherry gasped.

"You see, Nurse," Frank cut in. "There's a war going on— a war for the minds and hearts of free men everywhere. In the past, Father has helped the government uncover acts of treason and subversion lurking around every corner. But apparently that war has *yet* to be won."

Cherry shivered. Suddenly the room seemed icy cold. Jackie put her arm around the frightened nurse and held her tight. As Cherry snuggled close to the strong girl, she felt a warm surge racing through her body. It was a surge of pride: pride for the brave citizens engaged in the struggle for truth and justice so all Americans could enjoy the benefits of good schools, fresh air and lots of attractive outfits!

"I won't fail these brave soldiers," Cherry stiffened in determination. She made a vow to nurse as no one had ever nursed before!

"Hello?" they heard Nancy call from the den. "Where did everybody go?"

"We're in the closet," Cherry informed her. Nancy followed her voice, and when she stepped inside the room Cherry could tell, by the stunned look on her face, that she hadn't known of the existence of the Command Center either.

"You certainly kept this a secret all these years," Nancy exclaimed as she plopped down on a straight-back wooden chair.

"It was to protect you, Nancy," Frank told her. "And it has to remain a secret," he added hastily.

Nancy laughed bitterly. "Don't worry," she said. "If anyone can keep a secret, I can." The room grew quiet. Nancy seemed unusually distracted and perturbed, Frank thought, although her hair did look nice brushed back like that, and she had shaken almost all of the plaster dust from her outfit.

"Where were we?" Jackie asked, breaking the silence.

"Oh, yes," Frank snapped to attention. "This is our Radar-O-Scope," he said, pointing to a black box, resembling a television set, with its many dials. "It's just like the ones used in submarines, only ours is smaller. Father carries a transmitter in his pocket when he's out on a case so we can track him anywhere within a radius of one hundred miles. Plus, we have wristwatch tracking devices." Frank switched on the screen. After a few minutes of crackling and humming, it glowed an eerie greenish color.

"Father must not have the transmitter with him," Joe sighed. "Or else an orange blip would appear. Maybe he's called in to the reel-to-reel," he suggested helpfully.

"What's that?" Cherry asked.

"The reel-to-reel is a tape recording device hooked up to the Command Center telephone. A special motor attached to the telephone activates the tape so that incoming messages can be recorded and listened to later." Frank snapped the device into replay mode to see if there were any messages.

"What a marvelous invention," Cherry remarked.

"We have one very much like this at detective headquarters," Jackie said. "You could call and leave me a message any time you like," she murmured to Cherry.

Nancy pouted. All she had was a private line to the pink princess telephone in her bedroom.

The boys jumped when their father's unmistakably calm voice came over the tape loud and clear. "Caramel bread pudding, mushroom spread, chili con carne, steamed cauliflower hearts, wilted lettuce-leaf salad, baked Alaska, deviled crabs."

Cherry looked alarmed. "That's a recipe for dyspepsia!" she was about to cry when Frank suddenly blurted out, in a gleeful tone,

"Father hates those dishes! This must be a secret-coded message!"

"But what does it mean?" the others chorused.

"We'll run it through the Hardly Decoding Machine," Frank declared, leaping into action. He flipped the master switch on a massive machine, the size of a two-door Frigidaire, that stood against one wall of the little room. The contraption came alive as lights flashed, knobs twirled and a mechanical whirring sound filled the little room.

"This artificial brain is set up to recognize, analyze and transcribe over one hundred and thirty-seven known codes of the modern world," Joe explained as Frank typed the list onto a special typewriter that turned the letters into a series of dots and dashes on a paper tape. Next he fed the tape into a slot. "Now we wait," Frank breathed excitedly.

"As one of the most brilliant detectives the world has ever seen, Father knows every code imaginable," Joe pointed out. "Why, he could have used any one of them when devising this secret message. This machine saves us the hours of drudgery we used to spend hunched over the worktable, sweat pouring down our brows as we figured these things by hand."

A bell sounded and a moment later the machine spit out a piece of paper. On it were seven cryptic lines:

> *in closet under stairs*
> *secret map*
> *watch your step*
> *things are not what they seem*
> *underneath Lake Merrimen*
> *what goes up*
> *must come down*

"Is there a closet under the stairs that lead to the second floor in this house?" Jackie wondered.

"No," Nancy answered authoritatively. "There's a lovely built-in credenza under the stairs."

"And we don't have a cellar," Joe mused. "Father does have a detective's office downtown, but it's in a one-story building."

"Maybe it's at one of your father's hangouts," Jackie persisted. "His favorite bar, a gymnasium or the local men's club."

Frank shook his head. "Father doesn't mix much with other fellows," he told her. "When he's not solving a case, he's home with us."

"Where could it be?" the boys wondered.

"The only other place Father ever goes is the cottage, and there's no closet there, save a small one in the master bedroom," Frank said.

A funny look came over Uncle Nelly's face. All this talk about closets had jogged his memory. "Those two horrid men who tied us up asked me if we had any closets," he remembered. "Boys, where are those architectural plans we took from them?"

"Right here in my pocket, Uncle," Frank said. He pulled the tube out of his trousers pocket and laid the plans on the table.

Uncle Nelly flicked on a table lamp, took his reading glasses from his shirt pocket and closely examined the blueprint. Soon a wide grin lit up his youthful face. "Aha!" he cried. "I remember now—there *was* a closet under the stairs at our charming cottage at Lake Merrimen. Your father and I would play games in there on rainy afternoons, and use it for a hiding place when it came time to eat our vegetables," Uncle Nelly remembered, chuckling. "Mother was forever urging us to come out of the closet, so in 1923, when she redecorated the cottage, she had it boarded up."

"So those thugs weren't looking for antiques to steal, they were looking for whatever is in that hidden closet," Jackie concluded, saying what was on all their minds. "But how could those poodle-snatching thugs be connected to the Russian agents who kidnapped your parents?"

CHAPTER 24

A Chase

"Sputnik!" Frank spat out, his keen hazel eyes narrowing in anger.

"Gesundheit," Cherry cried as she reached for a fresh hankie.

Trust Cherry to lighten the mood, Jackie thought with a little grin. "Frank, what does the Russian satellite Sputnik have to do with the hidden closet?" Jackie quizzed him.

While the others listened attentively, Frank pieced together the case. "First, prized poodles are kidnapped, then the dognapper and an accomplice try to strong-arm their way inside our cottage, with architectural blueprints showing the location of a secret closet. That same day, Mother and Father are kidnapped by Russians, and Father's code specifically mentions that very same closet that may contain some kind of secret map."

"Something just doesn't make sense, though," Cherry admitted aloud. "Who would want that many poodles?"

Frank's next words were chilling: "One month after the successful launch of Sputnik I, the Russians launched an even bigger and better satellite, only this one had as its passenger *a small dog!*"

"Are you saying the Russians are stealing our top dogs for use in outer space?" Cherry gasped. "Poodles in space? What kind of people would do such a thing?" she cried in horror.

"The kind of people who would go to any length to get what they wanted," Frank said darkly.

"Could the thugs have been looking for the secret map in the secret closet?" Nancy wondered aloud.

"We'll see soon enough!" Frank cried. Within minutes, they had piled into their vehicles and were speeding toward the Hardly cottage at Lake Merrimen. Nancy shifted into third gear as she made the ascent up the main dirt road leading to the small house; by her side, Frank was mulling over the shocking events of the past hour. Jackie and Joe followed behind at an even clip, grimly rehashing every aspect of the queer case. They barely noticed the picturesque scenery of the breathtaking lake, so intent were they on getting to the cottage and discovering the meaning of Fennel Hardly's cryptic list.

Frank shivered. This was their most perplexing case yet, and if they didn't solve it—and fast—they would lose the best parents two fellows ever had. "Step on it, Nancy," Frank directed. "Hang the traffic laws, goshdarnit! We've got a mystery to solve; probably the most important of our young careers!"

CHAPTER 25

A Lulu of a Revelation

"Stand back, Joe," Willy ordered as he picked up the crowbar and jammed the tool into the wall. Sweat glistened on Willy's thick corded neck as he pressed his broad powerful shoulder against the rod. He rocked back and forth until he had created a deep vertical groove. Willy pulled the heavy bar out of the wall, and with his feet firmly planted on the floor, found another soft spot in which to insert his tool. "Oomph," Willy grunted as he continued.

Joe's jaw dropped in admiration as sweat poured down the wedge of the man's back, causing his snug tee-shirt to cling to his broad torso. Willy stripped to the waist, and barely pausing to wipe his glistening forehead on the damp tee-shirt, he threw the shirt to Joe, catching him squarely in the face. "I'm almost there!" Willy cried.

He thrust his sturdy tool into the pliant wood over and over again. The panel groaned and creaked with each powerful probe, bringing it closer and closer to bursting wide open. "Just a little more," Willy cried. "This one ought to do it." Harder and harder he slammed the bar into the wall, each time coming closer to whatever lay beyond its barrier.

Joe was so excited he could hardly breathe! He clutched the shirt to his chest and watched with bated breath as the muscular man worked. How long could Willy keep it up? Finally there was a shudder and a heave, and the crowbar found its mark. The entire wall, molding, floorboards and all, seemed to explode and fell in splinters around Willy's boots.

"Look, Frank! A door!" Joe cried. Joe gasped as Willy flung open the warped wooden door only to reveal...*an empty closet!*

"There's no secret map in there!" Cherry cried in dismay.

"Not at first glance," Nancy warned. She rushed inside the small musty space and began running her hands over the wallpaper looking for lumps or bumps that would indicate something had been hidden behind it.

"Uncle, do you recall any hiding places in here?" Frank asked.

"I'm sure there's nothing special about this closet," Uncle Nelly told them in a rueful tone. "Why on earth those men wanted inside it so badly I'll never know. It's small and cramped and smells like wash left too long on the line. Not only that, the wallpaper is far more hideous than I remember," he shuddered, noticing that the floral Victorian pattern clashed dreadfully with the pleasant rose-colored living room walls. Uncle Nelly vowed that when renovation of the cottage began anew, the closet under the stairs would be put back to its original use. "But not with that dreadful wall covering!" he pledged.

"I'm getting a chair so I can examine the ceiling," Nancy determined.

"Watch your step," Cherry warned. Why, Nancy might twist an ankle or break her collarbone!

"Watch your step? That's a line from Father's secret message!" Frank cried. He got to his knees and started to examine the worn wood floor. The warped boards creaked under the weight of the lad. Soon he found a small notch just big enough for the tip of his trusty Boy Scout penknife. A plank of wood pulled away, revealing a dark space.

"There *is* a hiding place in this closet," Joe breathed excitedly as he shone his flashlight into the hole. The beam of his light glinted off a rusty metal box tucked into one corner. The boys shared a look of triumph. Surely they had found their father's secret map!

"Hurry, Joe," Frank urged as his brother snatched up the old box and brought it into the light of the room.

"Any minute now, we'll have the map in our hands," Joe hooted triumphantly as he used his own handy Boy Scout penknife to break open the lock. "Ah-ha!" he cried as the lid popped open. Then, in a keenly disappointed tone, he added, "Oh, it's only old family snapshots."

"Old family snapshots?" Uncle Nelly cried in alarm. "Joseph, give them to me!"

"Perhaps there's one of Uncle Nelly in an unflattering hairstyle," Joe grinned to his brother. "Here's one of Grandmother

Hardly standing in front of the lake wearing a funny bathing costume," he said. "But who's this pretty little curly-haired girl holding her hand?" he mused. "Why, she looks just like Father!"

"No, boys," Uncle Nelly pleaded. "Forget you ever saw that photograph!" When Joe saw the alarm on his uncle's face, he dropped the box, scattering the sepia snapshots all over the rug.

"Sorry, Uncle," he cried. Joe hadn't meant to upset his uncle; he had just been acting like his boyishly curious self.

Uncle Nelly knelt to gather the photographs, growing misty-eyed when he gazed fondly at the little girl in the picture. "I suppose it's foolish folly to try and keep the truth from you boys forever," he murmured. "And if, heaven forbid, we can't find your father, I'm sure he'd want you to know the whole truth."

The boys gasped. Their family had a secret?

Uncle Nelly looked mighty serious. "Boys," he said, "I've got something to tell you. And I only hope you're grown-up enough to understand." He looked fondly at the little girl in the photograph.

"Boys, this was your father, Fennel P. Hardly, as a child."

"What?" gasped Frank.

Uncle Nelly nodded. "Fennel P. Hardly, world-famous detective and husband to Mrs. Hardly for twenty-seven years is really my older sister, Fanny P. Hardly."

Frank and Joe were stunned into silence. Uncle Nelly continued.

"You see, boys, when Fanny and I were young, there was a lot of prejudice against girls. People thought they weren't as smart as boys, weren't logical or strong."

Frank gasped. "Prejudice against girls! Why, I've often wished I could be as strong and smart as a girl!" cried the lad.

"And I've often wished I *was* a girl," Joe admitted. The Hardly boys looked at each other in open-mouthed astonishment. "How could people be so stupid?" they chorused.

"Well, boys, people *were* pretty stupid back then. More than anything, Fanny wanted to be a detective, and she knew that there would never be a place in that world for a girl dick, so she decided to dress as a man, at least until she got established and made a name for her, er, himself.

"And pretty soon she discovered she *liked* pretending she

was a man and since your mother didn't mind, well, the rest is history!"

"It's really true," Frank murmured in shock. "Father is a girl!" He bit his lip to hold back the tears, jumped up and raced to the closet.

"Francis—" Uncle Nelly started after his nephew. He stopped when he saw how truly upset the usually unflappable Frank was. The lad was pacing back and forth in the closet. Frank stopped and faced his uncle. "Uncle Nelly, how could Father keep this from us?" he cried, stomping his foot on the warped wooden floor.

"Frank, be careful," Uncle Nelly warned. "That floor dates back to the turn of the century." But his warning was to no avail, for just then, they heard the dreaded sound of old wood splintering as the floor under Frank's feet gave way.

"H-e-l-p-p-p-p!" Frank cried as he started to fall. Everyone rushed to the closet just in time to see the top of Frank's crewcut disappear into the darkness!

CHAPTER 26

A Daring Leap

 "Jumping crickets!" Joe exclaimed as he knelt on the jagged closet floor and stuck his head in the hole left by his brother. "Can you hear me, Frank?" he cried out. His voice echoed in the tunnel that had swallowed his brother. He took out the emergency flashlight he always carried in his pants pocket and shone his light down the dark hole. "Frank!" he cried again, but there was no answer.

The minute Cherry heard Frank's plaintive plea, she had snapped into action. Cherry Aimless, Disaster Nurse, barked out orders right and left. "Jackie, go to the car and get my first-aid kit. Willy, tie that quilt to two poles for a makeshift stretcher and then go in the kitchen and boil water. Nancy, get me clean, fresh towels—and plenty of them! And Uncle Nelly," she added, handing him a fresh handkerchief from her pocket, "blow your nose!"

Uncle Nelly did as he was told.

Joe leaned perilously over the hole, almost slipping in himself. Uncle Nelly yanked the lad back by the collar of his freshly laundered sporty summer shirt; Joe gave a start, dropping his flashlight. He listened for it to hit bottom, and using his glow-in-the-dark radium wristwatch, timed its descent. "It took approximately point four-five seconds to hit bottom," he declared, doing a quick calculation in his head. "That's a drop of sixteen feet; surely Frank couldn't have been badly injured, seeing as how he's athletically inclined and all."

"We'll have pots of boiling water in no time," Willy came back from the kitchen to report. Joe grabbed a nearby rope and threw one end to Willy. "Grab ahold and I'll shimmy down," he instructed his uncle's strong chum. "But first, let me get my back-up flashlight from the trunk."

The moment Joe was gone, Nancy put down her stack of

linens. "Do you have a firm grasp on the rope?" Nancy asked. Willy nodded.

"Good," Nancy said. Then before anyone could stop her, she tucked her hem into her belt, grabbed the rope with one hand and her pocketbook with the other, jumped into the hole and was gone!

CHAPTER 27

The Science Lesson

 "Frank, are you down here?" Nancy called out. As she listened to her voice echo in the tunnel, she groped in her pocket book for her flashlight. It wasn't there! "Oh, I left it in my alligator clutch!" she moaned. The girl sleuth crept bravely forward through the pitch-black darkness, a little bruised and shaken and fearing her stockings were snagged, but more concerned about her chum Frank than about her own troubles. Where could he be?

Nancy shivered as she gingerly made her way through the dark, damp cave with no light source to make out the pits, sharp drops, or protrusions that could spell instant injury to a girl without proper head protection. Frank could be lying on the ground in pain! As an avid spelunker, Nancy knew that while most accidents happened in the home, a cave was the second-most likely place for an accident.

"What's that?" she gasped as something flew above her hairdo. "It must be a bat," she told herself. Nancy was level-headed enough to know that, despite their reputation, bats seldom flew near enough to cave explorers to become entangled in their coiffures. She knew their keen echolocation perception enabled them to avoid all obstacles, even in total darkness.

"Frank," she called again. "Frank Hardly, where are you?" She was mighty relieved, yet somewhat alarmed, to hear a boyish groan as she almost stepped on the limp figure of her friend lying next to a stalactite.

"Oh, Frank, are you all right?" Nancy cried as she felt in her pocket book for her wallet-sized first-aid kit containing bandages and an aspirin.

"I'm fine," Frank said curtly as he brushed aside her attempts to help him up. He stumbled ahead in the darkness, then cried, "Oops!" as he tripped over a rock and fell, ripping the knees of his new sporty twill slacks. The lad sat in the dark cave and put his head in his hands. Hot tears raced down his handsome face. He tried to sniff quietly, but in the hollow cave, all sounds were magnified.

"Frank, are you upset?" Nancy asked softly as she took a fresh hankie from her pocket and thrust it at the boy, inadvertently smacking him in the head. "Sorry," she added when she realized what she had done.

"I'm fine," Frank insisted flatly. "Everything's just peachy."

Nancy sighed. She had known Frank long enough to know when he wasn't telling the whole truth. "I know you're worried about your parents having been kidnapped by Russian agents—who wouldn't be—but I suspect there's something else bothering you. Frank, are you upset about your father being a girl?"

"Of course not," Frank snapped. "I'm just busy thinking about our peculiar situation. If we're going to explore this cave safely, we'll need to shimmy back up to the cottage and drive to Feyport for the Hardly Boys Cave Exploring Kit. We'll need hardhats, miner's lights and lug-soled boots."

"We haven't time," Nancy insisted. "Precious minutes are ticking away." Besides, she could just picture the scene upstairs. "This little episode should tug on the nervous nurse's heartstrings for sure!" she thought with a secret smile. "Won't Cherry be impressed if I return with *the* clue that cracks this case wide open?"

"I'm not going back until we find something," Nancy proclaimed hotly. "Remember what your father's clue said? *All is not what it seems underneath Lake Merrimen.* Well, we're on the right track!"

"All right," Frank conceded. "But I still think it's sheer folly to traverse a cave without the proper equipment."

"Let's see what I've got in here," Nancy said as she plunged her hands in her purse. "I've got chocolate bars, a thermos of coffee and a sack of oranges," she reported.

Frank dug through his pockets and came up with a disappointing array of insignificant items. "A comb, my wallet and a piece of flint," he said dejectedly. "I can strike the flint against the wall and make a spark, but what are we going to light?"

"I've got a can of hair spray," Nancy realized.

"I'm sure your hair looks fine," Frank sighed.

"I don't doubt that," Nancy chuckled. "The point is, hair lacquer is made of flammable material, and if we can rig up a way to control the pressure flow, we can make a nifty torch." Moments later, the clever girl, with just a bobby pin and her own keen know-how, constructed a crude torch that would provide them with enough light to safely see their way about the dark cavern.

Frank was properly chagrined. "You don't have two hard hats in that purse of yours, do you?" he grinned.

"No, but I've got two thick cotton pads with strap-like tails at each end," Nancy showed him. "We can put the pads on our heads and loop the ends over our ears and at least have one layer of protection from unexpected bumps."

"What a clever device," Frank cried, making a mental note to add them to the Hardly Boys Cave Exploring Kit.

Nancy held the torch while Frank fastened the pad to his head. She then followed suit. "Nancy, you're top drawer!" Frank declared.

"Tell that to Cherry," Nancy grinned back. It felt good to be hard at work again, using just her wholesome good sense and the contents of her purse to figure her way out of a jam. "If only Cherry could be here to see us!" she thought ruefully as they made their way through the cave.

"This must be one of the secret caves old Miss Witherspoon was always talking about," Frank realized.

The two old chums raced through the dark cave, hoping there would be sufficient fuel in their torch for a thorough investigation. They gazed in wonder as they descended ever deeper into a subterranean world that had been right under their noses all along.

"Look, Frank!" Nancy cried. "There's a tunnel that branches off ahead." Keenly disappointed, they found the tunnel blocked by boulders. "There must have been an underground avalanche," Nancy guessed.

A queer look came over Frank's face as he examined the area. "One caused by dynamite!" he cried. "This filament is identical to the brand I found in our den!"

"Can we break through?" Nancy asked hopefully.

"We'll need ten Willies," Frank sighed. "I'm afraid this passageway is blocked for good!

"Why would Father send us to this dead end?" Frank cried.

"Maybe it wasn't a dead end when your Father drew that map," Nancy suggested. "Let's hurry and see what else we can find down here—quick, before I run out of hair spray," she urged.

Soon the unmistakable sound of water lapping against rock caught their attention. They reached a shallow drop and found themselves staring straight down into the placid water of Lake Merrimen. Frank checked his combination wristwatch and compass. "We're directly under our dock," he announced. "Want to go back or swim for it?"

"Swim for it," was Nancy's quick reply. "I've got a bathing costume in my purse." She slipped behind a rock to change, and soon the two were poised to make their leap into the watery, pitch-black pit.

"I'm awfully sorry things haven't worked out the way we planned," Frank said sadly as he took several deep breaths, getting his lungs ready for their underwater swim.

"It's not your fault your parents were kidnapped," Nancy pointed out. "Besides, if I crack this case, I may still win Cherry's adoration." She made the international Good Luck sign and plunged into the cold water.

Frank followed close behind. The water seeped through his clothes and quickly chilled the lad, but what really chilled Frank were the horrible thoughts swirling in his head—terrible ideas he hadn't been able to shake since hearing Uncle Nelly's shocking announcement.

If he wasn't the son of world-famous detective Fennel P. Hardly and his wife Mrs. Hardly, whose son was he?

"But I *am* a Hardly boy!" he told himself, over and over. "And Fennel P. Hardly's my dad—the best dad a guy ever had!" But deep down, he knew that it couldn't be true. They had covered human reproduction in health class and something just didn't seem right.

"I can't possibly be Fennel's son!" Frank realized in true and utter anguish. *"I'm not really a Hardly boy!"*

CHAPTER 28

What Luck!

"I don't know how you kids stand the suspense of detective work. Why, I can barely attend an auction without fainting in anticipation during the bidding," Uncle Nelly admitted as he paced up and down the living room all atwitter, practically wearing a path in the antique Turkish rug. "Oh dear, oh dear," he fretted whilst wringing his hands together. "What if Frank and Nancy are lying in a heap, all broken and bruised?" he wailed.

"Uncle, you know Nancy and Frank are seasoned detectives," Joe consoled the nervous Nelly. "Why, they've been through far worse than this and always return victorious with nary a hair out of place."

Still Nelly couldn't rest. "If anything should happen to either one of you boys, your father would never forgive me. Why, you're the apples of his eye!"

"Nelson, why not sit down and have a hot soothing drink?" Willy urged as he came into the room with a tray of nourishing snacks and steaming hot coffee. He had busied himself in the kitchen making a selection of sandwiches in case the errant detectives required sustenance after their underground ordeal. "And I've brought a plate of your favorite anise cookies," Willy tempted his touchy chum.

"I couldn't possibly eat a thing," Uncle Nelly protested. "Well, maybe just one," he murmured, adding, "This may be a long night; I'd best keep up my strength." Uncle Nelly took a cookie from the plate and nervously nibbled at it. "Drat!" he exclaimed as he dropped some crumbs on the carpet. He raced to the kitchen and returned with a small whisk broom and a dustpan.

"While I'm at it, I might as well get to these dirty windows." He took a bottle of window-cleaning solution and a clean cotton rag from his pocket and feverishly attacked the front picture-glass. "Oh, dear, I liked this fabric when I picked it out, but now I think it looks all wrong in this room," he bemoaned as he glared at the chintz drapes. "Will, do you think we need new curtains?" he cried.

"It's up to you, dear," Willy said. "Your uncle always redecorates when he's upset," he added in an aside to Joe. It was best, Willy knew, to keep out of Nelly's way in times like these. "How's your ladder coming along, Joe?" Willy asked, eager to lend the lad a hand. As an ex-merchant marine, Willy knew practically all there was to know about hitches, knots, slings, splices and lashings. He carefully checked Joe's work and found it to his liking. "This will hold you for sure," he said approvingly as he examined Joe's handiwork. Joe was turning out to be a lad after his own heart!

While Joe anchored the ladder with an anvil, Jackie slipped on a knapsack containing food, medical supplies and extra flashlight batteries. They had called down to Frank and Nancy but received no response, so Jackie and Joe were going down after them.

"You'll need a warm, sensible sweater," Cherry reminded Jackie softly. If truth be told, she was a little nervous about Jackie going down the hole. Cherry swallowed her fear. "Jackie's a professional, and if I'm contemplating being her girlfriend, I'd better get used to a life of danger!" she realized.

Jackie gave Cherry a wink that told her everything would be okay.

"I've got a thick, warm sweater sure to fit your broad shoulders," Willy offered. "And one for you, too, Joe. I'll be right back." He raced upstairs to his wardrobe. Luckily he had packed a soft gray cardigan that would look awfully nice on Jackie, and a red v-neck pullover that would bring out the cherries in Joe's cheeks.

"Oh dear, oh dear," Uncle Nelly fretted as he examined the hole in the closet floor. "We're going to have to redo this entire area." He took his reading glasses from his shirt pocket and studied the inside of the closet. "This wallpaper appears worse every time I look at it," he shuddered.

He aimed his nozzle at the wall and squirted. As he scrubbed, faint blue lines began to appear. He stopped when he realized his efforts were only turning the scrawls a darker shade of blue.

Uncle Nelly scratched his head and murmured, "How queer! I swear this drawing wasn't here a minute ago! We'll just have to paper over it," he sighed. "Although it's beyond me why anyone would draw on our closet wall."

His uncle's observation struck a chord in Joe.

"Oh, Uncle, stop at once!" Joe cried. "That sounds like invisible ink! You might have found the secret map we've been searching for." He raced into the closet and whipped out his magnifying glass. It *was* a map, and it was in his father's distinctive, neat hand.

"Your father must have drawn this before Mother had this old closet boarded up," Uncle Nelly guessed excitedly.

Joe made long rips in the wallpaper with his knife and peeled the map from the wall. "This appears to be a topographical map of a lake and a nearby resort town—why, it must be Lake Merrimen!" he gasped after a moment's inspection. "See?" he showed the others. "The kidney shape in the middle is the lake; here's the main drive into town; these squares represent lakefront homes—and the one with the *X* must be our charming cottage," Joe guessed.

"But I don't understand the sense of scale," Joe mused, "The River Depths Sanitarium is practically in our backyard and it's actually three miles northwest of here. Plus there are roads connecting the lake, the sanitarium, and our cottage where none exist."

"Those triangular shapes could be either hills or caves," Jackie suggested.

"Could they be the legendary underground caverns of Lake Merrimen?" Joe hooted with excitement.

"Is there a map of Illinois handy?" Jackie wondered out loud. "We'll compare the two for scale and come up with a reasonable facsimile of the area."

"I'll get one from Nancy's car," Cherry volunteered. She flung open the front door but froze as she spied frightful shapes in the dim light of the moonlit porch.

"Eek!" she cried as two long-legged creatures dripping water and oozing a brown substance climbed the porch steps. "It's sea monsters!" she cried, raising her hands to her face in fright. "Oops!" she tittered when she snapped on the porch light and found it was *really* Frank and Nancy.

"Very funny," Nancy glowered as she stepped through the doorway, with Frank right behind her.

The chums had a million questions for the detectives.

"Where have you been?"

"Are you hurt? Any cuts or contusions? Do you feel dizzy or nauseous? Would you like a pain reliever?"

"How did you get from the closet to the front door?"

"Do you think that mud will come out of your nice swim costume?"

"And what's that on your head?"

Nancy fled for the washroom, leaving Frank behind to explain their strange adventure. Willy grabbed a clean towel while Uncle Nelly went to put the kettle on for a pot of warming tea. "Golly," Joe cried, with not a little envy, as he watched the powerful Willy give the dripping wet lad a vigorous rubdown. Frank had all the fun!

Frank's words tumbled out all willy-nilly as he explained their exciting discovery. "There's a cave under our charming cottage that leads to the lake. It goes somewhere else, too, but the tunnel's been dynamited. Do you know what that means?" he asked the others.

Uncle Nelly clapped with glee. Why, the cave could very well be the answer to all of their storage needs and the site of any number of fun theme parties.

"It means the triangles on the map we found *are* caves," Jackie cried.

"You found the map?" Frank gasped.

"Thanks to Uncle Nelly," Joe grinned. Uncle Nelly beamed with pride. It was the least he could have done! "You just have to know what it is you're looking for," he said modestly.

Frank poured over the diagram. "There appear to be three ways into the caverns," he announced. "The one we found, which is unfortunately blocked, one at the River Depths Sanitarium and another at a house on Shady Lane. Joe, get me the map from our car." A moment later, Frank had his answer. "The third entrance is at 37 Shady Lane."

"That's the address of the Meekses' palatial summer home," Nancy announced. She had had a quick bath and was now clad in a comfy mint-green terry cloth robe several sizes too large and had a matching towel wrapped turban-style around her trademark titian hair. Even in a borrowed bathrobe and a simple towel Nancy still looked picture-perfect.

Nancy filled them in. "In the mid-1940s, Myra Meeks received an unexpected inheritance from a distant relative that allows her and her family to live a lavish lifestyle far exceeding a judge's salary. The first thing she did was buy the lake home on Shady Lane. Funny thing is, the same publicity-mad Myra Meeks, who invites reporters to visit her suburban home every time she redecorates, refuses to let anyone step inside her summer house."

"Maybe it's where she goes to get away from the demands of being a successful society matron," Cherry guessed.

"I hear she has eggshell-white carpet," Uncle Nelly said in a knowing tone.

"So there's little chance she'll let us dig up her floor to look for an entrance," Joe sighed.

"Not even a matter of the utmost national security would convince Myra Meeks to let us inside that house," Nancy shook her head. "I know because once, when I was working on *The Case of the Lost Lawn Ornaments*, I tried to take a shortcut through her property and was almost eaten by fierce dogs."

"Besides, you know she's the biggest gossip in town. Why, if we tell her what's going on, in a matter of minutes it will be all over Lake Merrimen that our parents have been kidnapped by Russians," Frank warned.

CHAPTER 29

A Dire Warning!

 The doorbell rang, then a thin yellow envelope shot under the door. It was a telegram for the Hardly boys!

"A telegram at eleven o'clock at night; it must be important," Cherry cried.

"Perhaps it's from Chief O'Malley," Joe said hopefully, "with a vital clue for our investigation." He eagerly ripped open the flimsy envelope and read the brief missive aloud.

"To Hardly boys. Stop. Stay away from secret caves! Stop. **Danger!** *Stop. Signed, a friend. Stop."*

"This cinches it!" Frank cried. "Someone's trying their best to scare us away, but it's not going to work!"

"But how are we going to get down there?" Joe groaned.

"Frank, would you agree that if there's one underwater cave leading to a tunnel, there just might be another?" Nancy wondered.

"That's exactly what I was thinking, Nancy," Frank admitted. "Those underwater formations often occur in multiples. Joe, let's strap on our new scuba gear and make a thorough search of the lakeshore wall for another cave," he proposed.

"We'll cover more ground by breaking into pairs," Nancy agreed with a furtive look Cherry's way.

"Nancy's right," Jackie added. She took her gold detective's shield from her pocket and pinned it to her tee-shirt, then checked to make sure her gun was loaded. It was. "I'm going to the Lake Merrimen jail and interrogate that thug. We haven't time to sit around and wait for the chief to question him."

"Right!" Nancy enthused, relieved to be getting the dashing detective out of her just-washed hair.

"That guy might need a nurse when I get through with him," Jackie added, looking straight at Cherry.

"You know I'll go wherever the call to duty takes me," Cherry cried. "But first, let me get my sweater."

"Wait!" Nancy cried. "I have a—er—plan, and I need—uh— *a nurse* in order for it to work!"

"I'm a nurse!" Cherry gasped.

Jackie crossed her muscular arms over her broad chest and looked annoyed. What was Nancy up to? "Oh, really?" she asked Nancy in a suspicious tone. "What's this plan of yours?"

"Cherry and I are going to search for a way inside those hidden caves, too," the quick-thinking detective replied. "We're going undercover at the River Depths Sanitarium!"

"Are we *both* going to be nurses?" Cherry wondered. Golly, if she had known this was going to happen, she would have packed *two* Travel Nurses' uniforms.

Nancy shook her head. "You'll be a private nurse traveling with Miss Darcy New, a movie actress who's suffered a recent nervous collapse."

Joe was puzzled. "Who's this Darcy New, and can we trust her to keep a secret?" he wondered.

Nancy giggled, slipped on dark glasses and clip-on earrings from her pocketbook and said, in a husky tone, "You mean you don't remember me from my starring role in the smash hit *Chit Chat?*"

Joe was impressed. Using just a few props and her own innate abilities, Nancy had transformed herself into a glamorous actress!

"It's an alias I used while returning to River Depths," Nancy further explained. "In Dust Bin, Nebraska, we fooled some nosy reporters into believing that I was an actress suffering from a nervous breakdown, headed for the world-renowned River Depths Sanitarium, and not girl detective Nancy Clue headed home to confess to the murder of my father."

"And I said I was her nurse, which wasn't *really* a lie since I *am* a nurse," Cherry added.

"As a nurse, you can move through the sanitarium virtually unnoticed," Nancy pointed out, "while I'll be able to mingle with the patients and subtly quiz them about secret tunnels. It's the perfect solution, but I'll need a Companion Nurse to cinch the charade."

"I'm your girl," Cherry promised. "I mean, I'm your—er—nurse," she hastily amended when she saw the pained expression in Jackie's eyes.

"It's too dangerous," Jackie objected. "I don't want anything to happen to you, Cherry," she added in a softer tone.

"Cherry will be in good hands with Nancy," Frank reassured Jackie.

Jackie was none too happy to hear that. A look of fierce determination spread across her face. If she could crack this case tonight, she could stop this sanitarium misadventure of Nancy's from ever starting! "I'll be back—and soon," she told the others as she raced out the door.

"Good-bye and good luck," Cherry called as she flicked on the porch light and waved to the departing detective. Jackie hopped into Joe's jalopy, gunned the motor and pulled out of the driveway. A few seconds later, the car screeched to an abrupt halt, the back door flew open and a chagrined-looking Midge and Velma tumbled out of the back seat. Midge exchanged a few quick words with Jackie, then the car roared off, leaving the bedraggled couple standing on the front lawn holding their shoes.

"Midge! Velma! Where have you been?" Cherry cried as she raced over to her chums. She hadn't seen them for hours!

Midge looked a little sheepish. "During the party, we snuck away to take a nap in the back seat of Joe's jalopy and when we woke up, we were here," she explained, adding, "Wherever this is." She tucked the tail of her short-sleeved shirt into her trousers and buckled her thin leather belt. Velma ducked into a dark corner of the porch to smooth on her stockings and otherwise straighten her mussed outfit.

"What's happened?" Midge quizzed Cherry. "Why is Jackie going to talk to the poodlesnatcher now? She looked pretty upset."

"Nancy and I are going to the sanitarium," Cherry reported.

"Things *are* bad," Midge muttered. She shook her head. And everything had been going so well at the party. "Honestly, we can't leave you kids alone for a minute," she sighed.

"You don't know the half of it, Midge," Cherry exclaimed. "The Hardly parents have been kidnapped by Russian agents, Frank and Nancy fell through the closet floor, and now we're all searching for a way into some secret caverns where we believe there might be even bigger secrets."

Midge stared at Cherry. "Is that all?" she asked dryly.

"Oh, I almost forgot," Cherry cried. "It turns out Frank and Joe's father, Mr. Hardly, is *really* a girl," she said confidentially. "Only don't mention it in front of Frank, as it seems to have upset him."

Nancy poked her head out the door. "Oh! Midge, Velma. Where have you two been?"

"In another world, apparently," Midge shook her head.

"Tell me all about it later," Nancy cried. "Cherry, we need you in here now. We're scheming." Cherry eagerly obeyed.

Midge raised one eyebrow in alarm and shot Velma a worried look. Velma calmly took out her compact and applied powder to her shiny nose. Then she snapped it shut. "Don't interfere," she warned Midge as she went into the house, adding, "You've got lipstick all over your neck."

Midge hastily scrubbed her neck with her handkerchief. Once inside, the boys, busy testing their scuba gear, quickly brought Midge and Velma up to date.

"What can I do?" Midge wondered when she realized the gravity of the situation.

"You can come to the lake with us," Joe offered. "I'm sure Mother wouldn't mind if we loaned you one of her bathing costumes."

Midge looked horrified. "I couldn't just go in what I'm wearing?" she asked hopefully, looking down at her rumpled trousers and scuffed wingtips.

Frank shook his head. "Those shoes would sink you in a minute," he said.

"I'll go to the sanitarium with Nancy and Cherry then," Midge offered.

"Me too," Velma piped up.

"No way," Midge said. "It's too dangerous."

"I'm sticking to you, Midge Fontaine," Velma stubbornly declared. "I'll be a nurse. Cherry can show me what to do."

Cherry wondered if this was going to be her last outing as Cherry Aimless, Registered Nurse. What was the penalty, she wondered, for helping someone impersonate a nurse? Would she lose her license? Have her crisp cap and cunning cape taken away? She squared her shoulders and pushed those thoughts out of her head. Her chum Nancy's friends' parents were in trouble and that was all that mattered!

"Midge, you can't come with us because it's a *women's* psychiatric hospital," Cherry explained. "You'd either have to check yourself in as a patient and submit to a thorough physical examination—"

Midge shuddered.

"—or put on a nurse's uniform and pretend to work there," she finished.

"Me in a dress?" Midge raised one brow in alarm. "Can't I just sneak in and stay close at hand in case you need me?"

"The place is crawling with staff," Nancy told her. "It's a *very* private institution with the best care and newest treatments." Her mind was racing a mile a minute as she planned a suitable wardrobe for the adventure ahead. Conservatively speaking, she'd need a glamorous travel outfit, several pairs of lounging pajamas, a few cute bed jackets, and sports outfits suitable for prowling the grounds in search of tunnels.

"I guess we're stuck here," Midge sighed to Velma, who gave her a little squeeze. There was no one she'd rather be stuck to than Midge!

"I'll need help manning the Hardly Command Center at the Hardly house," Willy pointed out. Once Willy had explained exactly what that was, Midge readily agreed to be second-in-charge of the vital electronic gizmos.

"It's all settled, then," Nancy declared. "I'll go home and select my wardrobe. Since the stores closed hours ago, I'll have to make due with what I've got," she said resignedly. "I'll just have to alter some of my own outfits if I'm going to pass as a glamorous movie star."

"What kind of movie star are you going to play?" Joe wondered as he checked the oxygen level in his air tank. "The bubbly all-American girl-next-door who goes to the big city and gets her heart broken only to realize life on the farm isn't as bad as she thought, or the pretty young ingenue with stardust in her eyes who'll do anything to be that one-in-a-million who makes it in a tough industry?"

"Good question, Joe," Nancy mused. "I'll have to look through my wardrobe and see what I've got."

"I'm a whiz with a needle and thread," Uncle Nelly offered, eager to contribute.

"I'm a pretty good seamstress myself," Velma volunteered. She gave Midge a kiss. "You go play with Willy, and I'll see you later," she directed.

Satisfied that the teams would function like a well-oiled watch, Frank and Joe raced upstairs to don their lake gear. "It seems I've gained a little weight from all that rich French food," Frank admitted to his brother as he wriggled into the wet suit that would protect him from the cold during their pre-dawn plunge into the lake, "not to mention all the wienies I had today." Why, the suit was so snug he couldn't even wear his usual modest bathing costume underneath.

"Golly, my suit's so tight it shows every bulge," Joe cried, finding himself in the same spot. "Well, it's dark and nobody will be able to tell we've nothing on underneath," he consoled himself.

"Good thing," Frank whistled, "as this fits me like a second skin!"

They threw gaily printed cotton beach jackets over their outfits before going downstairs to have a quick cup of coffee with the others. Before leaving for their short walk to their speedy craft, the *Sea Princess*, Frank pressed a small transmitter into Nancy's hand. "When you get to the sanitarium, hit this switch and you'll appear as a blip on our radar screen," he told her. "That way, we can always find you. Whatever you do, don't let it out of your reach."

"I'll hide it in my muff," Nancy promised, integrating the device into the glamorous outfit she would wear for her entrance at the River Depths Sanitarium. "No one will ever know it's there."

"The minute we find an entrance to the caverns, we'll activate our transmitter," Frank promised Willy. "That way, you'll know we're on the right track."

Willy gave each lad a manful handshake while Uncle Nelly wiped away hot tears. "Frank—Joe—be careful," Uncle Nelly begged. "If anything should happen to you boys—" he gasped sharply, then continued in a shaky voice, "—your father would be devastated."

Frank hugged his uncle to him.

"You know he loves you with all his heart," Uncle Nelly whispered in his ear. Frank gulped. Uncle Nelly knew how hard these adjustments could be!

"Sew as you've never sewn before, Uncle," Frank answered in a husky voice. "Nancy, don't take any unnecessary risks," Frank then cautioned his chum, realizing that his warning would go unheeded. Nancy would do whatever she had to do to crack the case, and Frank knew it.

"Bet you a shiny new penny we get there first," Nancy grinned. Frank could tell she was as taut with excitement as he was.

"You're on," Frank grinned back. Then a look of somber determination settled on his handsome features. "Let's go, Joe!" he told his brother.

The boys left in high spirits, certain that they were close to cracking the case. Why, with the Hardly boys *and* Nancy Clue on the job, what could possibly go wrong?

---- CHAPTER 30 ----

A Lucky Break!

The quick shrill of the telephone startled Willy, who had been concentrating on the latest issue of *Physique Magazine*. He snatched up the receiver. "Hardly Command Center," he said in a crisp tone, "Willy speaking." His action awoke Joe's cat, Creampuff, from her nap atop the Radar-O-Scope. She strolled across the Command Center table and hopped in Willy's nap. Willy patted Creampuff on her little head. "State your name and business," Willy said briskly.

"Willy, it's Jackie. I'm at—"

"Jackie! How are you? Any news to report?" Willy asked excitedly. He took his ear from the receiver and called over to Midge, who was chain-smoking and browsing through old copies of *Midwestern Spy*.

"It's Jackie," he said. "She's calling with news."

"Tell her 'hi,' " Midge said.

"Willy—" Jackie's faint voice came through the receiver.

"I'm back," Willy said. "Midge says 'hi.' What did you find out?" he quizzed her excitedly. "Did you get that man to talk? Did he tell you exactly where Fennel and Mrs. Hardly are hidden?" Just then, Creampuff jumped onto the table and, with a swish of her long, furry tail, knocked over Willy's cup of hot cocoa.

"Hold on, Jackie. We have a problem!" Willy cried as he threw the phone down, snatched up the cat and quickly sopped up the hot liquid with his handkerchief before it could damage any of the sensitive spy equipment.

"Willy, can you hear me?" Jackie cried out in an urgent tone. "Willy, I need help. I've been—"

"I'm sorry, your time is up," a burly cop with thin red hair and a pasty face announced, yanking the phone from Jackie's hand.

138

"Wait! This is important!" Jackie cried. "I didn't get through."

"Your time's up," the man repeated. He grabbed Jackie by the collar and propelled her past a row of cells. The prisoners jeered at the girl, calling out names that made even a streetwise officer like Detective Jackie Jones cringe.

"You know the chief won't be at all happy to find the likes of you in his town. Why don't you tell me where you swiped that badge and gun?" the officer demanded gruffly as he shoved Jackie into a cell.

"But I *am* a detective," Jackie insisted angrily. "Call the San Francisco Castro Street Police Station—" But the sound of the heavy metal gate clanking shut was the only reply. Jackie pounded her fists against the gate until they were bruised, but the only response she got were threats from the other prisoners.

"Quiet!" they yelled.

"I can't *believe* they took away my badge and gun and arrested me," Jackie fumed as she sat down on the hard cot and buried her head in her hands. She wished now she had insisted Cherry come with her. "But what if they had arrested her, too?" she wondered. As bad as this place was, it would be far worse for someone of Cherry's delicate nature.

"At least we would have had some time alone," Jackie dreamily thought, imagining herself locked in a cell with Cherry and a bed.

Jackie shook her head in disgust. "Here I am a prisoner in a small Midwestern town and all I can think about is unbuttoning the top of a certain nurse's snug-fitting uniform," she scolded herself. "Still, she did look great last night in that sexy number." Jackie closed her eyes and imagined she was running her hands up Cherry's creamy thighs. She knew she should be planning her next move, but she couldn't take her mind off her dream nurse.

"There are worse ways to pass the time," she told herself as she stretched out on the cot and tried to relax.

"Lights out," a guard called. A moment later, Jackie was left in the dark with her thoughts. The dashing detective soon drifted off to sleep, tossing and turning as she dreamt of Cherry. Jackie moaned imagining Cherry in her arms, their lips just about to meet when suddenly Nancy burst into the cell with a rack of fashionable frocks. "Do you like it?" Nancy cried as she twirled around to show off her outfit. "There's one for you in cherry red!"

Jackie awoke with a start. "What a nightmare," she groaned to herself. "What if Cherry chooses Nancy?" she then thought in horror. She tried to slow the wild beating of her heart. "What can Nancy give her besides a life of luxury?" she thought angrily. Bitterness and fear coursed through her body as she remembered the look of delight on Cherry's face when Nancy presented her with her very own poodle skirt. "I'll never be able to afford a wardrobe like that on my salary," Jackie groaned.

The now-despondent detective shut her eyes and tried to ignore the horrible thoughts churning in her brain. But it was no use, for every time she was on the verge of falling back asleep she would picture Nancy and Cherry dressed in matching frocks. Jackie gave up on the notion of sleep and went to the small barred window for a breath of fresh air. She was surprised to hear a man's voice right outside. Someone was outside the jail, speaking to the prisoner in the next cell. When she heard the man mention secret caves, she pricked up her ears. She was in the cell right next to the thug she had been planning to interrogate!

"I planted the fingerprints and the sticks of dynamite at the Hardly house, all right," the man said.

"False clues?" Jackie gasped inwardly.

"Once that thing blows and the explosives are found at the Hardlys', it'll be curtains for Fennel P. and his nosy sons!" the prisoner cackled gleefully.

Jackie had to stop herself from crying out, "What explosion?"

"Don't worry. The show's set for three p.m. Wednesday. Why, when Judge Meeks' plan is complete, the Hardly name won't be worth a nickel!"

CHAPTER 31

A Watery Grave?

The *Sea Princess* purred to a halt. Frank lowered the anchor, slipped his oxygen tank over his broad shoulders and strapped his oilskin bag around his waist. The waterproof pouch contained a first-aid kit, an underwater camera, a transmitter so Willy could track them on the Radar-O-Scope, assorted necessary tools, a thermos of hot cocoa, four ham and cheese sandwiches wrapped in wax paper and a tin of healthful prune cookies thoughtfully prepared by Willy. Frank knew the cookies would provide the kind of quick energy a boy needed on an adventure such as this.

"Are you ready, Joe?" Frank queried his brother. Joe nodded and tugged on his underwater suit. He was growing tense with suppressed eagerness. Soon it would be light, and the boys would be unable to move about as freely as they wished. By mid-morning, the lake would be jammed with water sports enthusiasts who would surely stare with curiosity at two well-known sleuths wearing snug rubber suits.

"Bon voyage," Joe joked as he put on his tank and mask and dropped backward off the boat. Eager to begin exploring, Frank was right behind him, his underwater lantern firmly in hand. The boys, top-notch swimmers both, descended to the bottom, their well-developed muscles rippling under the black rubber of their outfits. Soon they were at the inky-black bottom of the deep lake. Joe touched down, stirring up the silt floor. He stepped gingerly, knowing that the only creatures that could survive in this icy, dark habitat were earthworms, blood worms and small clams.

Joe and Frank used their lantern to examine the shoreline wall. For almost two hours, the boys searched, but to no avail. When they resurfaced, Joe didn't have to check his waterproof radium-dial wristwatch to know dawn was approaching.

The boys climbed into the boat for a quick energy-providing prune cookie. While they munched, Frank got out their nautical map and marked the territory they had covered.

"There's not much area left to explore," Joe pointed out with a little sigh. His spirits were beginning to flag.

"Nonsense, Joe," said the ever-optimistic Frank. "We've nearly a quarter of the lake shore left." He opened the Hardly Boys Ship Set and took out two underwater emergency whistles. "I say we split up. That way, we'll cover more ground before the sun is full in the sky. The first one to find something interesting gives a blow."

The boys moored the *Sea Princess* near some thick cattails and lowered themselves into the water. Joe went off to explore new territory while Frank stayed near the boat. Once in the water, Frank spotted a queer red blinking light from beneath the cattails. He trained his underwater binoculars on the light and gasped at what he saw. A round octopus-like creature with many tentacles and strange glowing eyes was darting around the vegetation! The creature was unlike anything Frank had ever seen in Illinois waters, and it sent a chill of terror down the lad's spine.

"Jeepers!" Frank gasped when it started to move toward him at top speed. "Lucky thing I was a varsity swimmer all through Saint Sebastian School for Boys," Frank thought as he retreated, his muscular arms chopping through the water. The lad soon realized that even Superman couldn't outdistance this foe. The creature forced him toward the center of the lake, then stopped and trained its red glowing eyes on its prey. Frank grabbed for the whistle around his neck but found to his horror that it had fallen off its chain. The creature closed in on the lad and grasped him around the torso with its tentacles.

"I'm going to drown!" the boy thought frantically, dropping his lantern. The creature pulled him deep into the dark lake. Frank tried his darndest but found his efforts feeble compared to the strength of the mighty monster. Why, this creature was stronger than any fellow he had ever wrestled to the ground!

In his struggle, Frank's air mask popped off. He watched helplessly as it floated to the surface, the life-sustaining oxygen bubbling out.

"Is this festive place where I've spent many a gay summer's day going to be my watery grave?" Frank thought in anguish as he sunk ever nearer to the bottom of his beloved Lake Merrimen.

CHAPTER 32

Mission Accomplished

 Frank frantically beat against the creature with both fists and, in the process, made a startling discovery. "Why, this is a *robot* built to look like a water creature!" Frank realized as his hands made contact with the aluminum skin. He groped in his oilskin pouch for his underwater welding arc. Luckily he had earned his Boy Scout Badge in Underwater Bridge Repair and, as the *Sea Princess* was a metal-hulled craft, he always brought along his welding equipment while on water missions.

With his last surge of energy, Frank switched on his oxyacetylene torch and blasted the creature. It melted before his very eyes. Its tentacles lost their grip and fused to the now-softened mass that was once its body. Frank wriggled free, jetted to the surface and took deep, life-saving breaths. Luckily, his air-mask was within arm's reach. He popped it back on and, with the remaining oxygen, dove back under. The robot was still thrashing about on the bottom of the lake, but this time its mighty arms were fused to its side. Frank took a screwdriver from his pocket, located the control panel on its underbelly and, with a flip of his wrist, opened the panel, ripped out some wires and stilled the once-powerful creature.

Frank used a rope and hook to tow the creature to the boat. When he surfaced, Joe was bobbing up and down, frantically looking for him. Joe got a quick look at Frank's welding job and instantly surmised what had happened.

"It's the sea monster the chief told us about," Joe cried as he helped his brother pull the misshapen mass into the boat.

"It's made of some new kind of aluminum alloy which makes it light enough to stay afloat yet sturdy enough to withstand most assaults," Frank determined. He continued his investigation of the creature. "Joe, what we have here is not just a sea creature capable of scaring tourists but a sophisticated piece of technology rarely seen at lakeside resorts," he told his brother with some excitement.

"But who has the knowledge to build such a beast *and* the ruthlessness to turn it into a death-dealing monster?" Joe wondered aloud.

"Who else?" Frank spat out angrily. "The very same people who engineered the theft of the top poodles from the Dog Show *and* kidnapped our parents!"

"Isn't it enough that they've proven their superiority in space? Now they want Lake Merrimen? Golly, is nothing sacred?" Joe swore angrily.

"Joe, the entrance to the caves must be near the cattails where I first spotted the robot," Frank realized. The boys quickly wove a cover for their craft from the tall reeds lining the shore. Soon the boat and its strange cargo were completely hidden to the casual viewer.

"We've got to keep this discovery a secret," Frank told his brother. Joe nodded. Just thinking of what a contraption like that could do if let loose on lake resorts all over the Midwest made him shiver with fear.

"Let's hurry back down before we meet up with any early-morning boaters," Frank urged. They replaced their oxygen tanks with fresh ones and dove back into the water. Swimming below the cattails, they used their remaining strong-beamed underwater lantern to search the side of the rocky lake wall.

"Golly, Frank," Joe signaled his brother using the Hardly Boys Secret Sign Language System. "I don't see any cave entrance. We've hit a dead end! What do we do next?"

Frank was sweating under his rubber suit. "It's got to be here, Joe," he frantically signaled back. "That creature wasn't just out for an early morning swim—it was guarding something!" As the boys swam, they shone their light along the bank, but saw only the typical underwater things one finds in a summer lake teeming with activity. Dragonfly nymphs darted on the surface of the water in a kind of strange water ballet. A three-foot long Queen Snake shot past Joe and grabbed onto an unsuspecting crayfish.

Joe swam a little closer to his brother, then pointed frantically as a school of Illinois striped bass swimming overhead seemed to disappear before his very eyes. "Did you see that?"

he signaled his brother. "Those fish swam into that clump of pickerelweed and vanished." Joe had immediately identified the heart-shaped leaf with its spike of attractive blue flowers, as they grew wild along the Hardly dock.

Luckily, Frank had earned his Boy Scout badge in Pond Plant Identification, and knew instantly something wasn't right. Pickerelweed grew above water level, not under water! Frank stuck his hand into the thick foliage and a look of delight washed over his face. The flowering weed was made of plastic! "It's a decoy shielding an opening in the rock!" Frank signaled Joe.

The boys shared a triumphant smile. They had found the entrance to the hidden caves!

CHAPTER 33

A Clever Ruse

"Hurry, driver," the glamorous titian-haired girl in the back of the taxi commanded. She pulled her compact from her jeweled pocketbook and powdered her pert little nose. Next she applied a thick layer of shocking bright red color to her full lips. Satisfied with her appearance, at least for the time being, she sighed, leaned back and tossed her white velvet satin-lined muff on the floor along with her jewel case, cosmetics travel bag and stack of fashion magazines.

"I'm so v-e-r-y bored," the girl cried in a peevish manner. She slumped in the wide back seat of the taxi cab. "Please let me go back to California," she wailed. "This place is so dreadfully Midwestern!"

"Why don't you just enjoy the lovely scenery?" Cherry suggested helpfully. Nancy rolled down the window of the cab, lit a cigarette, peered outside and groaned.

While Cherry was secretly impressed with Nancy's movie star performance, she had to act the part of the disapproving Companion Nurse. "You know that Doctor doesn't like you to get too much damp morning air, Miss New," Cherry admonished her.

"Doctor doesn't like me to do anything," Nancy pouted, hewing perfectly to her role as a spoiled actress. "There I was, all set to star in a major motion picture, when I'm shipped off to Illinois for a rest! Who can rest here?" she cried. "All these endless acres of green fields and this wide expanse of blue sky are enough to give me the jitters!"

"Miss New, you're getting yourself all excited," Cherry said in a soothing tone. She snuck a look at the driver. They were hoping to catch his attention so they could, without his knowing, involve him in their little charade. Cherry made an elaborate pretense of checking her sturdy nurse's watch. "It's time for your medication," she announced as she reached in her first-aid kit and took out a vial of sugar pills. She unscrewed the cap on a plaid thermos and poured Nancy a cup of water. Nancy grudgingly put out her cigarette, swallowed a pill and then stretched out on the seat, pretending to doze off.

"We're almost there, Miss," the driver said. He was a large burly man with a sun-burnt face and very nice manners. He peeked in the rearview mirror and saw that Nancy was asleep.

"Actresses are quite a handful, aren't they?" he said with a chuckle.

Cherry smiled. They *had* caught his attention! "They certainly are," she agreed. "Do you know many movie stars?" she asked the man.

"Oh, lots," he replied. "I've driven dozens of actresses to the sanitarium, only I don't ever recall having seen yours in a movie," he was forced to admit. "I take my mother to the picture show every Saturday night," he continued. "We saw *South Pacific* just last week.

"*I'm—going to wash—that—man—right—out—of—my— hair,*" he sang in a rich baritone. "Now *that's* a movie. Funny, though, I don't remember seeing her in anything, and like I said, Mother and I go every week."

Cherry was a little shaken by his comment. Oh, dear, was this going to be a problem at the sanitarium, too? She leaned across the seat. "Can you keep a secret?" she whispered to the man in a confidential tone. He assured her he could.

"Miss New *was* up for the lead in that film," Cherry told him. "When she didn't get it, well, she completely collapsed! You see, she has a great deal of talent, but is cursed with thin blood and shaky nerves. Every time she's cast for a movie that is sure to make her a star, she has another collapse and loses the role. The studio finally decided to send her to the world-renowned Dr. Fraud to see if he can cure her." Cherry could see by the man's expression that he believed every word she said. She felt instantly guilty, and strangely, a little thrilled.

"It's such a shame," the driver said, clucking his tongue. "But I'll bet anything, Dr. Fraud can help her. Why, folks around here say he works wonders with nervous women. All the best people send their daughters to him."

"It's not just a rich and rewarding career in motion pictures that hangs in the balance," Cherry added dramatically, "but her very sanity!" She had been practicing that line all night, along with many others sure to convince people that Nancy was the genuine article.

While Nancy, Velma and Uncle Nelly had spent the time sewing and basting, Cherry had written an official case history for patient Darcy New based on a real actress she had treated at Seattle General Hospital. Luckily the actress had been a fascinating case, and Cherry had spent many hours by the attractive woman's bedside. She was confident that her written record would stand up under anyone's scrutiny, even that of the incomparable Dr. Fraud.

There was one thing bothering Cherry, however. Doctor Fraud, like any reputable physician, was sure to check the girls' identities. Cherry's own credentials didn't worry her, as she was not only a high-ranking graduate of a top-notch Idaho nursing school, but she had also served as a Cruise Nurse aboard an ocean liner bound for the South Seas, a Dude Ranch Nurse at a Western resort, a Shoe Store Nurse for a Seattle shop specializing in sensible shoes, *and* she was a card-carrying member of the highly respected Nurses of America Club. But what about Nancy? She had nothing besides her glamorous good looks and fancy affectations to prove *she* was who she said she was.

"What if the doctor calls Hollywood and finds out nobody there has ever heard of an actress named Miss Darcy New?" Cherry wondered worriedly. "We'll cross that bridge when we come to it," she decided.

She tried to relax, and sat back in the comfy seat to take in the spectacular view of the passing landscape. Past fertile farms and rolling hills, grassy meadows and lovely lakes, the taxi and its precious cargo sped toward the sanitarium. Soon the driver had pulled through a stone entryway and was heading up a winding tree-lined path that led to an imposing white stone mansion set back among stately elms.

Cherry recalled what Nancy had told her about the institution. "It used to be the Frenshaw estate, and until twenty-two years ago, people from town went there regularly to perform skits and otherwise lift the spirits of the patients. Then suddenly, the ghostly figure of a woman in white began appearing on the grounds, and the citizens of River Depths began to hear the most ghastly screams. Since then no one's dared venture beyond the gate.

"The place," Nancy had added, "is guarded by fierce attack dogs!"

Cherry shivered a bit, and pulled her regulation nurse's sweater close as the taxi drew near the sanitarium. Nancy yawned, sat up and gave her a wink. "Good luck," she mouthed. Cherry smiled back and crossed her fingers in solidarity. The taxi came to a halt.

"All out for River Depths Sanitarium," the driver announced as he hopped out of the cab and took Nancy's many bags from the trunk.

Cherry brushed the wrinkles from her uniform, straightened her cap and got ready to begin what she hoped would be one of the most rewarding episodes of her nursing career— her stint as Cherry Aimless, Sanitarium Nurse!

CHAPTER 34

The Plot Thickens

"What do you think happened to Jackie?" Midge wondered aloud for the tenth time in as many minutes. Velma gave a big sigh and rolled off her girlfriend. In all the years they had been together, she had never seen Midge so preoccupied.

It was early morning and Velma, after a night of sewing and hairstyling, had returned with Uncle Nelly to relieve Willy and Midge at their post in the Command Center. Velma and Uncle Nelly had found their mates drinking coffee and smoking cigars while keeping their eyes glued to the Radar-O-Scope, anxiously awaiting the sign that Joe and Frank had successfully entered the cave system.

Willy had declared himself much too anxious to leave the Command Center until he had heard from the boys, so Midge and Velma decided to use the opportunity to take a refreshing nap. But Midge had been too restless to sleep, and apparently, too anxious to do anything else!

"This is unlike you, Midge," Velma asked as she sat up and slipped her lacy black bra over her full, rounded breasts. "You're really worried, aren't you, honey?" she said as she did up the snaps.

Midge sighed, propped herself up on one elbow and fished a cigarette out of the pack on the nightstand. "It just strikes me as odd that Jackie called in and then hung up without telling us a thing," she admitted between puffs.

"Maybe she's chasing a lead," Velma reasoned as she slipped on her matching panties.

"Maybe," Midge said. But she didn't sound the least bit convinced.

Velma shrugged into her blouse and skirt ensemble and hopped into her high-heeled summer sandals. "Let's go to the police station and see for ourselves," she suggested as she ran her fingers through her short dark hair, which only further rumpled her adorable mass of curls.

"I'll make this up to you," Midge pledged as she climbed out of bed, zipped her trousers and pulled Velma close. "Okay, honey?"

Velma put one hand between Midge's muscular thighs and rubbed softly. "You sure will," she promised with a sly grin.

Midge groaned aloud, forgetting for a moment why she had gotten out of bed. She nibbled Velma's neck.

"Later," Velma said, grabbing her purse and heading for the door.

"How much later?" Midge cried as she chased after her.

Soon they were in Nancy's car heading to the Lake Merrimen jail, a sack of snacks prepared by Nelly on the back seat. Midge had decided to resume her earlier charade and let people think she was Frank Hardly. That way, she was sure to get the answers she was looking for.

"So remember—I'm Frank and you're my wife," Midge warned her.

Velma smiled. She had called Midge many things in their time, but never Frank. She snuggled close to Midge and gave her a kiss that left Midge grinning. The grin disappeared, though, when they arrived at the jail and discovered why their friend hadn't made it home the night before.

"What do you mean you *arrested* Detective Jackie Jones?" Midge erupted in anger when the desk sergeant told her the news.

"Is she a friend of yours, Frank?" the fair-haired fellow cringed.

"Not only a friend, but a colleague sent here to help with an important investigation," Midge told him with considerable irritation.

"Free prisoner Jones *immediately*," the officer barked into his intercom. "We didn't know she was *really* a detective," he stammered. "Oh dear," he added worriedly. "The chief isn't going to like this one little bit." Why, everyone knew the Hardly boys and Chief O'Malley were as close as three fellows could be!

Golly, being Frank was fun, Midge thought as she watched the man squirm nervously. "You didn't think to investigate?" she asked indignantly. "No fingerprint check? No telephone call to San Francisco?"

"Believe me, I don't know how this happened," the sergeant cried, throwing up his arms in dismay. "You have my personal assurance that an investigation will be conducted immediately," he promised. "I'll have a full report on the chief's desk this afternoon."

"I don't think we need to inform the chief about this," Midge hastily told the man. Surely an intimate chum like the chief would realize Midge was an impostor, plus he had left specific instructions to stay away from the prisoner.

"This will be our little secret," Midge winked at the man.

The sergeant blushed with relief. "Gee, thanks Frank, you really *are* a swell guy! Say, is there anything I can do for you?" he offered. "Would you like a fresh donut? A ticket to the Policeman's Ball?" He leaned across the front desk and asked with a wink, "An escort home?"

"There *is* something I'd like, Sergeant," Midge told the man. She gave Velma a little grin, then leaned across the desk and whispered in the man's ear. A few minutes later, the girls emerged from the Lake Merrimen jail into the bright sunshine with their friend Jackie by their side. Midge had a satisfied smile on her handsome face and a brand new pair of shiny silver handcuffs in her pocket.

"I've had enough of this town to last me a lifetime," Jackie scowled as she strapped on her gun. "I'm tempted to leave this very minute," she declared, her black eyes flashing with anger. "Maybe even sooner!"

"I know a pretty nurse in a snug uniform who will be disappointed to hear that," Midge remarked.

Jackie's expression grew softer. A lovesick look came into her eyes, only to be replaced by one of heartbreak. Midge knew she was picturing the kinds of things that can happen when two normal, healthy girls are thrown together under emotionally stirring circumstances. Anything could happen! "They've already left, haven't they?" Jackie asked with some trepidation.

Midge nodded. "We saw them off about an hour ago," she told her.

"Damn," Jackie swore. "I wanted to talk to Cherry before she left. I'm worried about her going undercover with Nancy. After all, she's not a professional."

"But she is a Registered Nurse with lots of experience with mental disorders," Velma reminded her.

"True," Jackie said.

Midge could tell this was little comfort to the smitten detective. "Don't worry, Jack," she said in a reassuring tone. "Nancy's got nothing up on you."

"There's no time for my personal problems, anyway," Jackie replied. "Midge, Velma, you won't believe what I overheard!

"Those clues at the Hardly house were planted!" she exclaimed. "And that's not all. I'm not so sure the Russians are behind this kidnapping. If they are, they're not alone. Judge Meeks figures in somehow."

"Myra's husband?" Midge cried.

Jackie nodded. "I'm afraid he's planning to ruin Fennel Hardly's reputation by declaring him a Russian spy and blaming him for some blast that's planned for Wednesday."

"Good detective work," Midge was impressed.

Jackie flushed modestly. "All I did was overhear a conversation between some corrupt men," she admitted.

"Well, we won't tell Cherry that," Midge said with a wink.

Velma rolled her eyes. "While you two stand here trying to think of ways to impress girls, I'm going inside to ask that thug exactly what is going to explode."

"Three G-men came during the night and sprung him," Jackie told her, "and when I asked, the guard denied that there was ever a prisoner in that cell. Either Chief O'Malley is in cahoots with Judge Meeks, or the government is involved in this investigation and keeping it secret. Either way, it looks like anything we find out, we've got to find out for ourselves."

"So let's go to Myra's house and find her connection to the tunnels," Midge exclaimed.

"But you heard what Nancy said. She never lets anyone inside," Velma reminded her.

"We'll force our way in, then," Jackie said with determination.

"Oh, good," Midge smiled. "I can't wait to see the expression on Myra Meeks' face when we break down her door."

"We'll have to do it on the sly," Jackie countered. "We don't want to bring all the judge's forces down on us."

Jackie had another concern as well. "We've got to crack this case before bedtime at the sanitarium!" she thought urgently. "That leaves us about ten hours to break into Myra's house, find the entrance into the caverns, warn Joe and Frank about the explosion, rescue the Hardly parents and then race to the sanitarium and spring Cherry and Nancy before they turn in for the night," she realized.

"Follow me," Jackie commanded as she hopped into Joe's jalopy and headed for the main road. Midge and Velma took off after her in Nancy's car. Luckily Jackie was possessed with more than a strong physique and a confident manner; she also had a keen sense of direction enabling her to find Shady Lane with nary a false move. Jackie cut the engine and stopped her car behind a grove of weeping willows across the street from a stately house set back behind a tall wrought-iron gate grandly embellished with the initials *MM*.

"It's an awfully fancy cottage," Velma remarked as she and Midge joined their chum in surveying the imposing two-story home painted sparkling white with elegant pilasters.

Before they could head across the road, Midge spotted two German shepherds patrolling the grounds. The girls ducked behind Nancy's convertible. "Maybe Nancy's got some binoculars in here," Velma suggested as she popped open the glove box of the speedy vehicle. A jumble of assorted items tumbled out. "Sun-tan oil, sunglasses, a complete cosmetics kit with Nancy's initials on it, a manicure set, an assortment of gloves— long silk gloves, short cotton gloves and rabbit-lined leather ones, for winter, I suppose—," Velma said aloud, "—hair spray, a rain bonnet, a nice-looking compass in an attractive leather case, also with her initials on it—a Parcheesi set, a swim cap, road flares, a deck of cards, and oh!" she cried in triumph, "Opera glasses!"

Jackie whistled when she got a close-up view of the gate surrounding the house. "That's electrified wire along the top," she told her chums.

"Mrs. Meeks *really* doesn't want anyone on her carpet," Midge joked darkly.

"There's a man with a rifle at the second-floor window," Jackie gasped. "An electrified gate, an armed guard and patrol dogs all add up to one thing," she declared. "They're guarding that tunnel entrance because something *very* important is going on down there." She trained the glasses lower. "There's a basement, but the windows have been boarded up," she announced. "That's where we want to be. I'm going to check out the back of the house to see if I can find a weak spot in their security."

"I'll go with you," Midge offered. She tossed Joe's car keys to Velma. "Honey, go home."

"I'll do no such thing, Midge Fontaine," Velma pouted.

"I won't leave you here alone," Midge shot back. "It's too dangerous."

"You *both* stay here and watch the front," Jackie said. "See who comes and goes. Make note of any passing car."

"Be careful," Velma warned Jackie.

"Yeah, don't take any chances," Midge reiterated. "Remember you've got a great girl waiting for you over at that sanitarium."

"Do I, Midge?" Jackie's eyes met her chum's. "I'll be back soon," she promised as she stuck her service revolver in the waistband of her trousers and started off.

Midge and Velma made themselves comfortable in the wide back seat of Nancy's convertible. "When Jackie gets back with her plan, you've got to go home to Willy and Nelly," Midge said in a no-nonsense tone as she flung her long legs over the back of the seat and put an arm around her girl.

Velma didn't reply. Midge settled back in the seat and tried to keep her eyes on the gate but found them wandering instead to the soft curve of her girlfriend's neck. She leaned over and gave her a little nibble. Velma jerked away.

"Forget it, Midge," she said.

"It's because I'm sending you home, isn't it?' Midge groused. "I am not going to argue with you about this, Velma," she said in a tone of voice that let Velma know that, golly, she meant business!

"That's good," Velma retorted, "because you're not going to win."

"I don't want anything to happen to you," Midge pleaded earnestly.

"Well, I don't want anything to happen to *you*," Velma shot back.

"It's different," Midge insisted.

"How?" Velma cried.

"First of all, I'm wearing shoes I can run in," Midge pointed out. "Not those flimsy high-heeled sandals of yours."

"I thought you liked me in high heels," Velma gasped

indignantly, adding, "I'll remind you of this the next time you beg me to—"

"Don't change the subject," Midge warned, her temper rising.

"I am *not* going home," Velma declared.

"You *are* going home if I have to carry you there myself, Miss Velma Pierce," Midge promised angrily.

"Yes, dear, whatever you say," Velma mocked her in a high-pitched feminine voice. "Gee, married life sure is swell," she added sarcastically. "Remind me to recommend it to my friends."

Her remark stung Midge like a slap. Golly, the last seven days had been the happiest of her life knowing she and Velma were truly as one. "I didn't know you felt that way, Velma," she said sadly. There was no trace of sarcasm or anger in her voice now.

"Oh, Midge, I love being your wife," Velma cried in all sincerity as she climbed in Midge's lap. She gave her a kiss that made all of Midge's doubts instantly melt away.

"Oh, Velma," Midge gulped. "I love you."

"I love you, too," Velma smiled back. "That's why I can't let you go in there without me. Why, I'd die of worry!"

"You're not going in there, Velma," Midge said flatly.

"Yes, I am," Velma said as she unbuttoned Midge's shirt and ran her manicured nails over her tee-shirt clad chest.

"No, you're not," Midge said, this time in a softer tone.

"You know what I could really go for right now?" Velma sighed in Midge's ear.

"Me, too," Midge moaned as she slid her hands up Velma's skirt.

"I was thinking of an early lunch," Velma giggled as she wriggled off Midge and snatched up the sack of food Nelly had prepared for them. "I was also thinking we should probably keep an eye on that gate."

Midge reddened. "You're still not going," she told her girlfriend.

Velma stuck out her tongue. "What would you like to eat?" she said as she breezily ignored her mate. "We've got carrot sticks, cream cheese and jelly-nut sandwiches, butter split hard rolls, pickled beets, deviled eggs, pears, a bag of figs, brownies and a thermos of coffee."

"Nothing," Midge glared at her, but soon changed her mind when she got a look at the delicious spread. "I am a little hungry," she admitted. Velma gave her a deviled egg and a kiss.

After ten minutes of happy eating, Midge lit a cigarette and gave a great big satisfied sigh. "Where do you think Jackie is? She wouldn't try to go in there without us, would she? Do you think Frank and Joe have made it into the caverns yet? And, more importantly, do you think Willy and Nelly will adopt me?"

"Me, too," Velma smiled, thinking of the lovely creations Nelly had thrown together using Nancy's basic wardrobe, some scraps from his sewing kit, safety pins and his keen sense of style.

"Nancy has never looked lovelier than she did this morning when she left for the sanitarium dressed in that snow-white satin gown with its white velvet stole and matching muff," Velma remarked. "I especially liked the paste diamond necklace and brooch set Nelly whipped up for her. Why, she really *did* look like a movie star!"

Midge groaned. "Don't tell Jackie that," she warned Velma. "Besides, I don't think Nancy's all that good looking. I mean, she's a pretty enough girl in a collegiate sort of way, if you like that type," she grumbled.

"Nancy's a charming girl and you know it," Velma scolded her. "You just don't want her to be Cherry's type, that's all."

"I just want what's best for my friends," Midge retorted. "And I think what's best for Jackie and Cherry is each other. You don't really think Cherry's going to pick a high-strung debutante over a big strong, handsome cop, do you?" Midge baited her girlfriend. "Would you?"

"You have to ask?" Velma arched one plucked brow.

"What has Cherry told you about Jackie?" Midge asked, scooting close to Velma.

"I won't say," Velma said stubbornly, adding, "It's top secret."

Midge could tell she meant business! "I hate it when you get like this," Midge complained. She moved to the far end of the seat and pretended to ignore her girlfriend.

"Well, I hate it when you sit so darn far away," Velma shot back.

Midge grinned and slid back. She put her arm around her

girl and nuzzled her neck. "You are the most aggravating girl I've ever met, Miss Pierce," she said softly.

"And you, mister, are one big busybody."

"I like to be informed," Midge said in her own defense.

"What would the gang back home say if they knew what a gossip you really were?" Velma giggled. Midge shot her a withering look. Velma started to laugh even harder.

"What's so funny?" Midge cried.

"Nothing," Velma said quickly. "Just something silly that popped into my head. It's gone now."

"What was it?" Midge wondered.

"I can't remember," Velma told her with all innocence.

Midge didn't believe her. "I'm going to pester you until you tell me," she threatened.

Velma sighed. "You *really* want to know what was making me laugh?" she wondered.

"Uh-huh," Midge said.

"You sure?"

"Sure I'm sure," Midge retorted. "And don't lie. I know when you're lying. Your bottom lip quivers."

Velma grinned. "I was just wondering what the gang back home would say if they knew, well, if they knew who *really* gets to keep the keys for all the handcuffs you bring home," Velma giggled.

CHAPTER 35

And Brains, Too!

Midge gasped. "Velma! You promised you'd *never* tell!" she exclaimed, throwing up her arms in alarm.

"Honey, of course I'll never tell," Velma reassured her. "Now see, you wanted to know what I was thinking and now that you do, you're hurt!"

"I'm not hurt," Midge moped.

Velma could tell she was lying. "Midge, I would *never* tell anyone about how you like to be—"

"Shhh," Midge warned her. "People can hear."

"What people?" Velma wondered, looking around the deserted area.

"People on vacation," Midge shot back lamely.

Velma stifled a giggle. She hopped into her girlfriend's lap. "Honey, you know I would never say *anything* that would get you kicked out of that little club of yours back home," she teased.

"Oh, Jesus," Midge groaned. She covered her eyes with her hands. "I don't even want to think of how fast information like that would travel through the bar. I can just see it written on the washroom door in great big letters. Midge—Fontaine—likes—to—be—"

"Midge Fontaine likes to be *what?*" Jackie's voice rang out.

"Oh, good, you're back," Midge cried, eager to change the subject. "Did you see any way in? What's the back of the house like? Any more armed guards?"

"Midge Fontaine likes to be *what?*" Jackie asked Velma, ignoring Midge. Midge turned scarlet and shot Velma a warning look.

"Midge Fontaine likes to be *right,*" Velma laughed.

"Midge usually *is* right," Jackie grinned, jumping into the front seat of Nancy's smart car.

"We saved some food for you," Velma told her, handing her a cup of steaming coffee and three cream cheese and jelly-nut sandwiches.

"I'm starving," Jackie admitted as she wolfed down the food. Then she told them what she had found. "The electrified gate rings the entire property, but there is a service entrance in the back. If we can convince the guard to open the door even a crack, we can muscle our way in. I'm sure between the two of us we can overpower any guard in there."

"The three of us," Velma added.

"I stand corrected," Jackie said with a grin. Midge groaned.

"The only question is how to get past Myra Meeks without raising any suspicions," Jackie mused.

"We could lure her away," Midge suggested.

"Or just tie her up and take the consequences later," Jackie added. "Of course, she'll eventually have to be let loose and then the whole Lake Merrimen police force will be swarming around down there."

"Oh, Myra will be going out soon," Velma blithely informed them.

"She will?" Jackie and Midge chorused in amazement.

"How do you know that?" Midge wondered.

Velma grinned. "It's simple logic, darling. I read in yesterday's newspaper that tonight is the annual Wives of the Atomic Age Dress-up Ball. Myra is sure to be there, seeing as she's the president of the organization."

"But that's hours from now," Jackie pointed out.

"Pay attention, kids," Velma said brightly. "Tonight Myra is going to a dress-up ball and you know what *that* means."

Midge and Jackie exchanged puzzled looks. "No we don't!" they cried.

Velma rolled her eyes in mock disgust. "It means she's going to the hairdresser's, and someone of Myra's stature is sure to have the first appointment of the day, which is always ten o'clock." Velma checked Midge's watch. "That's eleven minutes from now, and since it takes seven minutes to get to downtown River Depths—" As if on cue, the gate opened and a spiffy black Thunderbird with white leather seats emerged. Behind the wheel was Myra Meeks, clad in a smart summer suit, dark glasses and a white chiffon scarf. At her side was her poodle Precious, wearing a red rhinestone-studded collar.

The two girls looked at Velma with frank admiration.

"She can cook, too," Midge bragged.

"Now we've got to keep Myra Meeks away from the house for as long as possible," Jackie declared.

"We could send Velma to detain her somehow," Midge suggested. Velma gave her a little kick in the shins. "Ouch," Midge cried.

"No good," Jackie nixed the notion. "She knows Velma and might suspect something is up. Although I *do* like the idea of sending a girl. Now if we could only find just the right girl. Who do we know that we can trust, has similar interests to Myra, plus has the talent to pull this off?"

CHAPTER 36

Nelly to the Rescue

"I'd be delighted to help!" Uncle Nelly cried into the phone. If truth be told, he was getting a little antsy waiting around the Hardly house for something to happen. So far he had rearranged the den, wallpapered the guest washroom, sewn some darling tieback curtains for the kitchen and had just started to cut a pattern for a nifty new housedress.

"Swell, Uncle Nelly," Midge said into the telephone outside the diner where Velma was refilling their thermos with strong coffee. Caves were notoriously cold and damp and the girls would need all the fortification they could get. "All we know is, she's gone to get her hair done but we don't know where," Midge told him.

"No problem," Uncle Nelly assured her. "I know for a fact that Mr. Francis does her 'do. I'll call and have him prolong her comb-out, which will give me time to select just the right outfit, hop in my car and race downtown to head her off."

"Do whatever you have to do to keep her occupied," Midge urged him. "We've got to have plenty of time to get into her summer house and find the entrance to the caverns. Have you heard from the others?" she then asked.

Uncle Nelly confirmed that both teams had apparently reached their destination and that the transmitters were blinking away on the Radar-O-Scope.

"Good luck with Mrs. Meeks," Midge cried. She had decided against telling Uncle Nelly about the impending explosion. He would need his wits about him when dealing with Myra Meeks.

"All systems go for Operation Stop Myra," Uncle Nelly replied.

"The boys found a way into the caverns, and Nancy and Cherry are inside the Sanitarium," Midge reported.

"All the more reason for us to hurry," Jackie exclaimed. When Velma returned from the diner, the girls headed back to the Meekses' summer house, gulping coffee and discussing their strategy on the way. The very first thing they had to do was find a way inside the guarded house, even if it meant using the gun strapped to Jackie's side!

Midge noticed "Secret Love" was playing on the radio. "A song about unrequited love is the last thing we need," she thought. She turned the dial, searching for a new station when she heard Fennel Hardly's name.

"What's that?" Jackie cried. Midge turned up the volume. A man's voice crackled over the radio.

"Judge Milton Meeks today issued an arrest warrant for well-known detective Fennel P. Hardly, charging him with espionage and consorting with known Russian spies. According to NASA officials, the plans for the latest rocket project, the Maxx-Thruster, reported stolen last week, were found in Fennel P. Hardly's possession early today after investigators searched the detective's pockets."

"I hope they didn't search his pockets too closely," Midge muttered as she remembered what Cherry had told her about Fennel's true identity.

"If those plans were found on him, they were planted," Jackie growled. "And if it's a lie, Judge Meeks is really playing hardball. But why? What's his gripe with Fennel?

"We've got to be really careful," Jackie added a warning.

"I hope we're doing the right thing," Midge muttered as they sped along the lakeside road. She took a good, long look at her girlfriend. If anything ever happened to Velma, Midge didn't know what she'd do!

"I know what you mean, Midge," Jackie said. "Uncle Nelly's an awfully nice fellow. I feel bad sticking him with Myra. But I have confidence in him. Besides, my experience with self-important people like Myra Meeks is that they're all talk; the minute something threatening happens, they fold like a leaf in the wind."

"I don't like that Myra Meeks," Midge admitted. She scowled as she remembered the meddlesome matron's manipulative manner during Nancy's murder trial.

Jackie shook her head. This was becoming much more than a simple kidnapping. Somewhere in this pleasant lakeside resort town, a bomb was going to go off, and they had to find it! "If we fail, a great many people could be in grave danger," Jackie thought glumly. "And the good name of Hardly will be forever besmirched!"

CHAPTER 37

To the Tunnels!

"Those extra cream-cheese jelly-nut sandwiches sure came in handy," Midge grinned. They stood back as Jackie used the butt of her gun to smash a first floor window. "Let's hurry before those dogs finish that sack lunch," Jackie proposed as she looked over her shoulder. The two German shepherds were fighting over a butter split hard roll, but they wouldn't be for long!

"And my new handcuffs were just what we needed for that guard," Midge added. "Although it's a darn shame to waste a perfectly good set of cuffs like that."

"You have more at home, honey," Velma consoled her.

Jackie gave a little laugh, put her jacket on the window ledge to guard against shards of glass and pulled herself over. Midge helped Velma through, then pulled herself up. "We broke into this place in record time and with no casualties," Jackie praised them.

"Except that guard," Midge smiled.

"He'll be okay once someone gets him out of that tree," Jackie assured her. They were in a room filled with comfortable plaid-covered furniture and a fully stocked bar. "This must be Myra's play room," Midge remarked as she took a look at the plaques covering one wall. "Wow. She's the head of the Literary Society, the Etiquette Club, the Dramatic Club *and* the Wives of the Atomic Age. Oh, and she volunteers at the River Depths Sanitarium," Midge added. She read a plaque aloud:

Awarded to Mrs. Myra Meeks
for her meritorious service as
A Friend of the Insane

"—and it's signed, Dr. Fraud, River Depths Sanitarium."

"I hope Myra Meeks doesn't go there today. Why, she might blow Nancy's cover," Jackie said worriedly. "Let's get to the cellar and find that tunnel entrance." They raced out of the den and were halfway through the living room when they heard the front door open.

"Quick," Jackie whispered as she pointed to a door. "Let's hide in here!" They found themselves in a closet practically bursting with fur coats. Leaving the door open a crack, they listened in nervous anticipation as someone entered the house and walked across the marble flooring of the hallway.

"There's two of them," Velma whispered in a barely audible tone. "One is wearing wingtips and the other is in high heels. Three-inch spikes with a very narrow toe."

Midge and Jackie exchanged worried looks. Could it be that Myra Meeks and her husband had come home? The footsteps abruptly stopped. The intruders were mere feet from the girls!

"Good thing my mother's not home," they heard a girl exclaim. "Funny, though, there's usually a guy with a gun out there."

Midge's mouth dropped open. Why, it was Myra Meeks' daughter, Micky Meeks, who had proven such a help in their last mystery. "Phew," Midge thought.

"Does your mother always have a guard?" Micky's feminine companion asked.

"My mother's really paranoid," Micky chuckled. "She thinks there's a communist hiding behind every bush." A hi-fi was switched on and soft music filled the room. "I didn't come here to talk about my mother," Micky said in a low tone. "Let's dance."

"It's Micky Meeks—and she's got a date with her," Midge grinned in admiration. "And it's not even noon!"

Jackie relaxed. She would have jumped a judge if she had to, but she wouldn't have liked explaining it later!

"Should we let Micky know we're here?" Midge wondered.

"Let's wait and see if they go upstairs," Jackie suggested. From the giggles and groans, she suspected it would be just a matter of minutes.

"What do you think, Velma?" Midge asked her girlfriend, who was pressed up against the door peering through the little slit.

"I think Micky's a pretty smooth operator," Velma giggled.

"She's already unzipped the back of that girl's dress!"

"We'd better make our presence known," Jackie realized.

"Too late," Velma informed her. "There goes her slip!"

"Oh, Micky, you're such a bad girl!" they heard Micky's date exclaim happily.

"What's happening?" Jackie wondered.

"Do you want details or just the general picture?" Velma grinned back. Then Micky's date moaned, loudly, "Oh, Micky!" and the three chums knew they were going to be in that closet for a while.

Midge blushed hotly as she tried not to listen to the ardent lovemaking happening just feet away. Twenty uncomfortable minutes passed. "Think they'd notice if I had a cigarette?" Midge wondered.

Velma peeked out the door. "I don't think those two would notice an earthquake," she replied.

"I say we make a run for it," Jackie proposed after taking a look for herself. All she could see were two sets of feet dangling over the edge of the high-backed davenport. "Here's the plan. If we crawl out of here and stay low, I think we can get to the hallway."

"I'm game," Midge said. "I don't know about you two, but it's getting awfully hot in here!"

The three chums made sure to keep their heads down as they crawled past the sofa to the hallway and into the kitchen. They found the cellar door not a minute too soon, for just as it closed behind, them they heard a girl scamper into the kitchen.

"This isn't a cellar—this is a bomb shelter!" Velma gasped when they had tumbled down the narrow stairs and switched on the light. They looked around the utilitarian cement-floored room with its stainless steel miniaturized kitchen appliances, narrow cots and simple shelves loaded with canned goods, a battery-operated radio, walkie-talkies, the complete *Reader's Digest Condensed Books* series and board games.

"These walls are steel-reinforced concrete," Jackie reported. "This isn't a simple cellar converted into a bomb shelter; this is a feat of modern engineering. Look at the ceiling—it's also made of steel. The Meekses really are expecting an attack here in central Illinois!"

"The bomb they're detonating must be huge," Velma said in awe.

"You don't think—Judge Meeks wouldn't dare drop *the bomb*—would he?" Midge gasp incredulously.

"Not even Meeks could be that nefarious. Besides, I distinctly heard those thugs discussing dynamite," Jackie assured her.

"Maybe Myra just uses this as her private getaway," Velma suggested hopefully. "After all, here's a year's supply of her famous rose perfume and a five-gallon drum of cold cream. I guess what Cherry says is true. 'A girl must always look her best and be prepared for the worst.' "

Midge picked up one of the peculiar-looking silver packages stacked on the shelves. "Not only will Myra look good, she'll eat well, too," she quipped, adding, "I didn't know they made freeze-dried Apple Betty."

Midge read the label aloud. "Contains sugar, bread crumbs, stewed apples, monotrigludimate, phosphorus monogylserine, sodiacarbonate, tartaricerian, cellulosand and other preservatives. Expires August 1974. And look—there's meatloaf, tuna-noodle casserole, chili con carne, clam chowder and an assortment of gelatin fruit salads. *Serve straight from package*." Midge ripped open the chili con carne and took a big bite of the rust-colored bar. "Yuck," she said as she spit it out. "Who would eat this stuff?" she wanted to know.

Velma looked queerly at the package in Midge's hand. "Do you see what's stamped on the back? *Property of NASA*. Midge, this is astronaut food!" she cried.

"Where did Myra Meeks get experimental food meant for use in outer space?" Jackie wondered. "This stuff is strictly top-secret cuisine."

"And how can a government that can't make food taste any better than this put a man on the moon?" Midge grimaced.

"Ssh," Jackie warned her. "I hear footsteps up there. We'd better find that entrance before we're discovered. It may be cleverly disguised," she warned them. "Leave no stone unturned."

"I bet it's behind these shelves," Midge said, "or under these cots. Or behind that green metal cabinet."

As Midge and Jackie grunted and groaned, putting their well-developed muscles to work, Velma said, "Or maybe it's the door over there marked *To Tunnel*. "

She walked across the room and opened the door to reveal

a steep set of stairs carved into rock. Small white lights hung from wires strung along the wall. "Yep, this is it," Velma grinned. "But, brrr," she shivered as a gust of cool air hit her. "It's cold down there."

"Maybe there's something in that cabinet we can put on," Midge said. She opened the door to find a pile of starched white laboratory coats.

"This is odd," Velma pointed out. "If this is Myra's personal bomb shelter, what is she doing with dozens of matching laboratory coats?"

"Maybe she likes to dress up like a scientist," Midge joked as she unfurled one and held it up to herself. *Dr. Oskar Ottoman* was embroidered in red script above the left breast pocket.

"Isn't Ottoman that rocket scientist who came here after the war?" Jackie remembered. She grabbed a coat. "*Dr. Ernst Early*. This name rings a bell, too."

"But what do the tunnels have to do with these scientists?" Midge wondered.

"Something *very* suspicious is going on down there!" Jackie cried.

"Let's disguise ourselves with these coats," Velma proposed. She picked one from the pile and slipped it over her summer frock. "I don't think I look right," she said worriedly as she fussed with her costume.

"Honey, don't belt it like that. It gives you too much of a figure," Midge pointed out. "If anyone's going to believe you're a guy, we'd better fix your hair, too." Midge took a can of pomade from her pocket and got to work. Velma reluctantly wiped off her eyeliner and lipstick.

Midge stepped back and surveyed her girlfriend. With her dark curly hair slicked off her winsome face and the baggy white coat hiding her voluptuous figure, Velma looked like a sweet-faced boy scientist. "You look pretty darn cute like that," Midge had to admit.

"But I have no shape," Velma flushed prettily.

"*I* know what's under there," Midge murmured as she grabbed the front of Velma's baggy coat, pulled her close and planted a big kiss on her lips. Midge then shrugged into her costume and placed her pack of cigarettes in the plastic pocket protector in the breast pocket of the lab coat. Midge checked

Velma one last time and gasped when she realized whose name was on her girlfriend's coat.

"Dr. Fraud!"

"Is there nobody in this town we can trust?" Jackie cried as they raced through the door to the tunnel and started down the stairs.

CHAPTER 38

The Strange Case of Darcy New

"Dr. Fraud, your new patient is here for her evaluation." The crisp nurse clad in a snow-white uniform and a jaunty cap hit a switch on the black box on her desk and spoke in clear, concise tones.

"Everyone here is very efficient," Cherry thought in admiration. "And I do so love her unusual round, fluted cap with its midnight blue stripe. I've never seen such a unique design." Cherry was about to ask the Receptionist Nurse where she had received her training, but before she could open her mouth, it was their turn to finally meet the world-famous psychiatrist Dr. Fraud, whose work with unhappy women was known far and wide.

"Doctor will see you now," the nurse told them. Cherry wiped her damp palms on the handkerchief in her pocket and took a deep relaxing breath.

"Leave everything to me," Nancy said with a little wink as they crossed the threshold and stood face to face with the nattily dressed middle-aged man smoking a thick cigar.

"Do you mind the cigar?" was the first thing Dr. Fraud asked them.

"How courteous," Cherry thought, smiling.

"I like the smell of a good cigar," Nancy replied.

"Excellent," the man grinned. "Sit." He gestured toward a thickly-upholstered leather chair facing his desk. "Nurse, take a seat over there," he said, pointing to a wooden straight-backed chair against the wall. "And take notes."

"Yes, Doctor," Cherry demurred. She flipped open her nurse's notebook and poised her pen.

The doctor took his time reading the case history on his desk. Cherry had constructed a psychiatric background for Nancy, one she prayed would hold up under such expert scrutiny. Why, the incomparable Dr. Fraud had studied thousands of

171

women over the years. One flaw in her report and their charade would be over!

"So, Miss New, you're an actress suffering from nerves and you've come to my sanitarium for relief," he finally said. "It says here you suffer from hysterical attacks, mood swings, nervous exhaustion and fainting spells."

Nancy nodded but said nothing. She was watching the doctor watch her. She selected a cigarette from her silver case, put it between her ruby-red lips and waited. The doctor, expressionless, leaned across the desk and offered her a light.

Nancy quickly slipped the silver case back in her purse. She had forgotten her new name when she packed her monogrammed cigarette case! "Thanks," she said in a breezy tone that implied she was accustomed to such treatment. The hand that held the cigarette shook, though, and the doctor made a notation in his report.

Cherry smiled. Nancy had practiced her cool manner and shaky hand all night. Her act as a disaffected actress suffering from a deep-seated nervous disorder was perfectly realized, Cherry thought. She couldn't help but admire the aplomb with which Nancy was handling herself. She realized with a start that Nancy could fool practically anyone into believing practically anything!

"Have you ever suffered from amnesia, Miss New?" Dr. Fraud asked.

Nancy flicked her ash in a crystal ashtray. "I don't remember, Doctor," she said with a smile in her voice.

The doctor chuckled. "How's your health?" he asked.

"Fine," Nancy shrugged.

"She's anemic and suffers from heart palpitations, Doctor," Cherry interjected.

The doctor frowned. "There's plenty of sun out there in Hollywood yet you're pale as a ghost," he remarked. "You look as though you spend a lot of time indoors. Do you, Miss New?"

"Pretty much," Nancy said in a vague tone. She yawned. "Will this take long, Doctor?" she sighed. "It's time for my mid-morning nap."

"How's her appetite, Nurse?" the doctor asked abruptly, turning his attention toward Cherry.

"Poor," Cherry replied, guiltily thinking of the wieners, pickled onions in bacon, fried chicken, sweet potato croquettes, pear salad, lemon bread pudding *and* a double-fudge cake decorated with gay sugar roses she had seen Nancy tuck away at yesterday's patio party.

Patient eats like a bird, the doctor wrote in his report. "Now I'm going to ask you a series of questions meant to probe the innermost areas of your psyche. Just answer 'yes' or 'no.' "

He began. "Have you ever dreamt you're being chased by a man with a knife?"

"No."

"Ever dream you're flying?"

"No."

"Invisible?"

"No."

"Naked in public?"

"No," Nancy said. Cherry blushed. She had once had a dream like that! "Except I was wearing my cap," she remembered.

"Ever dream you're swimming in a warm ocean with another girl?"

Cherry blushed even harder. She *often* had dreams like that about her nurse chums, only lately her companion was always Jackie.

"Not really," Nancy smiled.

"What do you mean?" the doctor asked.

"I did have a dream like that once, but I was with two girls," Nancy explained.

"Two girls?" the doctor's thick brows shot up in alarm.

"And then we were on a train," Nancy continued. "It was going faster and faster until suddenly—"

"Yes?" the doctor leaned across his desk in eager anticipation.

Nancy shrugged. "I woke up."

"Oh!" the doctor said as he took a handkerchief from his suit pocket and wiped his damp brow. "That's very interesting, Miss New. Very interesting." He scribbled at length in his report.

Nancy turned to Cherry and gave her a little wink. Cherry shot her a grin, then grew wide-eyed in alarm when she realized the doctor was observing them out of the corner of his eye. He had seen their exchange! "We're going to be discovered for sure," Cherry thought frantically.

But the doctor acted as though he hadn't seen a thing. "Miss New, do you have any secret vices?" he wondered. "For example, do you ever take alcohol to excess?"

"Never," Nancy said, although her face reddened a bit at his suggestion.

"Do you spend money recklessly, never saving for a rainy day?"

"Only when the fall fashions arrive in the stores."

The doctor smiled. "Drive too fast?"

"Only when I'm late."

"Have unnatural attachments to other, more passive girls in which you play a domineering role?"

Nancy blanched.

"Miss New," the doctor continued. "What exactly *is* your relationship with your *private* nurse?" he asked.

"She's an employee," Nancy quickly replied. Perhaps too quickly. A spot of color appeared on each cheek.

"Anything else?"

"Sometimes I help her coordinate her outfits," Cherry explained.

"I can't help you if you persist in lying to me, Miss New," the doctor said curtly as he closed Nancy's folder.

"I'm *not* lying," Nancy protested. "Why, Nurse Aimless means nothing to me."

"I explicitly saw you wink at Nurse Aimless just now. Why? What secret do you two share?"

Nancy flushed to the roots of her upswept hairdo. Cherry gasped. Was her stint as an Undercover Nurse about to come to an abrupt end? She must do something—and fast!

"Doctor, I have a confession to make," Cherry jumped up, her first-aid kit clutched to her bosom.

Nancy drew in a quick breath. Cherry had crumbled so quickly! "Nurse," Nancy cried sharply. "I think you should leave the doctor and me alone."

"I can't," Cherry cried nervously. She walked over to Dr. Fraud's large impressive mahogany desk, her heart pounding with trepidation. Cherry was about to do something she thought she would never do. She was going to lie to an eminent doctor!

"Miss New is a *closet drinker!*" Cherry cried as she reached in her first-aid kit and took out a small dark bottle filled with medicinal whiskey. She put it on the desk and hung her head. "Although I was hired to take orders from her and her alone, I can no longer be a part of this deception." She looked him straight in the eye and pleaded, "Doctor, can you help her?"

CHAPTER 39

Second Thoughts?

"I'm so sorry," Cherry exclaimed, throwing up her arms in dismay. "I had no idea this was going to happen," she attempted to explain. "I was just trying to help. Oh, I'll *never* lie again. Mother was right. 'What a gnarled mess we make when we conjure up a fake.' Nancy, can you ever forgive me?" Cherry begged.

With considerable effort, Nancy tossed her trademark titian hair over one shoulder and gave Cherry a brave smile. "You couldn't have known that your confession would lead the doctor to diagnose me as suffering from an alcohol-related psychosis requiring such extreme measures as this straitjacket," she sighed.

"You're being really swell about this," Cherry said.

"I've been in tighter jams than this," Nancy assured her. "Now, we've got to make a plan. Tell me how to act and what to say to convince Dr. Fraud that it's safe to let me out of this thing so I can roam about and do some investigating." Before Cherry could think, the door to Nancy's room swung open, and in walked a crisply-uniformed nurse pushing a steel cart holding an ice bucket, drinking glasses, assorted liquor bottles, a pitcher of water, scallop-edged cocktail napkins and a plate of miniature meatball and stuffed-olive canapés. She set up a bar atop the bureau, dimmed the lights and switched on the radio to a station playing soft tunes. From under her arm, she took a thick rubber sheet and stretched it over Nancy's cot.

"Dr. Fraud will be in shortly," the nurse said curtly. Then she left.

"What's going on?" Nancy whispered anxiously to Cherry.

"It must be some new experimental treatment," Cherry guessed.

"It is," Dr. Fraud said. He stood in the door surveying

Nancy's transformed room. "What do you think, Miss New? Feel right at home?"

Nancy said nothing. She was too busy staring at the large hypodermic in Dr. Fraud's hand. "What's that?" she wondered aloud.

"You wouldn't understand even if I told you," the doctor assured her with a smile. "All you need to know is that this is going to help you get better. Nurse, remove the patient's straitjacket and have her sit on her bed," he directed.

"I'll need to know for my records what you're giving her," Cherry insisted.

The doctor ignored her.

"Let's stop this now," Cherry whispered as she bent over Nancy and loosened her restraining outfit. "What if he's going to inject you with a narcotic substance that causes you to cease being a productive member of society?"

"We'll proceed as planned," Nancy mouthed back. "Too much is riding on us. We don't know if Frank and Joe found a way in. We could be the Hardly parents' only hope!"

Cherry was flooded with tender feelings for the brave detective. "Ready, Doctor," Cherry said as she swallowed the lump in her throat. She gave a little smile as Nancy submitted to the injection.

The stern nurse who had brought the cocktail cart came back in the room. "Nurse Cramp will assist me today with the patient's Repulsion Therapy," the doctor informed Cherry.

Cherry froze. She hated to leave Nancy alone, even if she was in the capable hands of Dr. Fraud and Nurse Cramp! "Can't I stay?" she asked.

"Report to the Head Nurse on the first floor and she'll give you some light duties to occupy your time. Please return at exactly three o'clock," Nurse Cramp said, curtly dismissing her.

It was with a heavy heart that Cherry left the room. She hadn't meant to put Nancy through such an ordeal. "Nancy's such a sport," Cherry smiled. "She's so brave—so stalwart—so selfless. How can I even *think* of deserting someone so good?" she admonished herself.

───── CHAPTER 40 ─────

A Star Is Born!

Myra Meeks put one small white-cotton gloved hand to her powdered cheek and giggled. "Imagine *me* in *Life* magazine," she cried into the telephone. Her best friend Mrs. Thaddeus Tweeds was at the other end of the line, speechless with delight at the incredible news!

"A four-page spread on America's Most Beloved Matrons and *I'm* the centerpiece of the whole article! Imagine my surprise when, in the middle of my comb-out this morning, a reporter from *Life* magazine walked up to me and begged for an interview on the spot," she said with an unusual hint of modesty. "You should have seen the look of envy on everyone's face when I walked out of there with my new sophisticated beehive *and* that nice reporter! And to think that a moment before I was considering whether or not to tip Mr. Francis because he let me sit far too long under the dryer. I think he burned the back of my neck," she complained.

"There's no one who deserves it more," her best friend enthused.

"It's true," Myra Meeks agreed. "My years of dreary charity work are *finally* going to pay off," she bubbled happily. "All those hours at the Etiquette Club teaching table manners to the less fortunate haven't been for naught!"

"Not to mention your work at the Sanitarium as a Friend of the Insane," Thelma Tweeds pointed out.

"Thank you for reminding me of all my good deeds," Myra sighed. "I do do a lot for others, don't I?"

"We don't know how you do it," her friend said in admiration.

"Sometimes it's a burden," Myra admitted.

"You're not going to miss the annual Wives of the Atomic

Age Dress-up Ball tonight, are you?" her friend wondered suddenly.

"Certainly not," Myra promised. "I wouldn't miss it for anything on earth, especially since everyone will know I'm going to be in *Life* magazine next week."

"Oh, Myra, you'll be the belle of the ball," her friend gasped. "I'll start telephoning members of the Women's Club right away and break the wonderful news."

"Just ring Bea Gabske," Myra said. "You know what a gossip she is. Why, by tonight, it will be all over town that *I'm* going to be *famous!*"

"It won't come as a bit of a surprise to anyone who knows you, Myra," her chum said.

"True. Well, I've got to run," Myra twinkled. "Mr. Nelly's on a deadline and we've got photos to take after my interview. I think the sanitarium would be a picturesque backdrop, don't you? And isn't it fortuitous that I just had my hair styled this morning? By this time next week, my name will be on the tip of everyone's tongue," she confided. "This is the most exciting thing that's ever happened to me."

Thelma Tweeds agreed. Myra hung up the telephone, checked her lipstick in her compact mirror and skipped happily back to her table at the stylish restaurant where the interview was being conducted. She gave Uncle Nelly a blinding smile before waving down the waiter.

"Another dry martini," she ordered. "Shaken not stirred. Two olives." She turned her attention to her companion. "Where were we?" she cried.

"You were telling me about the Dramatic Club's highly successful production of *Oklahoma!* last summer," Uncle Nelly replied.

"I happen to have a picture of myself in the starring role as Laurie, the plucky farm girl, in my wallet," Myra cried as she dug into her handbag.

"Charming," Uncle Nelly murmured. "Who knew your many talents included acting ability?"

Myra flushed with pleasure. "To tell the truth, I stepped into the role at the very last minute," she confided. "It really isn't a part suited to my particular talents, but the lead actress came down with a sudden illness opening night and I selflessly volunteered to go on in her place."

"How brave of you," Uncle Nelly cried.

"I know!" Myra Meeks nodded. "And although I hadn't memorized the script and was forced to wear my street clothes on stage, the production went over quite well. I hear people are still talking about it."

"I imagine they are," Uncle Nelly told Myra with all sincerity.

CHAPTER 41

Frank's Anguish

BUCKSAW

SAWHORSE

"Are there any more of those yummy prune cookies?" Joe wondered hungrily. He was resting atop a pile of boulders overlooking an underground rivulet falling into a shallow pond while his brother was leaning against a thick stalagmite whilst reading their map and scratching his head over their next move. "Golly, what is it about spelunking that makes a fellow feel famished?" Joe asked.

Frank tossed his younger brother the last cookie. "How can you eat so much?" Frank groaned as he patted his own swollen stomach. "Three ham and cheese sandwiches and seven cookies is my limit."

"We'll need all our strength to traverse the tunnel ahead," Joe pointed out.

"I can't believe we've been exploring for hours and still haven't found the main cavern. Who could have guessed this particular cave system extended for so many miles?" Frank mused. To make matters worse, the boys were shod in their underwater diving flippers as Joe had forgotten to bring along their waterproof duffel bag containing suitable cave-exploring outfits.

Frank checked his compass. "Hmmn," he puzzled. "I'm getting no reading whatsoever. The needle just lies limply and doesn't move when I change position."

"It must be broken," Joe figured.

"Impossible," Frank insisted. "It's guaranteed virtually foolproof. Why, it's the same model the Mercury 7 astronauts will wear into space when that great day finally comes.

"There must be some strange force field wreaking havoc with our polarities," Frank surmised.

"At least our one remaining lantern's working," Joe said in relief. No sooner were the words were out of his mouth when the torch flickered and went out. Joe banged on it to no avail. Except for the soft shimmer of glowworms attached to the cave ceiling, the boys were left in total darkness! "Oh, no," Joe groaned. "I just remembered I put the spare batteries in the duffel bag I left on Uncle Nelly's love seat."

Luckily Frank always kept two double-D batteries in his oilskin pouch at all times. After letting Joe stew a moment, he handed him the replacements. "Phew!" Joe exclaimed. A moment later, the Hardly boys were back on the case.

"I'll never forget that duffel bag again," Joe swore as they walked toward the tunnel entrance, slipping on the slick ground under their flippers.

Frank smiled. "Sure, Joe, that's what you *always* say," he teased his younger brother.

"Hey, I'm a busy boy with a lot on his mind," Joe bantered back.

"I saw you eyeing Willy's cookies when you should have been double-checking our gear," Frank grinned knowingly.

Joe said nothing because Frank was frankly right. "I try to be level-headed like you and Father, but I'm afraid I'm given to flights of fancy," he explained.

"I'm not *all* that much like him," Frank quickly shot back.

Joe was puzzled. Why, Frank was *always* comparing himself to their father. "You're cut from the same cloth, and you know it," Joe teased back.

"Am not!" Frank insisted brusquely.

Joe gasped. Why, Frank sounded almost angry! He stopped in his tracks and turned to face his brother. The two lads stood flipper to flipper while Joe looked queerly at his brother. He could detect a pained expression in Frank's usually affable hazel eyes.

"Frank, you've been acting peculiar all morning," Joe declared. "What gives?"

Frank bit his lower lip and look down at the ground. "Ever since Uncle Nelly told us the truth about Father, a million different questions have been racing through my head."

"Mine, too," Joe admitted. He wondered, for example, if Grandfather Hardly was a girl, too.

"Why did Father have to lie to us?" Frank cried out.

"It wasn't really a lie, it was more like a fib," Joe pointed out. "And I'm sure he had a very good reason. I'll bet it's a matter of national security. Why, Father may be protecting us from something."

"Yeah," Frank said bitterly. "The truth about who we really are!"

Joe was puzzled. "We're the Hardly boys, Frank. Everyone knows that."

"Joe, *think,*" Frank cried. "If Father's a girl and Mother's a girl; well, don't you know what that means?"

Joe thought for a moment. "No," he had to admit.

"It means we're not really their sons! Joe, we're *not* the Hardly boys!"

Joe gasped. "Are you implying that we're *not* the fruit of the family tree?" cried the lad.

"We're probably not even *brothers!*" Frank was pulling no punches!

Joe gasped. His eyes filled with tears. Not Frank's brother? Why, he couldn't even begin to imagine not being Frank's brother!

"You're making this up," Joe insisted. "Stop it, Frank, you're scaring me!"

"Joe, has it ever struck you as peculiar that neither of us looks *anything* like Mother or Father, or anyone else in the Hardly family for that matter?"

"So?" Joe replied. "That doesn't mean a thing. Our chum Chick Morgan doesn't look anything like *his* parents."

"Chick was adopted, Joe. Like us!"

Joe took his waterproof hankie from the pocket of his wet suit and tried to sop up the tears racing down his boyish cheek. "I won't listen to another word," he sniffed as he grabbed the lantern from Frank's hand and headed into the tunnel. "We're on an important case and I haven't time to stand here and listen to your silly ideas." He stomped away.

"Hey, wait up," Frank cried. Joe slowed his pace but said nothing.

"Joe, I'm just trying to get you to look at the truth," Frank insisted, "instead of living in that dream world of yours. The truth is Father—"

Joe cut him off. "Frank, you don't know what you're talking about," he informed his older brother. "Of course we're their sons. Who else could we be?"

"That's what *I* want to know," Frank said in a foreboding tone.

CHAPTER 42

I *Before* E *Except After* C

Cherry paused at the doorway to Ward B to make sure her crisp cap was pinned securely to her mop of merry curls. "Aimless, you must keep your eyes and ears open at all times for anything unusual and not let on for a moment that you're here as an Undercover Nurse trying to find an entrance to some secret caves hiding dangerous kidnappers," she told herself, plastering an efficient smile on her face.

Although Cherry was mighty worried about Nancy, she knew this was her only chance to search the sanitarium. Cherry was hopeful she could pick up some all-important clues on her own. "Especially since I'm the reason Nancy's not available for sleuthing," she thought glumly.

She checked the sturdy nurse's watch on her right wrist. "It's one twenty-seven, which gives me exactly one hour and thirty-three minutes to race through my assignment and slip away to do some investigating. I wonder what my duties will be?" Cherry thought nervously as she opened the door to the ward and walked inside. A charming scene greeted her eyes. Ten nicely-dressed elderly women with freshly set hair were seated in comfortable chairs around a large wooden table, sipping tea and snacking on dishes of creamy sherbet and crisp-looking sugar cookies. A friendly discussion of commonly misspelled words was underway.

A cheerful, efficient-looking nurse with dark blond hair and shining brown eyes gave Cherry a big smile. "I'm glad to see reinforcements have arrived," she grinned.

"Where exactly am I?" Cherry asked, explaining, "This is my first day on duty at this particular sanitarium."

"You're in the Retired English Teacher's Wing, or Ward B, as it's more commonly called," the nurse informed her. "Starting from the far end of the table and working clockwise, that's

Miss Vivian Valencia, Miss Betty Lingo, Miss Antonia Lefler, Miss Evelyn Hoover, Miss Zena Wallace, Miss Grace Smith, Miss Myrtle Allen, Miss Bernice Bloom, and our two Marys, Miss Pratt and Miss Meredith. I'm Head Nurse Fern Fiscus and I'm in charge of this boisterous gang."

Cherry smiled. She could tell from the warm tone in her voice that Head Nurse Fern Fiscus held her patients in the highest regard. "I'm sure these ladies aren't at all difficult to handle," she said in a nurse-to-nurse tone.

"Just watch your grammar," Nurse Fiscus warned. "The last nurse the front desk sent me asked Miss Lingo to 'please go and lay down on your cot' and all heck broke loose!" The two nurses shared a knowing smile.

Nurse Fiscus showed Cherry the rest of the ward. It consisted of the lounge; a separate sleeping chamber with cozy cots and bedside tables, each with a good reading lamp and a stack of novels; a bathing facility that looked sparkling clean; and a small nursing station stocked with the most up-to-date medical conveniences.

"The more I see of this place the more impressed I am," Cherry enthused. "This is a very sanitary sanitarium."

"Our patients seem to find it very comfortable," the Head Nurse smiled. "In fact, a few of the patients came to the Institution as young women for treatment in the Career Gals Ward and upon retirement moved to this ward."

"Goodness," Cherry said. This was the most confusing mental institution she had ever been in. "But back at Seattle General, we classify people according to their illness, not occupation," she blurted out before she remembered she was not to reveal any information about herself.

"Here, we use Dr. Fraud's experimental therapies and approaches," Nurse Fiscus explained. "The female of the species is his specialty, you know. He classifies them according to type, like anxious adolescents, harried housewives, congenital career gals and so forth. Along with their private thrice-weekly visits with Dr. Fraud, our patients receive supportive therapies especially designed for their group. There's Occupational Therapy, Hairdo Therapy, Hydrotherapy, Wardrobe Therapy, and for the very worst cases, Shock Therapy."

"I've been involved in many applications of hydrotherapy," Cherry remarked, "and patients seem to find the hours spent in a tub with soothing warm water racing over their limbs quite refreshing."

"It's a favorite among the ladies in this ward," Head Nurse Fiscus agreed, adding confidentially, "If you ask me, some of my patients aren't really ill; they're just bored."

Cherry nodded sympathetically. She knew a great many people who were lonesome and suffered from social isolation. "It must be awfully hard to retire after an exciting lifetime spent teaching English," she murmured. She had a grand idea! "I'll bet what these ladies need is something interesting to do," she cried. For a moment Cherry forgot all about her all-important task of searching the sanitarium. "Let's have them write essays about the most influential person in their life, or given the choice, which animal they'd choose to be," Cherry suggested brightly.

"Splendid idea," Nurse Fiscus cried. "We'll need essay books, some number two pencils and gold stars," she declared. She took a ring of keys from her pocket and gave them to Cherry. "Would you go to the basement storeroom and get those things? Just take the main stairs three flights to the bottom level, turn left and continue east until you find the door marked *Storeroom*. You can't miss it."

"I'll be back," Cherry promised.

What luck being sent right to the basement where the entrance to the tunnel must surely be! She skipped out of the room and raced down the three flights of stairs, past nurses in crisply starched uniforms carrying trays of medications to various destinations. "Now that I have an excuse for being down here, I'll take a few extra minutes to poke around and then explain to Head Nurse Fiscus that I got lost," she schemed a little guiltily.

Ten minutes later, as she raced dizzily around the basement with its long winding corridors and numerous adjuncts, she realized she really *was* lost! Cherry had followed the head nurse's instructions to the letter and had quickly found the supply room. After filling her pockets with essay books, pencils and gold stars, she had ducked down a dimly lit corridor with a bright light at the end, thinking it might be the way to the tunnel entrance. She had instead found herself in another hallway, this one brightly lit, with black and white linoleum flooring, mint green walls and a steel door with glass windows threaded through with wire.

"Why, this is the only part of the sanitarium that looks like a real hospital," Cherry thought as she crept down the hallway, thankful that her regulation nurse's shoes had silent rubber soles on them. She would hate to make any undue noise and interrupt an examination!

"Perhaps this is where surgery is carried out," she thought as she peered through a window and saw a row of steel tables and trays of sterile surgical implements. "But why put it so far away from the other wards?" she wondered. Cherry suddenly remembered having seen a sign for the Surgical Ward on the second floor. "So what is this place?"

The sound of muffled footsteps let her know she wouldn't be alone for long. She grabbed the door knob and, relieved to find the door unlocked, raced into the room and hid behind a pile of cardboard boxes marked *Fragile*. The footsteps faded away.

Cherry jumped up to leave and clumsily sent the top box flying. She heard the sickening sound of glass breaking. When she opened the box, she was relieved to find only a few vials had shattered. "Maybe nobody will notice," Cherry hoped, "seeing as there are hundreds of vials in this box. I wonder what it is?" she mused, looking at the clear-colored liquid. Each vial was stamped with three letters.

"*LSD*," Cherry read aloud. "It must be some new medication," she reasoned. She froze when she heard the footsteps again, only this time they were much louder. "Uh-oh," she thought. "I'd better not get caught creeping around." She set the box upright and scurried out of the room. In the hallway, she glanced over her shoulder and saw the distinctive shadow of a man with a cigar clenched in his teeth. He was about to turn the corner!

"It's Dr. Fraud! If he finds me here, he might suspect something's up," Cherry thought worriedly. Another door a few feet away caught her eye. Cherry hurriedly found the skeleton key on the key ring, fit it into the lock, said a quick prayer and breathed a sigh of relief when she heard a click. She slipped through the door and quietly shut it behind her. She found herself in a dimly-lit stairwell.

"Oh, no," Cherry thought when she realized she was holding a vial of the mystery medication in her hand. "What if he notices a box has been opened?" she thought worriedly. "What if I'm found sneaking around down here while Nancy has been unmasked and is in trouble? Is there a law in Illinois against impersonating a psychiatric patient?" she wondered.

CHAPTER 43

A Sad Case

 "This is no time to think, Aimless," she told herself. "You've got to get out of here—and fast!" Cherry pushed the door open a crack and looked out. The hallway was deserted. The only sound besides the loud thumping of her heart was that of Dr. Fraud's deep, booming voice.

"Nurse Cramp, we are about to embark on an experiment that will free all of mankind from the confines of the human mind," she heard him say.

Cherry listened eagerly. That was something she'd like to know about!

"Yes, Doctor," Nurse Cramp replied. "Ward C is ready. The patients are looking forward to their vitamin shots," Nurse Cramp said with just a hint of gaiety in her voice.

"Once it's been tested here, the whole of Lake Merrimen can have a taste," the doctor promised. "You see, Nurse, just a bit of this in the water supply will produce amazing results."

"Phew," Cherry thought as she slipped the vial into her uniform pocket. "And I thought it might be something dangerous!" She took a deep steadying breath and opened the door, ready to make her escape, but jumped back when she saw Nurse Cramp standing in the hallway. She hoped desperately that she hadn't been spotted.

"Even if she did see me, she'll never be able to pick me out from all the other nurses here," she told herself. "I'd better get back to the ward before I'm reported missing!"

Hoping to find her way back to Ward B, Cherry scrambled up the narrow, winding staircase. To her consternation, the stairs kept spiraling upward. "I've climbed every stair there is to climb in all of Illinois," Cherry thought breathlessly when at last she came to a door. She realized she was in one of the twin towers flanking the Gothic-style mansion turned sanitarium. She fit the skeleton key into the lock of the old wooden door and flung it open only to find a sweet-faced middle-aged Private Duty Nurse sitting in an orange Naugahyde chair reading a magazine.

"Oh, good, my replacement's here early," the nurse said in relief as she dropped the magazine onto a nearby table, slipped into her regulation nurse's sweater, walked to the modern elevator not five feet away and pressed a button. "I've never seen anyone come up the back way before. You must be quite an athletic girl," she remarked. "Well, anyway, her medication's on the tray. I've left you a stack of magazines. Help yourself to some candy. Bye."

"Wait!" Cherry cried. "I'm not here to—" But it was too late. The nurse was gone. There was no one else on the floor; indeed, there were no other rooms!

"Oh, no," Cherry thought, all in a tizzy. "Now I *am* trapped, for I can't possibly leave the patient on her own. But how am I going to explain what I'm doing here when the right nurse comes along?"

Cherry shook herself to her senses. First and foremost, she was a nurse. "I'll check the patient's chart, dispense her medication and hope for the best," she decided.

She opened the door to find a woman about her mother's age, clad in silk lounging pajamas and soft slippers, sitting in a chair staring out the room's lone window. The woman didn't look up when the door opened. She just sat there looking all alone in the world.

Cherry's heart went out to the sad psychiatric patient. She scanned the simply furnished room for the woman's medical records, but didn't see any. "Excuse me, could you tell me where your chart is kept?" Cherry asked. She had no idea how many of the pink pills on the hallway table to give the patient.

The woman turned her head and looked straight at her. "Where have I seen that pert little nose and determined chin before?" Cherry wondered to herself. "And she has such lovely strawberry blond hair—it's a pity no one's styled it recently."

"Are you speaking to me?" the woman asked in a soft voice. "No one ever speaks to me. It's probably because I can't remember anything. I can't remember what day it is, or what I had for luncheon, or even my name." The woman's dramatic confession was delivered in a flat emotionless monotone. Her eyes seemed glazed over, as if she couldn't quite focus.

Cherry walked over to the woman and gave her hand a reassuring squeeze, but deep down she was disappointed. She would never find that chart now. It was clear, especially to a nurse of Cherry's vast experience, that she had an amnesia victim on her hands!

Cherry knew that light conversation on pleasant topics could be most helpful for amnesiacs. She searched her brain for something soothing to say. "I often can't remember the littlest things," Cherry confided. "And I'm a nurse!"

This seemed to startle the patient, so Cherry tried a different tactic. "I like your outfit," she said.

"It's very soft," the woman replied as she stroked the cream-colored fabric of her right sleeve, "but I can't remember what it's made of. Oh, I can't remember anything." Her bright blue eyes filled with tears. She turned away, clutching her hankie in her small white hands.

Cherry touched her shoulder. "It's shantung silk," she told her. "I know because a friend of mine has two sets of shantung silk lounging pajamas. They're hand-made and embroidered with her initials."

"Shantung silk," the woman murmured.

"Can you remember that?" Cherry asked her.

"I'll try," the woman said. "I try to remember things, really I do, only everything sifts through my brain like sand. Oh, what's wrong with me? It's as if I'm in a fog!" She began to weep.

"I mustn't let her get too excited, especially if she's past due for her medication," Cherry told herself. "I must say something to take her mind off her troubles. But what?"

"I was in a fog once in San Francisco," she chattered brightly. "You see, I had gone there to visit my beloved Aunt Gertrude and along the way I met the nicest girls—" The patient visibly relaxed while Cherry told the story of her past adventures, taking care to omit any parts that might unduly frighten the frail-seeming woman, who fell back in her chair and closed her eyes.

For five full minutes, Cherry talked, ending with, "—and then I met Nancy and we came here to Illinois and here I am."

The patient shot straight up. "Nancy?" she cried. Then she put a finger to her lips and furrowed her pretty brow.

"That name seems to ring a bell," Cherry thought. "And

it's the queerest thing. Nancy makes that very same gesture when she's thinking. It must be a Midwestern trait."

"Could *your* name be Nancy?" Cherry asked her.

"I don't know," the woman shook her head. "I hear that name over and over in my dreams," she remembered.

"Your name must be Nancy, then. It's the only logical explanation," Cherry cried in triumph. "We've certainly made remarkable progress in a very short time," she added happily.

The patient's face lit up when she heard that. "Do you mean to say you think there's hope for me?" she asked tentatively.

"There's no such thing as a hopeless case," Cherry scolded her. "Remember. Every cloud has a silver lining." Cherry decided then and there she would have to take this woman's case up with Dr. Fraud. Pleasant chatter and social stimuli obviously helped this patient—why, then, was she kept so far from the others? A moment later, Cherry's first opportunity to voice that question appeared when a strange nurse burst in. But before Cherry could say anything she was ordered out of the room in a most discourteous manner.

"Please don't go," the patient pulled at Cherry's arm.

"I must go," Cherry told her in a kindly manner. "I have other patients who need me. I'll come see you again," she promised.

Tears filled the woman's blue eyes. "Promise?" she asked.

"Scout's honor," Cherry said. "I will, too," she told herself, "just as soon as this case is cracked!"

Once in the hallway, Cherry received the tongue lashing of her career. "Were you authorized to have contact with that patient?" the new nurse angrily quizzed her.

Cherry shook her head. She didn't trust herself to speak. She was both scared and angry, plus she was unimaginably tardy! "I didn't think it could do any harm," she finally managed to say. "She seems so lonely shut up like that. She says nobody ever comes to visit her."

"That woman is a hopeless paramnesiac," the nurse explained curtly. "She tells terrible lies."

"What?" Cherry said in bewilderment. "She seems like an average amnesiac to me and not someone who has a memory of that which has never happened, refusing to believe her memory's anything but real and so goes on and on about a thing that has never occurred. Quite the opposite. Why, she couldn't tell me a thing about herself."

The nurse relaxed. "When she first came to this institution twenty-two years ago, she was housed with the general population," she explained, "but we had to put her here because she scared everyone so with her wild stories. She ran around the grounds wailing and moaning and telling everyone she was a ghost!"

"No!" Cherry cried. "How ghastly!"

The nurse nodded in sympathy. "She imagines she was brutally murdered by her husband. Nothing we say can convince her otherwise."

"I understand now why she's in isolation," Cherry said. "Paramnesiacs can be most upsetting to others. Still, it's so sad. How horrible to believe something as gruesome as that.

"I'm due back on Ward B," Cherry suddenly remembered. "I'm new here, and I got lost, and that's how I ended up in her room."

The nurse put Cherry in the elevator and punched a button. "When you get out, turn left, then right, then left again, and you'll be in Ward B," she directed. Cherry tried hard to memorize the path between that place and Ward B. As soon as she could, she would be back with more helpful conversation. Cherry wouldn't forget her promise to that lonely woman.

When at last Cherry arrived in Ward B, she was surprised to find Dr. Fraud and Nurse Cramp waiting for her. And they had the queerest expressions on their faces.

"I got lost!" Cherry cried. "Can they tell I'm lying?" she wondered as a deep flush crept up her neck. "Can they see the outline of the top-secret vitamin vial through the thin material of my uniform pocket?"

"We were worried about you, dear," Head Nurse Fiscus exclaimed.

"It's so easy to get turned around in this big old place," Nurse Cramp added with a knowing smile. "You should never have gone off on your own."

Cherry smiled cheerily. She hadn't been found out after all! "I got the supplies you asked for," she informed Nurse Fiscus. "Shall I begin the assignment?"

"We've got a new task for you, dear," Nurse Cramp told Cherry. "You're to go get Miss New and accompany her to Hydrotherapy."

"Think you can find your way there?" Head Nurse Fiscus teased.

"Absolutely," Cherry promised. Inwardly she breathed a sigh of relief. What luck! The Hydrotherapy Room was in the basement! "Now Nancy and I will *really* get a chance to investigate," she smiled to herself as she left the room. "And on the way down, I'll tell her about the top-secret vitamin potion I found, plus relay to her the tragic tale of that poor patient I stumbled onto." She realized with a start that Nurse Cramp was right behind her.

"Oh, you don't need to show me the way," Cherry assured her. "I'm sure now I know where I'm going."

"I bet you do, dear," Nurse Cramp smiled back. "Only I'd better show you how to operate the equipment."

"Oh, I've assisted with plenty of hydrotherapy treatments at Seattle General Hospital," Cherry assured her. She regretted her words the minute they were out of her mouth. Hadn't she told everyone she was a Hollywood Nurse?

Nurse Cramp didn't skip a beat. "Our way of doing things might be different. The pipes in this building are old; getting just the right water temperature is sometimes a tricky business. We wouldn't want our newest nurse hurting herself, now would we?"

CHAPTER 44

"Boy, Oh, Boy!"

"Do you see *that?*" Joe gasped in wonder as he peered through his binoculars, his mouth agape. Four burly guys stripped to the waist and glistening with sweat, large tools firmly in hand, were bent over an enormous machine spewing sparks and smoke. The boys were perched on a stone ledge overlooking the entrance to a vast cavern two-stories high and as wide as a basketball court.

"I sure *do!*" Frank whispered back as he trained his spyglasses on the scene below. He was agog with excitement about a discovery of his own! "Golly," he murmured as he brought his binoculars sharply into focus on a tall, clean-cut darkly handsome fellow not much older than himself. The man was clad in a simple charcoal-colored worsted wool continental-cut suit and owlish glasses, but even from this distance Frank could see the intelligent glimmer in his eyes. He was listening intently to his walkie-talkie, his handsome brow furrowing in concentration.

Frank gave a low whistle. This fellow would certainly bear watching!

"The electrical current from this generator must be what's interfering with our compass," Joe reported excitedly. "What's down here that requires that much juice?" he wondered.

"How are we going to get past these men?" Frank shivered to himself. "Why, those fellows are so manly and muscular they'll have us down on the floor in no time at all—and there's two for each one of us!"

Inch by inch, the Hardly boys surveyed the fascinating sights captured in their binoculars. Frank watched the handsome man's every move with the keen interest befitting a boy detective hard at work. Already breathless from their travels, Frank felt himself getting warmer by the minute. "Is it getting hot in here?" he asked his brother.

"It sure *is!*" Joe agreed. He unzipped his wet suit to the waist and fanned himself with his hand. That generator was conducting an awful lot of heat!

The darkly handsome man suddenly climbed down the stairs, spoke briefly with the four-man crew, strode purposefully across the floor and disappeared into an chasm in the cave wall.

"Let's follow him," Frank urged. "I'll toss a smoke bomb to the far side of the generator to create a diversion. They'll think it's coming from the equipment and won't be unduly alerted." Frank's scheme proved victorious and soon the boys found themselves creeping down a tunnel lit by flickering electric bulbs set high up on the wall. "Lucky for us, they're having electrical problems," Frank whispered, "The dim lighting makes it easier to hide."

The boys spotted two men clad in white laboratory coats coming their way. The men however were too engrossed in their clipboards to notice two boys in rubber suits quickly jump behind a metal cabinet. "Those men look very smart," Frank whispered to Joe.

"I bet they're math teachers," Joe replied. Frank nodded. He had expected to find some Russian agents and his parents blindfolded and tied to chairs, but it looked as if they had stumbled onto something *really* queer!

CHAPTER 45

What Goes Up Must Come Down

"Give me a blow-by-blow," Joe directed. "What do you see?"

Frank was standing on his brother's shoulders, peering through the transom in a windowless metal door. "It's a long room with man-sized tubular metal cylinders stacked horizontally," Frank reported. "There are all sorts of chains and hooks hanging from the rocky ceiling. It must be a pulley system to move these things. But why? What are the cylinders used for? Joe, stop wobbling," Frank ordered curtly. He could see the shadowy figure of two men amid the columns and he wanted to get a closer look.

"I'm trying to get comfortable," Joe grumbled. "Frank, you're going to have to cut back on your wiener consumption. You weigh a ton!" He gave a little cry as he lost his footing, and Frank came crashing down on his head. Luckily neither lad was injured, but they had attracted some unwanted attention. They could hear footsteps on the other side of the door. Someone was headed their way!

Without a moment to lose, the boys snatched up some sharp rocks and held them ready. The door flew open and two men strode out. Joe struck first, beaning a man clad in blue mechanic's overalls on the noggin. The man went down without a fight. Then Frank raised his rock, but froze when he realized his foe was none other than the handsome man they had been following. A look of alarm, then a flicker of recognition passed through the man's soft gray eyes. Frank flushed under his intense gaze. The boy went weak at the knees when he saw the little smile gathering at the corners of the man's plump yet manly lips.

Without a moment's hesitation, Joe stepped forward and clunked the handsome man on the back of the head. "Ooh!"

the man moaned as he fell right into Frank's arms.

"That's funny," Frank thought as his stomach did flip-flops. "He's the one who took it from behind, but I'm the one seeing stars!"

"Quick, Frank," Joe ordered. "Drop that guy, strip off his outfit and get into it. This is our chance to move about this place freely." Frank lost no time following Joe's orders, starting with the man's trousers.

Once costumed, the Hardly boys trussed up the unconscious naked men, dragged them into the room with the metal cylinders and deposited them among the tubes. Upon closer inspection, Frank realized that each cylinder had a small hatch and a circuit board with wires attached to its shaft. "These look familiar," Frank thought.

"Let's go," Joe urged impatiently.

Frank paused to loosen the prisoners' gags. Then he gently slipped the handsome man's glasses onto his face.

"Frank, stop fussing," Joe demanded.

"I don't want them to suffocate. Besides, he'll need his glasses when he wakes up," Frank explained.

"So he can *see* clearly when he comes after *us*?" Joe snapped. "Do you think they gave *us* one minute's thought when they kidnapped our parents?"

Frank remembered the look in the man's face before the blow. He gulped. He had captured a lot of fellows in his day, but this time he felt none of his usual pleasure. There had been a look in the man's eyes—one that Frank just couldn't forget. "Who knows," Frank murmured as he gazed at the handsome unconscious man. "Under different circumstances, in a world where all men are free, we could have been chums."

"Frank, what is *wrong* with you today?" Joe demanded to know. *"First* you act all peevish about Father being a girl, and *now* you're mooning over this Russian guy. I don't know who you are anymore," he cried in exasperation. "That fall through the closet floor must have loosened a few wires in your brain."

Something clicked in Frank's head. "Mooning—wires—?

"Oh, Joe, that's it! Now I know what this place is! We've stumbled upon a secret Russian moon-missile launching laboratory!" he cried excitedly. "These cylinders with the wires attached—they're Russian rocket bodies, and those men in the white coats are Russian rocket scientists!"

"That's right, Frank. These people are the enemy," Joe reminded his brother.

Frank nodded. He had come to his senses. "Let's get them," he cried, balling up his fists. "And when we do, why—"

"Why, they won't need rockets—we'll send *them* into orbit!" Joe promised.

CHAPTER 46

To the Moon!

"This proves my theory to the letter," Frank scribbled on the clipboard in his hands. He and Joe were striding manfully through the middle of enemy territory in their Russian agent disguises. All around them, men were hard at work: hunched over tables drawing rocket diagrams, heating chemicals in beakers, working with electronic gizmos, welding sheets of aluminum. So far, no one had even glanced at the two lads, who were furtively writing their communiqués instead of talking, so as not to give away their true nationality.

"What do you think that low roar in the distance is?" Joe penned.

"Wind tunnel," was Frank's guess. NASA had a wind tunnel the size of a city block where they tested the wind-resistance factors of all their missiles. No doubt there was one here, too. From what the boys could see, this was a fully operational space experimentation center.

Frank and Joe's mouths dropped open when they peered through a doorway and saw in the distance a full-sized model of a rocket ship, poised as if for takeoff. Joe whistled softly when he saw the acronym *NASA* painted on its side.

"They stole this stuff from us!" Joe scribbled hurriedly. Frank nodded. There was a very big leak at the National Space and Aeronautics Agency! Only then did Frank begin to fully understand the gravity of their situation. Not only were their parents' lives in danger, but the fate of the Space Race was in the Hardly boys' hands!

Joe elbowed Frank and pointed to a machine much like a giant cocktail shaker. Inside the huge plastic canister, two men in helmets and thickly padded suits were trying unsuccessfully to keep their footing while the machine rolled them about. A few yards away, a man was strapped in a chair attached to a long metal arm rotating faster and faster around a sphere until the centrifugal force flattened the man's features into one big blob.

"G-force test," Frank scribbled. He wondered how the Russians had found this spot in the first place, and how they had managed to infiltrate it without alerting any of the local citizenry. But before he could mention it to Joe, a glass-walled room at the far end of the laboratory caught his attention. Frank blinked and rubbed his eyes. For a minute, he thought he had seen a bunch of poodles floating in thin air! When he took a closer look, he gasped.

"Look, Joe, it's an anti-gravity chamber filled with dogs!" Frank scribbled. Joe looked up. Like buoys in an ocean, dozens of small fuzzy poodles were floating about unfettered, their rhinestone collars twinkling like stars. The mournful-looking animals were falling head over paws, bumping into one another like lost atoms.

Now Frank knew for certain who was behind the rash of dognappings in Illinois. His eyes filled with tears as he thought of Laika, the last dog the Russians had sent into space. She never came back!

"The Russians *do* want our top dogs for their space launches!" Frank cried, momentarily forgetting to keep his voice down. "Uh, oh," he then gulped. Everyone was staring at the two lads.

"Run for it, Frank!" Joe gasped. The boys threw down their clipboards and hotfooted it out of the room. Each knew what the other was thinking. It was worse than they could have imagined! If the Russians were willing to test gravity on poodles, *what* were they doing to their parents?

"We mustn't be captured and become victims to their cruel experimentation," Frank cried to Joe.

"Quick!" Joe cried, "Let's hide inside the life-size rocket ship model!"

The boys ran through the doorway and scrambled up the rungs of the needle-nosed titanium giant. They hurled themselves inside and secured the latch just as an alarm system began to wail. "We made it in the nick of time," Frank breathed with relief as he peered out the small round portal in the side of the spacecraft. Men were scurrying about, looking high and low for the intruders.

"They'll never find us here. We'll sit it out until the hullabaloo is over, find Mother and Father, then get out of here and immediately report this to NASA!" Frank schemed.

"Gouf imes," Joe said.

"What?" Frank asked.

Joe swallowed, then repeated, "I said, good idea. Hey, want a candy bar? There's a whole box here, and they're pretty good."

Frank frowned. Joe picked the queerest times to be hungry! "Here we are sitting on the biggest spy case of the twentieth century, and all you can think about is food!" Frank groaned. "Why, we've got information to win the Space Race single-handedly for our country. Think of it, Joe. We'll be the heroes of our generation. We'll be on the lips of Boy Scouts all over America!" Frank snapped out of his reverie. "Joe, what are you doing over there? Can't you sit still?"

"I'm just checking things out," Joe defended himself. "Look, there's a whole box of magazines just like the ones Willy reads. *Physique Magazine. Guy's Life. Indoor Sports.* I guess this goes to show you, guys are the same all over."

Frank frowned. He was intently studying the control panel of the craft. "This is an exact model of the experimental Maxx-Thruster Rocket NASA's been working on," Frank realized.

"Golly, you don't mean the latest rocket designed to take man into deep space?" Joe asked excitedly.

"Don't touch anything," Frank warned his brother. "We don't know if this thing is wired with alarms."

"Aye, aye, Captain," Joe grinned with a snappy salute to his brother. Just then the rocket began to rumble.

"Joe, what did you do?" Frank cried.

"Nothing," Joe gulped. "Honest." The boys tried to stop the engine, but it was too late, for inside the ship, things had begun to happen. Lights flashed; a data recorder clicked on; radarscopes beamed strange images on their screens. Frank looked out the window and saw a brilliant flash of light as the roof of the cavern appeared to open. There was nothing but blue sky above! "Do you know where we are, Joe?" he yelped. "The launch pad must be under Treasure Island!"

Joe grabbed the handle of the escape hatch and pulled it, but to no avail. "It won't open—we're stuck!" he cried.

"Lift-off minus two minutes. Lift-off minus one minute and

fifty-nine seconds—" a mechanical voice announced, starting the countdown.

The boys broke out in a sweat. "This can't really be happening," Frank cried over the roar of the engines. But he knew it was; for he could feel the rocket rumble and lurch. It was *really* taking off!

Were the Hardlys going to be the first boys in space?

—— CHAPTER 47 ——

Frank Sees the Light

"Joe—strap yourself in!" Frank directed. The boys flattened themselves on the horizontal take-off seats and buckled the safety straps. "Sure you're in tight?" Frank asked Joe tensely. Joe nodded.

Terrible thoughts were racing through Frank's mind. Their youthful bodies could be torn asunder during the high acceleration it would take to shoot this rocket past the Earth's atmosphere. Without safety suits, they could be burned to a cinder from the sun's intensive rays. Why, they could end up as a fiery shooting star! The Hardly boys were ill-equipped for space travel, and Frank knew it!

Frank and Joe shared a solemn look. "Joe—" Frank started, then stopped. He knew he didn't need words—not with Joe! He put out his hand. There was a long, firm handclasp as silent hopes were conveyed from the eyes of each.

"Lift-off minus two seconds. Lift-off minus one second. Blastoff!"

"What thrust!" Frank found himself thinking in admiration, despite their precarious predicament. As the engines roared and rumbled beneath them, thrusting the rocket ship up, up into the sky, Frank was flooded with emotion.

"Father will never know how much I really love him," he realized with a sob. "Oh, why did I have to come to this realization now, when it's too late to tell him? I hope nobody tells Father what a knucklehead I was!" he thought worriedly.

The G-force grew stronger, flattening the boys' clean-cut features until they were no longer recognizable as America's best-loved boy detectives. The pressure proved too great for the lads. They fell into deep faints. When Frank came around, he realized the force-field had abated. He unstrapped himself and walked over to the window. Darkness punctuated by the twinkling of stars greeted his eyes.

"Joe—we're here. We're really here!" Frank cried excitedly. "We're the first boys in space!"

Joe awoke, stretched and let himself loose. "How long do you figure we've been out?" he wondered.

"Hours, probably," Frank guessed. "Look—we're high above the Earth."

Joe peeked out the window and gasped when he saw the small revolving planet they called home. He gazed through his binoculars. "What a sight!" he whistled. "Why, the continents look just like they do on our globe at home. Africa is all pink, while Europe is yellow."

"Joe, don't be silly," Frank scoffed. "That's just the effect of gamma rays on the visible spectrum."

Frank checked the levels on the control panel. "We've got three tanks of rocket fuel left, just enough to circle the moon, fling ourselves back into the Earth's orbit and make a splashdown in some nice soft body of water like Lake Merrimen," he schemed. "Lucky for us, we don't seem to feel the effects of the sun's intensive rays. The aluminum body of this rocket must be triple thick, which is sure a relief." Frank knew that if the ship were to be pierced by a meteorite, their blood would boil like water in a tea kettle.

"Happily, NASA's solved the additional problem of weightlessness in space," Frank noticed, relievedly.

He began poking around the panel, which resembled the flight panel on the Hardly speedy two-seater airplane, the *Sky Princess*. He took hold of the throttle in an attempt to guide the craft's course, but found it wobbling out of control!

"Look, Frank," Joe gasped as he looked out the window and saw they were hurling toward a rocky orb pockmarked with craters. "We're going to crash-land on the moon!"

"Look out, Joe," Frank cried as he grasped his brother to him, hoping to break Joe's fall. The craft came to a sudden standstill, and the boys were thrown against the panel. Suddenly the hatch popped and two men strode inside, each grabbing a Hardly boy and yanking him to his feet.

Frank gasped when he recognized the man whose hands had him by the collar. It was the handsome fellow Joe had beaned with a brick, only now he was wearing a navy blue suit with a three-buttoned jacket with wide, sloping shoulders. A crisp white shirt and a simple carmine-colored tie completed his ensemble.

"Nice suit you've got on, Frank," the man quipped sarcastically, giving Frank the once-over. "Your father said you were a snappy dresser," he added in a low tone, giving Frank a little wink. A million butterflies started flitting around in Frank's stomach. He had a million questions. How did this man speak English with no trace of an accent? And what occasion had provided context for such a casual conversation with his father?

But before Frank could say anything, the boys were forced out of the rocket at gun point. As Frank was descending the rungs, he could plainly see that what he and Joe had experienced had been a clever simulation of a rocket launch. "Now that I've taken another look, I can see this rocket's not full-size. And there's a globe and a projector," he whispered to Joe. "And giant springs underneath caused us to feel motion—"

"No talking!" the handsome man ordered. *"Don't—say—a—word!"*

Joe and Frank exchanged fearful glances. Was this fellow friend or foe?

CHAPTER 48

Prisoners!

Midge read aloud the three signs. "Left is the Moonscape Simulation Hall, to the right is the Rocket-Propulsion Chamber, and straight ahead is the Cafeteria." They were standing on an observation deck overlooking a vast underground scientific laboratory, pleased that they had had the foresight to don disguises, as they blended right in. Why, except for the pocketbook dangling from the crook of Velma's elbow, they looked just like any of the industrious men below.

"This is just like Endless Caverns in Arizona, isn't it, Velma?" Midge exclaimed. "We went there a few years ago on our vacation," she told Jackie. "It's a huge underground cavern with a lake, a ballroom and a cafeteria. It looks like this, except for all these rockets and guys in white coats running around. That was a fun vacation, huh, babe?"

"It *was* a memorable trip," Velma noted, "especially the part where we were kicked out of the caverns for unseemly behavior."

"We were caught in a limestone crevice," Midge grinned. "The tour guide shone his light on us at a most inopportune time."

"A woman in our party fainted," Velma giggled, adding, "Midge and I have been thrown out of all the best places!"

Jackie smiled. She hoped some day she and Cherry would have memories like that! She swallowed hard. Better to stay focused on the task at hand and not let her mind wander to a certain dark-haired nurse with the sweetest lips and a curvy figure who was at this minute locked away with a devious titian-haired detective. "See? This can't be a Russian operation. Look—all the signs are in English."

Midge jumped in. "Look over there! It's Joe and Frank and they're being led away at gun point by two men."

Velma took Nancy's opera glasses from her purse and tried

to make out what the men were saying. "The guy in the blue suit is going to take the boys away for interrogation. And they're speaking English."

"And?" Jackie said excitedly.

"Now they're talking about lunch," Velma groaned. "The other man just mentioned some cheese—"

Midge's stomach grumbled.

"Wait," Velma cried. "I was mistaken. Not some cheese— the *big* cheese!"

"The big boss?" Jackie guessed.

Velma nodded. "Only I can't make out his name. Oh, no, don't put that stick of chewing gum in your mouth! Drat! Now I can't make out a word he's saying! Oh, darn, they just turned a corner. Sorry."

"You did just swell, Velma," Jackie said in admiration.

"You see why I never leave the house without her?" Midge bragged to Jackie.

Still, Velma was keenly disappointed, but there was no time for pouting. They had to follow the Hardly boys and set them free! They shimmied down a fire escape, dropped to the floor and blended unobtrusively with all the other white-coated men. They turned down the corridor where Frank and Joe had disappeared when Velma suddenly gave a little cry. Her left shoe was stuck to the floor!

Velma slid her foot out of her sling-back pump. "Gum!" she grimaced as she scraped the sticky wad from her shoe. "Further proof that this place is run by Americans. Besides, look at these life-size photographic portraits lining this hall-way. Aren't these the Mercury 7 astronauts?"

"I thought I recognized these fellows," Midge admitted.

"But what does Fennel Hardly's kidnapping have to do with this place?" Jackie wondered. "After all, isn't he working for these guys? Why would they kidnap him?"

"And why would Judge Meeks try to make him out to be a spy?" Midge wondered.

"Maybe he discovered something he shouldn't have," Velma guessed.

"And you know how dangerous that can be," came a deep threatening voice from behind. Midge whirled around to find a darkly handsome man in a snappy suit and horn-rimmed glasses. And he was holding a gun.

"Don't say a thing," the man growled as he cocked his revolver. "Just walk!"

They did as they were told.

"Security, this is Agent Anderson," the man spoke curtly into his walkie-talkie. "I've captured three intruders in quadrant seven. I'm taking them to the interrogation chamber with the others."

"Okey-dokey," came a cheerful male voice over the crackling wires.

Midge and Jackie exchanged grins. That sounded just like Joe! Midge cleared her throat. "Excuse me," she said. "I think you should know—"

"No talking!" the man said curtly. Midge was miffed but she kept her mouth shut. If Velma hadn't been there, why, she would have taken a swing at the rude fellow!

"Now do as I say or the little fellow gets hurt," the man snarled. Midge gulped. He meant Velma! She shot her girlfriend an anxious look. "You are never coming along on another adventure again, no matter how much you pout!" that look said.

"Get in that room!" the man said, pointing to a steel-plated door. They were ushered inside a chemical laboratory where the Hardly family sat lashed to bare metal chairs.

Midge suddenly leapt into action. She shoved Velma aside, then turned and socked the guy with the gun right on his square jaw. The man lurched backward against a table, and flasks, condensers and test tubes went flying in all directions onto the concrete floor, shattering to bits.

Jackie grabbed his wrist and squeezed until he shrieked in pain and dropped his gun. The strong girl then grabbed him by his lapels and shook him. "Who are you and—" But before she could continue, the Hardly family jumped up, their restraints falling away. They hadn't been tied up after all, only made to look that way!

Frank hurled his body between Jackie and the man. "Don't hurt him!" Frank cried. He took a clean hankie from his pocket and held it to the man's split lip. "Oh, Agent Andy, are you all right?"

"This is Secret Agent Dwight 'Andy' Anderson," Mr. Hardly rushed over to explain.

"He's one of us!" Joe crowed. The boys then tumbled all

over themselves trying to fill the girls in on everything they had learned.

"This place—" Joe started.

"—is a secret rocket ship and moon walk operation—" Frank cut in.

"—our own government—"

"—never any Russians—"

"—the clues were fake—"

"—they've run amok with the public's trust—"

"—spending millions developing rockets that won't even take off—"

"Wait a minute—I'm getting dizzy, fellows," Agent Anderson protested. He was still a little weak from the sock on the jaw he had just taken.

"Lean on me, Agent Andy," Frank urged. The good-looking secret agent guy looped an arm over Frank's shoulder and rested heavily on him. "Thanks, Frank," he said. "Say, this is much better. I ought to take you with me everywhere I go."

Frank beamed. The thought of entering government service was becoming more and more attractive as time went on.

While Agent Anderson caught his breath, Mr. Hardly outlined the strange case. "It's a complicated tangle of secret agents, double agents, faulty rocket ships, kidnapped poodles and hidden explosive devices," he said in a calm tone that let them know he would soon have the situation under control. Mrs. Hardly clutched her husband's arm. While he gave her a comforting hug, Agent Anderson began talking. The girls plopped themselves on chairs and listened to the man's incredible tale.

"I'm with a secret government organization. I can't tell you which one. This all started when I got a call from Fennel. We'd worked together on a case a few years back—"

"So this place *is* a United States government laboratory," Jackie said.

"That's right," Agent Anderson said. "It's been here since the war. For years, it's functioned without a hitch, first as a weapons research laboratory and then, in the last few years, as a space rocket laboratory." He gratefully accepted a cigarette from Midge. After a few puffs, he continued his tale.

"Fennel sends me a coded message. Something's queer here. He'd been following the dognappings and found the link to NASA. Then I get a call from my boss. Can't say who he is.

He wants me to come here and investigate a local detective—"

"He means our dad," Joe interjected.

"—who was rumored to have gone over to the other side—"

"Become a spy for the Russians!" Joe translated.

"I took on the case so I could protect Fennel and Mrs. Hardly, but I got here too late. Someone had already taken it upon himself to pull in the Hardlys, and they had done a pretty rough job of it, too," Agent Anderson continued. "I'm not sure who we can trust," he finished.

"Certainly not Judge Milton Meeks," Jackie announced. "He's issued a warrant for Fennel's arrest on charges of espionage. What's more, he had someone plant false clues linking Fennel to the Russians.

"But what's this blast that's scheduled for tomorrow?"

Fennel P. Hardly spoke up. "Girls, our government is planning to launch a faulty rocket ship manned by dogs, then blow it up over Lake Merrimen and blame it on the Russians!"

"We've got to save those dogs!" Midge cried.

"But that doesn't make any sense," Jackie exclaimed. "Why would we want to blow up our *own* rocket?"

"For the publicity?" Velma guessed cynically. "If we don't launch something soon, people might become wary of the space program. Funding would be cut. Instead it will *look* like we were ready, only our foes caused us to fail. Everyone will worry even more about losing the Space Race, and NASA's future will be safe."

Midge said nothing, but leaned over and kissed Velma on the top of her head.

"I never thought our government could devise something that devious, and that a court official would falsify evidence to help carry it out, but that's exactly what's going on," Frank sadly shook his head.

"Only they're going to blame it on you, too, Father," Joe cried. "We've got to stop the blast, find evidence that will expose Judge Meeks for what he is and clear your good name."

"*Our* good name," Frank said, giving his father a manful one-armed hug.

"But how do we get you out of here without alerting anyone?" Agent Anderson mused. "Meeks has to have cohorts down here working this end of his evil plan. I don't know who they might be. We've got to be very careful."

"You've kept us safe this far," Frank pointed out with adoration.

"How *did* you know to intercept us, anyway?" Jackie wondered.

"We contacted Willy on Andy's communications device, and he told us you were headed down here," Frank said. "It was sheer luck that Andy found you before one of Meeks' men did."

"When I saw Midge in that white coat I was afraid for a second that Frank had snuck out to do some investigating on his own," Agent Anderson admitted with a smile.

"Although Frank and I *could* be brothers, I'm just a friend of the family," Midge grinned.

"I am, too, now that I've gotten to know *all* of them," the man exclaimed, sneaking a significant look Frank's way.

Midge lit another cigarette and grinned. She gave her girlfriend a happy squeeze. They weren't the only ones in that room who were in love!

"Let's be speedy about this," Jackie pleaded. "We've got two chums working undercover at the River Depths Sanitarium and they've got to get out before nightfall," she told the man.

Agent Anderson's face grew rigid with concern. "They sure do," he cried, "for that place is unsafe!" He explained. "I've been investigating Dr. Fraud for months, and was going to move in on him after I cleaned up this operation. He's got a government contract to test space drugs, but I've uncovered evidence that he's really developing dangerous mind-control substances. See, I suspect—"

"Give us the details later," Jackie urged. "The girl of my dreams is in that sanitarium!" She was about to race out the door when Midge grabbed ahold of her. "If we get captured, who's going to rescue Cherry and Nancy?" Midge warned her.

"Is there any way to contact them? To tell them to get out?" Agent Anderson asked.

"No, but they are carrying a tracking device that could lead us to them," Frank announced. "My watch has a built-in receiver."

"I'm getting you all out of here right now," Agent Anderson decided. "But how to move seven people through the laboratory without raising any suspicion?" he mused.

At this, a clever look came into Velma's eye. "I have an idea," she said. "I'll need a sharp knife, some string, that bolt of silver fabric over there, those portraits from the hallway and seven glass fishbowls."

Midge grinned. She had a feeling this was going to be good!

CHAPTER 49

"It's John Glenn!"

"Why, it's the Mercury 7 astronauts come to pay us a visit!" a scientist cried. He put his work aside and waved hello to the brave men who would someday ride their rockets into space.

"Look, everyone! It's John Glenn!" someone else exclaimed. A cry went up throughout the caverns. Men everywhere put down their clipboards and rulers, protractors and compasses and blinked their eyes in profound disbelief. The seven bravest men in America, wearing their shiny silver suits and protective bubble-shaped headgear, were walking through their rocket rooms, accompanied by Agent Anderson!

Voices rang out. "Hi Wally!" "Hi Gus!"

A mathematician began to clap, and within minutes, the room was thundering with applause. The astronauts waved manfully before getting into the transport elevator.

"Did you see? Scott Carpenter looked right at me!" a rocket chemist beamed. "Now I'm too excited to get anything done today."

"Come back to Earth, Chip," his chum teased. "We've got that big launch tomorrow. You want to come out on top, don't you?"

The rocket chemist shook his head. "I still think it's premature to launch the Maxx-Thruster this early in the game. We're going to look like awful fools if this thing doesn't fly, plus we'll lose the public's confidence, and we can't afford to do that."

"Don't worry," his chum assured him. "You don't think they'd let it go up if it wasn't a tight ship, do you? Besides, if the government wasn't one hundred percent confident, do you think they'd bring the Mercury 7 fellows here?"

CHAPTER 50

To the Rescue!

"I can't wait to get out of here and into some fresh air and open sky," Midge complained as she yanked off her glass headgear and pushed up her John Glenn mask. "Phew. That's better. I'm beginning to feel claustrophobic from being down here, especially with this thing over my head."

"Better put your disguise back on, in case someone gets on the elevator," Joe warned.

Midge complied.

"Velma, you are brilliant," Jackie said through the air holes in her mask. "I've always suspected as much, but now I'm certain of it. Why, putting these photographs of the Mercury 7 astronauts over our faces was a stroke of genius."

"Finding that map and making your way into these caverns took acts of brains and courage far exceeding anything you've ever done," Mr. Hardly said to his sons. "I want you boys to know that I've never been more proud of you." Mr. Hardly's voice was thick with emotion. "I'm proud to be your father."

"We'll always be proud to be your sons," Frank assured him. Father and son exchanged strong, silent glances. No words were necessary.

"Father," Frank then said softly.

"Yes, son?"

"Father, I've got some things to tell you. So much has happened since I saw you last. You need to know—Father, I'm—I'm—not the boy I used to be."

Mr. Hardly glanced at the handsome fellow by Frank's side and smiled. "And I'm not the man you think I am," he told his eldest son. "As soon as we're back home, safe and sound, we'll have a good long talk over a piece of your mother's famous peach cobbler."

Frank smiled happily. Somehow he just knew everything would be okay!

"We're here," Agent Anderson spoke out as the elevator came to a halt. "Now, our aim is to get to the tunnel headed northwest. That's the direct link to the sanitarium. Word has no doubt spread that the Mercury 7 astronauts are visiting, so remember to wave but move quickly."

"People really like these guys," Midge remarked as men jumped out of their path, pointed and waved their handkerchiefs.

"In these get-ups, we could probably eat free anywhere in town," Jackie replied in a low tone.

"Or rob a bank," Midge chortled.

Agent Anderson gave them a look of mock horror.

Frank grinned. "You'll get used to these two," he whispered.

"I hope I have the chance," Agent Anderson murmured back. Frank turned scarlet under his Scott Carpenter mask.

Just then a green flashing light went off. "Intruders dressed as astronauts escaping cave. Intruders dressed as astronauts escaping cave," a voice cried over the loudspeaker.

"We've been found out," Agent Anderson gasped as they shed their costumes. "Now, quick—go!" He pointed to some motorcycles at the mouth of the tunnel leading to the sanitarium.

Midge jumped on the nearest motorcycle and switched on the starter. The bike throbbed under her as she gunned the motor. "Hop on, Velma," she cried.

"It's three miles to the sanitarium," Agent Anderson said in a crisp, efficient tone. "Just follow the white marker lines on the tunnel wall. You'll end up in the mouth of a cave hidden in the roots of a big oak. From there, you'll see the entrance to the sanitarium. I'm going to the rocket ship to dismantle the bomb. Are you with me, Fennel?"

All three Hardly men responded in the affirmative.

Frank tossed Jackie his watch. "Use this to find Nancy and Cherry," he said. "We'll rendezvous at the sanitarium."

Mr. Hardly helped his wife onto Jackie's motorcycle and then kissed her tenderly. "Hold on tight," he said.

"Be careful, darling," Mrs. Hardly murmured. Jackie started her engine.

"See?" Midge said to Velma as the fellows slipped away.

"Mrs. Hardly doesn't give *her* husband any gruff when he goes off to investigate."

"Mr. Hardly will get a good tongue lashing later," Mrs. Hardly promised with a little smile. Velma giggled.

Midge cleared her throat. "Well, now that that's cleared up, let's go get Jackie's girl out of trouble."

Jackie fervently hoped she still had a girl! With Mrs. Hardly holding on tight, Jackie hummed along on her motorcycle. Suddenly a terrible thought entered her mind. What if they got to the sanitarium only to find Nancy and Cherry in a compromising position?

CHAPTER 51

To Tell the Truth

"A-r-e yo-o-o-u f-r-e-e-z-z-z-i-n-g t-o-o-?" Cherry chattered through ice-cold lips. Cold water rushed over her bare limbs. Only a tarp stretched taut on top of the tub kept her naked body from view. Except for the crisp cap perched on her curls, Cherry was entirely unclothed!

"N-u-r-s-e-e-e C-C-C-r-a-m-p, w-e'-r-e c-c-c-o-l-d!" Cherry pleaded to the stern-faced nurse sitting in the corner reading a magazine. The dour woman ignored Cherry's cry for help.

"If only I could reach the hot water spigot," Cherry thought, but it was no use. The only part of her body sticking out of the tub, besides her head, were her toes, and neither was doing her much good at the moment!

Nancy shot her a helpless look. "C-h-e-r-r-r-y," she chattered. "W-e m-u-s-t n-o-t t-e-l-l t-h-e-m a-n-y-t-h-i-n-g"

"I can hear you," Nurse Cramp sang out. "Scheming won't do you girls any good. You'll just have to sit tight until the doctor arrives."

"B-B-B-u-t—" Cherry protested. Their hydrotherapy treatment was quickly turning to hypothermia! "A m-m-i-s-t-a-k-e—"

Nurse Cramp looked annoyed. "There's been no mistake. While you were out snooping your chum here had one too many martinis and bragged quite a bit about her sleuthing skills."

Nancy looked frankly chagrined and a little hung over. Then she hiccuped. Cherry shot her an understanding look. She didn't blame Nancy one little bit. Why, anyone could have slipped with that much inducement!

"Next time you go snooping, remember to take off your distinctive cap," Nurse Cramp cackled.

"Y-o-u'-r-e h-o-r-r-i-d!" Cherry cried. "W-W-W-h-a-t a-b-o-u-t y-o-u-r n-n-n-n-u-r-s-i-n-g v-o-w?"

"S-s-s-hut up!" Nurse Cramp mocked her, throwing her magazine down on the wet tile floor. Just then Dr. Fraud walked in, briskly strode over to the tubs and turned on the warm water. Cherry sank back in relief. Dr. Fraud had come to save them from the clutches of this nurse gone mad!

"Prepare them for their injections, Nurse," Dr. Fraud ordered.

"W-h-a-t i-n-j-e-c-t-i-o-n-s?" Cherry chattered.

"Nothing to worry about, Nurse Aimless, if that *is* your name. Just a little shot of truth serum and we'll have this nasty business cleared up in no time at all. Nurse, turn on the hot jets."

Dr. Fraud efficiently injected first Cherry, then Nancy. "In a few minutes, we'll know everything," he smiled at Nurse Cramp.

Cherry was sure now that she and Nancy would never leave the sanitarium. "We'll end up like that poor woman I met earlier; all locked away with no one to talk to!" she thought wildly. A sob caught in her throat. There was still so much she had left to do in her life! "I still owe Mother a letter—I never repaid that loan of five dollars I borrowed from Midge in San Francisco—Jackie has no idea how much I—" but before she could finish her thought, Dr. Fraud pulled his chair next to her tub. He leaned over Cherry.

"What's your real name?" he asked.

"Cherry Aimless, Registered Nurse," Cherry said without a moment's hesitation. Dr. Fraud frowned. The truth serum hadn't kicked in yet!

He waited a minute, then asked another question. "Who's this girl?" he asked, waving his hand at Nancy.

Cherry frowned. She had been asking herself that very same question for the past two weeks. Who was Nancy, really? Was she Cherry's one true love, or just a summer infatuation?

"I don't know!" was Cherry's truthful response.

"Nurse, are you sure you gave me truth serum?" the doctor wondered.

"Cherry, try not to say anything more," Nancy urged her. "You do have a tendency to prattle on a bit, you know."

"Don't I, though?" Cherry laughed. "I'm trying to keep my mouth shut but I just can't! Oh, Nancy, I've kept a terrible secret to myself these last few days. It's been burning in me and now it's just got to come out!"

Dr. Fraud grew all excited. "What's the secret?" he urged.

"I'm afraid, Doctor, the truth is *I don't love her anymore!*" Cherry announced.

"What?" Dr. Fraud cried.

"There. I finally said it. What a relief!" Cherry added happily.

"A *relief?*" Nancy cried. "Cherry, you can't possibly mean that! Why, girls *everywhere* want to be my girlfriend!"

"But they don't know you the way I do," Cherry pointed out. "I love you like a sister, and I'll always remember our night of passion, but I'm in love with another girl. I am truly sorry, but our romance has fizzled."

Nancy started to cry big fat tears that plopped onto her tarp and rolled down the side of the tub. "But *I* love *you,*" she wept. "Oh, I've told lots of girls that I loved them, but I never meant it before. Now I really, truly *am* in love, and the one I love doesn't love me back! How could this have happened to *me* of all people?

"It's because I kissed that nurse earlier after they got me tipsy, isn't it?" she demanded to know.

"Not Nurse Cramp?" Cherry cried in horror.

"Actually, a pretty little student nurse," Nancy smiled wickedly. "I think she likes me. Oh, but I'm too distraught over losing the love of my life to even *think* of another girl right now."

Cherry smiled. "Do you mean the brunette who was hanging around the front desk when we checked in? I noticed her, too."

"She was awfully cute, wasn't she?" Nancy boasted. "But you've already got a new girlfriend. You're going to move to San Francisco and play house with Jackie!"

"Play *hospital,*" Cherry corrected her, "for you know no matter where I go and who I love, first and foremost I'll always be a nurse."

Nancy sighed. "Is there anything I can do to make you change your mind?" she wondered. "How about a nifty convertible?"

"Nancy, you can't *buy* love," Cherry scolded her.

"Fine," Nancy scowled. "Go ahead, live in some cold-water flat and spend your nights ironing Jackie's uniform."

Cherry smiled dreamily. Nancy had read her mind! "But

if we don't get out of here, Jackie will never know how much I love her," Cherry fretted aloud. "Now that I think about it, I must have been in love with her right from the moment we fell through that tunnel in the convent during *The Case of the Not-So-Nice Nurse,* and I landed right in her lap."

Dr. Fraud and Nurse Cramp exchanged looks of alarm. What was *in* that injection he had given them?

CHAPTER 52

Hurry!

 "Do you think Cherry and Nancy have been found out?" Jackie asked as the little group crept closer to the sanitarium. They had arrived at their destination with great speed and were now formulating a plan to get inside.

"Nancy's a pretty good detective, and Cherry really is a nurse so their cover is foolproof, if you ask me," Midge assured her. They had reached the entrance and could see a nurse sitting at a reception desk. Three more nurses were lolling about, chatting over charts.

Jackie checked the receiver strapped to her wrist. "They're in there all right. Now we just need a way to distract those four nurses. Mrs. Hardly, how do you feel about jumping a nurse?" she asked, smiling.

The older woman laughed. "I wouldn't mind, but I'm not sure how Mr. Hardly would feel about that!" she said.

"I've got a plan," Velma said. She shook out the contents of her purse. A compact, two bottles of nail polish, a cake of eye liner and several tubes of lipstick fell to the ground. "Mrs. Hardly and I will pretend to be door-to-door cosmetics salesladies and see if we can distract those nurses long enough for you two to slip past."

Mrs. Hardly readily agreed. Midge and Jackie held their breath as Velma and Mrs. Hardly entered the sanitarium and engaged the nurses in conversation. Soon Velma was showing the front desk nurse her eyeliner tips, and Midge and Jackie were able to creep through the lobby, using a potted rubber tree plant as cover.

"In there," Jackie whispered urgently as she spotted a bevy of nurses coming down the hall towards them. They ducked into a nearby linen closet. Jackie opened the door a crack and assessed their situation. "It may be a while before we can get out of here, unless—" her eyes lit up when she spied a stack of crisply starched pink and white striped uniforms.

"Unless what?" Midge gasped. She had a funny feeling she wasn't going to like what it was!

"Unless we change into these outfits so we can move freely around the sanitarium."

Midge groaned. She knew it!

"I liked being an astronaut better," Midge complained as she shed her trousers and shirt and slipped on a ghastly pink and white striped uniform with a Peter Pan collar, scoop neckline and short puffy sleeves. Even the biggest uniform she could find was still pretty snug, especially around her biceps.

"Nice tattoo, Midge," Jackie exclaimed as she spied Velma's name in a heart on Midge's upper right arm. "Goes great with your dress."

"I almost can't look," Midge moaned as they stood in front of the mirror. She peeked through her fingers. "Eek!" she said. "We're candy-stripers!"

"Don't forget the little cap," Jackie smiled. "Lean over and I'll pin it on."

"No cap!" Midge declared.

"You're going to attract attention without it," Jackie pleaded. "First they'll notice your cap's missing and then they'll see the tattoo and finally those wing tips."

Midge rolled her eyes. "Do it and do it quick!" she ordered tersely.

"What did I tell you?" Jackie smiled a few minutes later as they rushed through the hospital carrying flowers they had stolen from a sleeping patient. Nurses nodded as the two earnest-looking candy-stripers strode past. Jackie checked her receiver-watch. "Turn left, then right, down these stairs, then through this door—darn it's locked!"

"Can I help you girls with something?" a pleasant-faced nurse inquired.

"We're supposed to deliver these flowers," Midge replied in a high-pitched feminine voice.

"Girls, the basement's off limits to candy-stripers. Didn't they cover that in your training?" the nurse wondered.

"We forgot," Jackie admitted.

"I'll take those flowers down myself," the nurse offered. "In fact, Dr. Fraud is just about to perform a shock treatment on a new patient and I was going to observe—" she quit talking when the lights dimmed for a split second. "There—he's testing the machine. I'd better go. It's the saddest case, really. A brand new nurse has had a complete and utter nervous breakdown. Those flowers must be for her." The nurse took her keys from her pocket and opened the door. "It's such a shame, too," she added. "I worked with her earlier in Ward B and she was an awfully sweet girl. Why, the patients loved her, although she did seem a little confused at times and had a tendency to go on about the silliest things."

Jackie gasped. She was talking about Cherry! She whipped out her gun and said, in a low tone, "Don't make a sound or I'll shoot! Get through that door." The nurse did as she was told.

"Now take us to that nervous nurse," Jackie ordered. "And hurry!"

CHAPTER 53

"Say Cheese!*"*

"This is the perfect place for my photograph to be taken," Myra Meeks exclaimed as she barged into the sanitarium with Uncle Nelly in tow and pushed past the Receptionist Nurse. Around his neck was a camera and on his face was a look of frank alarm. He feared his charade had gone too far!

Myra and Uncle Nelly had spent the afternoon driving around to local picturesque spots looking for suitable locations in which to show Myra Meeks in the best light. Unfortunately, Myra thought the sanitarium seemed like the perfect spot, and Uncle Nelly had been unable to convince her otherwise! "What if she sees Nancy and Cherry and gives them away?" he thought worriedly.

"This way," Myra said as she pushed open a door marked *Private—Dr. Fraud Only.* "This is a short cut and I've got the key," Myra smiled. "You see, I'm a special friend of Dr. Fraud's. I want you to get a shot of me next to his new shock machine. It's the modern way to cheer up people. Have I mentioned that I'm a Friend of the Insane? I come here once a month to comfort disturbed souls amid the Gothic Revival splendor of the River Depths Sanitarium. I think the shock machine will make a dramatic background for our photograph. It's got all these wires and blinking lights and—oh, I hope it's in use today. It will make for such an exciting, lifelike photograph!"

CHAPTER 54

What a Shock!

Cherry gulped as Nurse Cramp applied cold gelatinous matter to her forehead. She knew from experience that it was the material that would conduct the electricity from the electric shock machine to her brain. She squirmed about trying to get out of her wrist-restraints, but it was no use. There she was, naked as the day she was born, except for a thin sheet covering her body and her nurse's cap proudly pinned to her curls.

"You have one last chance to tell us everything you know," Dr. Fraud said with a sinister smile. "I'll give you ten seconds to start talking. Ten—nine—eight—seven—"

"I'll never tell you I found your stash of experimental medication in the basement!" Cherry cried.

An alarmed expression shot over Dr. Fraud's face. "This little nurse knows even more than I suspected," he cried. "We must make sure when we're through with her she doesn't remember a thing! That government contract I have to develop mind-controlling new drugs will be lost! Turn the machine up to full power!"

Nurse Cramp did as she was told, then picked up the countdown, her hand on the switch. "Six—five—four—three—"

Cherry stiffened as she readied herself for the shock of her life.

"Two—o—"

Suddenly the door burst open and the biggest gun-toting candy-stripper Cherry had ever seen raced in and yelled,

"*Stop!*"

"Too late!" Nurse Cramp cried as she hit the switch. The wires hummed as a double jolt of electricity headed straight for Cherry's brain!

Jackie took quick aim and with one shot destroyed the machine, which sizzled and came to a whining halt just in the nick of time. Cherry had received no more than a slight shock!

"Oh, Jackie!" Cherry sobbed. She writhed under her restraining straps, tears of joy coursing down her cheeks. While Midge rushed in to take care of Dr. Fraud with one good blow to the jaw, Jackie unstrapped Cherry and gathered the girl up in her arms.

Cherry lay limply against Jackie's strong chest. She could hear Jackie's heart pounding in concert with her own beneath the thin cotton-blend sheet. Although Cherry's head was still tingling, her mind had never been clearer.

"Oh, Jackie," she cried as she flung her arms around her rescuer. "I love you with all my heart!" Then she kissed Jackie with a fervor and sincerity of purpose she had never known before.

"We've got to save Nancy," Cherry then remembered. "She's up to her neck in hot water!"

"Midge rescued her—she's probably getting dressed," Jackie assured her. "Come here!" she said in a husky voice. She pulled Cherry close for another kiss.

A few minutes later, Myra Meeks strolled into the room. "Oh, no!" she cried when she got a look at the scene. Midge was buckling Dr. Fraud into a straitjacket; Nancy had arrived and was wrestling Nurse Cramp to the ground; and Cherry and Jackie were locked in each others' arms in the middle of a long-lasting kiss.

Uncle Nelly smiled happily, and delighted by the romantic moment, snapped a few pictures for Cherry and Jackie's album.

"What is going on here?" Myra Meeks demanded to know. "Dr. Fraud—get out of that straitjacket. And, you, Miss Candy-striper! You know very well you're not supposed to socialize with the patients!" No one paid Myra Meeks the least bit of attention.

"This place really *is* a madhouse!" Myra Meeks declared as she turned on the heels of her alligator pumps and raced out of the room.

CHAPTER 55

"Take Them Away!"

"Take them away, boys," Chief Mike O'Malley ordered. Two lads in crisp blue uniforms grabbed Dr. Fraud and Nurse Cramp by the back straps of their straitjackets and led them through the lobby of the sanitarium. Nurses did their best to keep patients calm while the evil doctor and his nefarious assistant were locked in the back of the waiting paddy wagon. "Frank—Joe—what can I say?" the chief turned to the well-known boy detectives with a look of genuine chagrin on his chiseled features. "If Milton Meeks hadn't insisted that I hold off on interrogating that prisoner and follow the lead on Mad Dog MacDougal, I could have been tracking the real criminals.

"Never in a million years could I have guessed that Milton was capable of such a devious plot as the one you've just outlined, boys," the chief then shook his head. "Myra, maybe."

"I think you'll find both Meekses equally guilty," Frank said. "Myra must have known all along that innocent dogs were being put in peril."

"Mother and Father are free, and we've disarmed the bomb that was set to go off, pulled the plug on that defective rocket, and saved the good Hardly name!" Joe crowed happily. He crossed his arms over his broad chest, leaned against the Receptionist Nurse's desk and looked around with a satisfied smile on his face. "With the door open and sunlight streaming in, this place doesn't look half-bad," he declared.

"Now that Nurse Fiscus is in charge, this place will change for the better," Cherry piped up. She was curled up in Jackie's lap at the far end of the reception-room sofa. Nurse Fiscus had already offered her the prestigious job of Nurse-in-Charge of Hairdo Therapy, but Cherry had more important things in mind! "Everything's turned out for the best!" she murmured happily as she cuddled close to Jackie.

"*Almost* everything," Nancy muttered.

Cherry felt a small pang that was barely soothed by the reassuring warmth of Jackie's arms.

Frank and Joe exchanged regretful glances. "I'm awfully sorry you've lost the love of your life," Frank said in a sympathetic tone.

Nancy shrugged. "I'll get over it," she said bravely. "It's just that without someone by my side, I feel so alone in the world!" Nancy buried her head in a hankie and started to cry.

"You'll always have us," Frank gulped.

"We couldn't love you any more if you were our own daughter," Mrs. Hardly comforted the weeping girl.

"And we love you like a nephew!" Uncle Nelly assured her.

"But you're not *really* my family," Nancy pointed out through her tears.

Frank jumped to his feet and turned a critical eye Nancy's way. "What is a family, anyway?" he cried. "It's a group of people who love you through thick and thin. They're always there for you no matter what! Who comes to the rescue when devious criminals carry you off? Who's there when you stand accused of murder? Who gives you fashion advice whether you need it or not?

"Nancy, your family's been right by your side all along, only you didn't know it. There's one thing I've learned in solving this case: it's not blood but fellowship between people that makes a *real* family," Frank admonished her.

Nancy dried her eyes. Why, Frank was right! She had Frank and Joe and Mr. and Mrs. Hardly, Uncle Nelly and Willy, and Hannah, too! And even if she didn't have a girlfriend, well, in time she would!

A relieved look spread over Fennel P. Hardly's handsome face. "I'm sure glad to hear you say that, Frank, for I've something along those very lines to discuss with you."

At this Uncle Nelly burst into tears. "Oh, Fennel, when I feared you weren't coming back, I told your boys all about you being a girl and I'm afraid I've made a mess of things," he wailed.

"No you didn't, Uncle," Frank jumped in. "Father," he started, "we do know the truth about you, but we don't care one fig. Nothing will *ever* change the way we feel about *you!*"

"You'll always be Dad to us," Joe assured him.

Mr. Hardly took a fresh hankie from the inside breast pocket of his natty, box-cut wool-blend jacket and blew his nose. He appeared to be overcome with emotion.

Mrs. Hardly put her arm around her husband's waist. "When your father and I were first married, we had little hope of having the kind of family we dreamt of. But then one day, your father came home from investigating a corrupt Chicago orphanage run by the cold-hearted Newton Gangrene. In your father's arms were two little boys—one fair-haired with a serious expression in his hazel eyes, the other with curly brown locks and a sunny smile. They had been abandoned and ill-treated."

Joe gasped. "She means us, Frank!"

Mrs. Hardly nodded. "Fennel said he knew the moment he laid eyes on you two that he would raise you as his own—that you would never know the horror of your early years, never want for anything.

"We kept meaning to tell you boys the truth—the whole truth—about your origins and who Fennel really is—but somehow the years kept slipping past and we were all so happy.

"All these years, your father's lived in fear that you'd find out his secrets and wouldn't understand," she explained. "That you'd be ashamed to be his sons."

"We'll always be proud to be the Hardly boys," Frank cried out, "only now we're men, too. Father, we're just sorry you had to carry the burden of these secrets for so long."

"People can be awfully queer about the truth," Nancy piped up.

"It's true. People are often afraid of what they don't understand," Mr. Hardly said knowingly.

Joe nodded. "It's just like that movie, *The Ghost and Mrs. Muir*. A young widow goes to live in a lighthouse home of a long-dead sailor, setting the stage for a heartwarming romance."

Frank looked queerly at his brother.

"Everyone else was afraid of the ghost except for Mrs. Muir who took the time to listen," Joe blushingly explained.

"That makes sense to me," Cherry said. Then she gasped. "Speaking of ghosts, I just remembered something! There's a patient in one of the towers, a lonely woman whom no one ever visits. I met her earlier today; her name is Nancy and she suffers from paramnesia, and she's all alone in the world. I'm the first person to visit her in years and before I left, she made me swear I'd come back. I can't go without at least saying good-bye," Cherry said. "She has no friends, no family, nobody but me. Does anyone want to go along?"

"I *do* need to get my luggage," Nancy realized.

"I'm too tired to even think of going anywhere right now," Midge admitted. She was sitting cross-legged on the tile floor, her head on Velma's knees. "You sure missed a show, honey," she told her girlfriend. Midge was still chuckling at the sight of Myra Meeks racing from the shock treatment room with her arms flung up in alarm.

"I took pictures of the whole thing," Uncle Nelly assured them.

Midge looked alarmed. "Not of me in my—er—costume?" she fretted.

"You mean the candy-striper's uniform you were wearing when you rescued us?" Cherry wondered innocently. "You didn't look half bad, but really, Midge, I'd stay away from Peter Pan collars if I were you," she advised helpfully before hopping on the elevator to the top floor, Nancy by her side.

Midge blushed and buried her face in Velma's lap.

Velma grinned and ran her hands through Midge's close-cropped hair, "Take me home, honey," she sighed. "It's been an awfully long day in awfully high heels."

"It's been a long *month,*" Midge replied. She got up and held out her arms. Velma fell into them. "Do you want to go home? Really go home, I mean?" Midge murmured.

Velma nodded. "I miss our old boring life," she admitted. "Promise me something, Midge. No more chasing after cunning crooks, evil priests, mad scientists or power-mad matrons. Promise?"

"Promise," Midge said softly. They headed for the door.

"I'd better go see if Agent Andy needs me," Frank cried. The secret agent was in Dr. Fraud's office gathering evidence sure to keep the evil doctor behind bars for years to come. Frank first checked his reflection in the washroom mirror. He smoothed his crew cut and brushed the wrinkles from his slacks.

"Oh, brother," Joe said as he sank into a chair. "Love!"

He turned to Mrs. Hardly. "Don't worry, Mother. I won't ever go running off all starry-eyed like Frank."

"It's true," Mrs. Hardly thought. "Frank is the image of his father, but Joe, well, Joe will always be *my* boy!"

CHAPTER 56

A Tearful Reunion

When Cherry flung open the door to the private room, she got a pleasant surprise. The patient seemed happier and more relaxed than when Cherry had visited her last. "Nurse, you forgot to give me my pills," the woman scolded when she saw Cherry. She laughed when Cherry blushed with alarm. "And I'm feeling better than I have in years!" the patient cried happily. "I'm going to ask Dr. Fraud to change my medication."

Cherry gasped. "You remember Dr. Fraud's name?" she cried. "You *are* getting better. Before I leave, I'll speak to Nurse Fiscus and have her schedule you for the various therapies sure to set your mind working again," she promised. She decided not to tell the woman about Dr. Fraud's arrest until she was sure she could handle the shock.

Cherry hoped she could get the woman an appointment in Hairdo Therapy that very day, for if she were going to rejoin the general population, she would need an updated look.

Cherry took a few hairpins from her own coiffure and twisted the woman's thick reddish-gold hair into a simple upswept hairdo. "There. With your hair off your face, I can really see your distinctively charming features. And the fog has disappeared from your lovely blue eyes. Why, with a fashionable suit, a set of pearls and a new hairdo, you'll look just as well put together as any of the River Depths smart set!"

The woman flushed with pleasure. "Oh, Nurse," she cried happily.

"Oh, Nancy!" Cherry cried back clapping her hands in glee. This was her most successful case ever!

"Yes?" Nancy asked as she stuck her head through the door. She had gotten her suitcases, slipped into a fresh travel suit, and was engrossed in juggling all thirteen-pieces of her matching grosgrain leather luggage set. "Guess what!" she cried as she clung precariously to her cosmetics travel case. "I can laugh about it now, but we were doomed from the start! I forgot to scrape my monogram off my luggage!"

"Oh, I wasn't calling you," Cherry told her. "I was exclaiming over my patient, whose name also happens to be Nancy."

The woman tugged at Cherry's uniform. "My name's not Nancy," she said. "I remembered right after you left. My name is—"

At the sound of the soft, lilting voice, Nancy looked up, gasped and lost her grip on her bags. A hat box spun crazily out of control. A shoe case burst open and a pair of baby alligator sling-back pumps skittered across the floor. But Nancy didn't notice her wardrobe had run amok, for she was fixated on the sweet-faced woman at Cherry's side.

"Mother?" Nancy cried in wonderment. For a split-second, she stood frozen in the doorway. Then she raced across the room, dropped to her knees and buried her head in the woman's lap. She began to sob.

"Mother, it's you, isn't it? It's really you!"

"Yes, Nancy," the woman murmured as she stroked her daughter's soft shiny hair. "It's Mother."

CHAPTER 57

"Shall We Dance?"

"Another canapé?" Willy offered the handsome young secret agent seated on the Hardly davenport. As soon as Willy had heard the news that the whole family was safe and sound, he had started whipping up an array of delicious treats for the hungry detectives.

"These are *d-e-licious!*" Agent Andy cried as he took a bite of a yummy creamed-crab puff. He delighted Willy by asking for the recipe.

"Oh, it's a family secret," Uncle Nelly said.

"There will be no more secrets in this family," Mr. Hardly warned with a good-humored tone.

Uncle Nelly gave Willy a happy hug. "Everyone's safe, the bad guys have gone to jail, and Mrs. Hardly likes what I did to the guest washroom," he sighed.

"I never liked that Carson Clue," Fennel shuddered. "But to think he staged a fake car accident and put his wife away in a sanitarium all these years, not to mention the reprehensible manner in which he treated his own daughter—" His voice broke off.

"That's all over," Midge assured him. "Nancy's made remarkable progress just this week, and seems happier than ever now that she's got her mother back. Plus the poodles are on their way home!"

"Case closed," Joe cried.

"Except for Myra and Milton Meeks, that is," Chief O'Malley grinned. They had decided that that evening's annual Wives of the Atomic Age Dress-up Ball was the perfect place to arrest the Meekses. While the detectives sat in the living room discussing their strategy and snacking on tasty treats, their dates were upstairs changing into party outfits.

"So this is the plan. We'll get into the dance and wait for just the right moment, then slap the cuffs on the Meekses," Jackie schemed.

"Maybe we can goad Judge Meeks into publicly admitting his plot to blow up a rocket ship and ruin Father's good name," Joe added.

"I can't wait to see the expression on Myra's face when she finds out the jig is up," Midge grinned.

Just then Cherry came running downstairs in her stocking feet, clad in an off-the-shoulder evening dress of rich crimson that left bare her creamy white shoulders. "Velma needs her lipstick," she told Midge.

Midge blushed and fumbled in her pocket for the tube. "It's a spare," she explained.

"Cherry, that color is you!" Uncle Nelly exclaimed.

"It may be too revealing," Cherry confessed. But from the look on Jackie's face, Cherry knew that the risk was well worth taking.

"It was nice of Nancy to loan it to me," Cherry acknowledged. Before Nancy had taken her mother home to rest, she had given her chums her sanitarium outfits to wear to the Ball. Velma was upstairs slipping into a sophisticated bare-back emerald satin dress with a silk stole while Mrs. Hardly had reached into her closet for a chiffon creation of striking sapphire.

Uncle Nelly reached for a needle and thread. "I'll just take up the hem a half-inch so when you dance, everyone will see the ruby slippers on your feet. Myra's going to be pea green, for her coral-colored gown can't even begin to compare with this creation. Oh, I *almost* feel sorry for that woman!" Everyone laughed.

"Do you think Myra is as evil as all that?" Joe wondered.

"Myra's crime is worse in a sense," Fennel Hardly said. "She looked the other way while her husband broke the law because of the financial benefits. And I suspect Myra knew all along that the paramnesiac in the tower was Rebecca Clue. The commitment order we found in Dr. Fraud's files was signed by Judge Meeks. They both have a lot of explaining to do and a lot to atone for.

"When people shut their eyes to what's happening around them, they're just as guilty."

Joe nodded. "I understand, Father. What do you think will happen to them?"

Agent Anderson answered. "Judge Meeks will be charged with tampering with the space program, a federal offense that carries a stiff prison sentence; and libel for his lies about your father. Myra will no doubt get off with a lesser punishment, but she will do time in jail."

"Do you think there are Women's Clubs in prison?" Joe wondered.

Jackie hooted and shot Midge a sly grin.

"There's plenty of them. I'm sure Myra will climb to the top in no time," Midge laughingly replied.

When Velma, Cherry, Mrs. Hardly and Frank came down the stairs resplendent in their best evening outfits, their dates jumped up and whistled in admiration. While the girls made sure their purses contained hankies and compacts, Chief O'Malley checked to see he had the right equipment in his pockets.

"All set," he declared. "I've got handcuffs with the Meekses' name on them."

"Do you have a pair with my name on them?" Midge wondered wistfully.

The chief laughed and tossed her a shiny new set, "Courtesy of the Lake Merrimen Police Department for a job well done." Midge stowed her reward in her pocket, then swept Velma out the door and into the Hardly's top-notch sedan. The others followed.

Chief O'Malley gave Joe a wink, then held out his arm. "Looks like you're my date, Joseph," he grinned. Joe looked the strong man in the eye and blushed at what he saw. Although the chief had a light tone in his voice, Joe could tell he was dead serious!

Joe gulped. "Okay, chief," he whispered.

"Call me Mike," the chief smiled as he gave Joe's hand a little squeeze. Joe blushed. How many nights had he dreamt of just this moment?

CHAPTER 58

"And the Winner Is..."

 "Our first dress-up ball together," Cherry sighed happily as she and Jackie alighted from the back seat of the Hardly family sedan. Cherry felt a sudden stab of guilt when she saw the lavish hotel where the dance was taking place. "If only Nancy were here," she cried.

Jackie looked none too pleased to hear this.

"I mean, it's so sad that her nice dress is here without her," Cherry explained.

Jackie gave her a hug. "Cherry, you don't even know what you've done for Nancy, do you? You're the reason she has her mother back," she said proudly. "Cherry, you're amazing!"

Cherry blushed prettily. "I was just doing my duty," she protested. But before she could go any further, Jackie stilled her objections with a kiss.

"Say *cheese*," Uncle Nelly cried as he snapped a commemorative picture of the happy couple. Cherry clung to Jackie's arm as they made their way into the ballroom of the lovely downtown Merrimen Arms.

Agent Anderson was right behind them with Frank, dressed in a sharp Palm Beach dinner jacket, on his arm. Bringing up the rear were Midge and Velma, the Hardly parents, and Uncle Nelly and Willy, too! Joe and the chief were just pulling up in the patrol car, with big grins on their faces.

Nobody, it seemed, wanted to miss the social event of the season!

"Excuse me," a haughty fellow in a tuxedo stopped Jackie at the door. "Do you have an invitation?" he sniffed.

Jackie opened her coat to show him the gold detective's shield pinned to the lining. "This is my invitation," she said sternly. She pushed him aside. Next Agent Anderson flashed his badge. "Secret Agent," he said curtly.

Frank felt a little thrill course through his lean yet sturdy frame. Agent Andy was a man of few words, but when he did speak he was pithy!

"Oh, it's beautiful in here!" Cherry gasped as she got her first look at the grand ballroom. Blue velvet curtains with hand-sewn silver stars sparkled under shimmering lights coming from rocket ship-shaped lanterns hanging from the ceiling. Dozens of couples were already on the dance floor, gliding about to the tuneful melody of a jazz orchestra.

"There's Myra over there," Cherry exclaimed. Just in time, she remembered one should never point whilst wearing elbow-length gloves. "By that papier-maché model of the atomic bomb," she added.

"Let's wait before we drop *our* bomb," Agent Anderson suggested.

"We should time this just right for maximum embarrassment," Jackie proposed.

Agent Anderson agreed with a grin. "I'm going to check out the exits and see how many we need to cover. I want to make sure no one leaves before we make our arrest." He turned to Frank. "I'll be right back," he promised.

"Let's lose ourselves in the crowd," Fennel Hardly proposed to his wife. He was already getting stares and whispers from people who had obviously heard the radio broadcast fingering him as a Russian agent!

"Look, Willy," Uncle Nelly cried as he spotted a buffet table loaded with all sorts of delicious dishes. "They're about to light the mushroom flambé! Let's have a taste."

Jackie grabbed two champagne cocktails from a passing waiter and handed one to Cherry. "There's no crime in having a drink and enjoying ourselves in the meantime," she said.

"You know what happens when I drink," Cherry giggled.

"Yeah, and I can't wait!" Jackie grinned. "Cheers!"

Three champagne cocktails later, Cherry was swaying to the music in Jackie's arms. They made a handsome couple as they glided around the dance floor, but halted mid-step when they heard a familiar shrill shriek. It was Myra Meeks, and she had just spotted Frank!

"Stay out of the line of fire," Jackie instructed. She made her way over to her chums.

"What are you doing here?" Myra Meeks hissed to Frank. "Your mother's not an Atomic Wife!"

Mr. Hardly raced to his son's side. When Myra saw the world-renowned detective, she gritted her teeth angrily. "You *must* be in the wrong place," she said haughtily. "This is hardly the place for a Russian spy to appear! Have you no sense of decorum, Fennel? Well, I see Chief O'Malley is here, too. I imagine with intent to get you!"

Frank noted with pride that his father didn't debase himself by exchanging cruel accusations. He just smiled and said in a charming manner, "It's nice to see you, too, Myra."

Myra turned pink with anger, unfortunately clashing horribly with her coral-colored gown. She opened her mouth to reply, but shut it quickly when she spotted Uncle Nelly and his camera over by the refreshment table. She pasted a big smile on her face, grabbed onto Uncle Nelly's arm and cooed,

"Mr. Nelly! I see you accepted my invitation to come to the Ball! You should have called; I would have sent my driver to fetch you," she scolded him lightly. "I'll deal with you Hardlys later," she hissed over her shoulder.

"You're just in time to see me accept the Atomic Wife of the Year Award," she informed Uncle Nelly as a man in a tuxedo walked on stage, flicked on the microphone and held up his hands for quiet.

"It's Judge Meeks," Frank whispered to Jackie. He scanned the crowd for Agent Andy and was relieved to see him approaching the stage. They exchanged delighted looks. "It's almost time," that look said.

"Good evening," Judge Meeks said, "and welcome to the 1959 Wives of the Atomic Age Dress-up Ball. Tonight I have the honor of presenting the Atomic Wife of the Year Award." He showed them the gold-plated statuette shaped like an upright Maxx-Thruster rocket.

"The nerve!" Joe whispered to his brother. "That's a replica of the very rocket he was going to blow up! Little does he know, his plan's been thwarted."

Judge Meeks took an envelope from the pocket of his tuxedo and as the drummer beat out a drum roll, pulled out the name of the winner. A look of feigned surprise crossed his face. "Why, it's my own lovely wife, Myra Meeks!"

Everyone cheered. "This award comes as no surprise, seeing all that Myra's done for this town," Joe heard a woman remark.

Myra hitched up her gown, and with Uncle Nelly firmly in her grip, jumped on stage to accept her award. "This is both an honor and a surprise," she cried. "And speaking of surprises, I have one for you. The gentleman by my side is none other than prize-winning writer Mr. Nelly, currently on assignment for *Life* magazine. He's doing a cover story on me for the next issue!" she squealed.

Frank and his father looked at each other with merry eyes as a murmur went through the crowd. Nicely dressed party-goers shot envious glances Myra Meeks' way. "Perhaps Mr. Nelly would like to say a few words about me?" Myra thrust the microphone in Uncle Nelly's face.

Uncle Nelly blushed nervously. He was much more a home-body than a public figure, and a whole day of pretending to be a reporter for a national magazine had left his nerves frankly frazzled.

"Go on. Say something," Myra begged. "Just one little thing."

"Myra, you and your husband are under arrest for attempting to blow up a rocket ship and saying untrue things about Fennel Hardly!" Uncle Nelly blurted out. Then he snapped a commemorative photo of Myra gasping in surprise.

"This must be a joke," Myra cried shakily. Her eyes bugged out in horror as Detective Jackie Jones and Agent Anderson leapt on stage.

"Hello, Myra," Jackie smiled. "Remember me?" She whipped out her handcuffs and cuffed Myra just above her thick gold bangle bracelet. "You have the right to remain silent—" Jackie began.

"It's all the judge's fault!" Myra screamed. "I told him it was a bad idea to plant a bomb on that rocket ship and make everyone think Fennel did it. I said to him, 'Milton, if you think people around here are going to believe Fennel's a Russian spy, well, you're crazy!'"

"Judge Meeks, you're under arrest for espionage and libel, and transporting stolen poodles across state lines, among other things," Agent Anderson intoned.

Myra looked at her husband in shock. "*You* stole the poo-dles?" she gasped. "What kind of monster are you? I knew nothing about those dogs. Do you hear me? I'm innocent!"

She was still protesting her innocence when Chief O'Malley

put her in the patrol car. Judge Meeks maintained a stoic silence as he was taken away.

"That was smooth," Midge patted Uncle Nelly on the back. She and Velma had observed the whole affair from behind the atomic bomb model.

"Good work, Nelson," Fennel gave his brother a hug. Uncle Nelly fanned himself with his hankie. "Can we go home now, honey?" he begged Willy.

"Nelson, you've been a pip. I'll take you home for some of my banana cream pie," Willy smiled.

Frank grasped Agent Anderson's hand to his chest. "Our first arrest together," he sighed happily.

"Not our last, I hope," Agent Anderson murmured back. He swept Frank up in his arms and waltzed him to a private corner of the dance floor.

"Golly, Frank," he gulped as he slipped off his thick horn-rimmed glasses, and pulled the boy detective close for a deep, satisfying kiss.

Mrs. Hardly glimpsed the tender moment out of the corner of her eye. "Our boy has grown up," she smiled as she plucked a lace hankie from her satin evening bag and wiped away a happy tear.

"One more spin around the dance floor and then—*home?*" Jackie whispered in Cherry's ear.

"I'd love to go home with you," Cherry murmured.

Jackie took Cherry in her arms. "You're going to love San Francisco," Jackie promised, hoping that was the home Cherry meant.

"I already do," Cherry smiled back.

"You mean you'll go?"

Cherry nodded happily.

"I love you," Jackie murmured.

"I love you, too," Cherry sighed.

"No doubts?" Jackie wondered anxiously. "Speak now or—"

"Not a one," Cherry assured her. Then a flit of concern crossed her pretty face. "Although, I *am* worried about something."

"What is it?" Jackie cried.

Cherry flushed. "I did the silliest thing earlier. I was at the refreshments table drinking some delicious fruit punch, and when you arrested Myra, I got so excited I accidentally dumped the contents of my evening bag in the punch bowl!"

Jackie grinned with relief. "I'll buy you whatever you need," she promised.

"I managed to fish out my lipstick and thermometer, but I had to leave my powder puff," Cherry admitted ruefully. "But what worries me is that I had a vial of that new extra-strength vitamin I found at the sanitarium in Dr. Fraud's laboratory, and now it's in the punch. Do you think I should warn people not to drink it?"

"Surely a few vitamins won't hurt this crowd," Jackie assured her.

"One can never have too many," Cherry agreed. She closed her eyes and rested her head on Jackie's chest. "I worry too much," she decided, "and about the silliest things, too!"

—— CHAPTER 59 ——

A Happy Ending

"Mayhem in the Midwest!"
by Mamie Eisen
Midwest Correspondent

When prominent River Depths society matron Myra Meeks peered into the mirror to admire her new coral off-the-shoulder gown just minutes before making her entrance at the annual Wives of the Atomic Age Dress-up Ball, little did she suspect that before the evening's end, the force of the federal government would soon fall down upon those very shoulders.

All eyes turned to Myra as she made her way through the grand ballroom that night. And why shouldn't they? After all, the prominent matron and her husband Judge Meeks were among the most influential and prosperous people in town and oft the object of many an admiring gaze. Little did Myra realize that among those eyes were those of the keen-hearted sleuth Fennel P. Hardly, and his detective sons, Frank and Joe, hot on the trail of a space age crime that led them right to the Meekses' door.

"Myra's finally gotten the kind of publicity she deserves," Midge chuckled as she closed the latest issue of *Life* magazine, wriggled comfortably on the cushion-laden porch swing and yawned. After two days of hair-raising adventure and another few days of press interviews, Midge was finally able to relax and engage in one of her favorite pursuits. She was flat on her back with her head in Velma's lap.

"How nice for her," Cherry smiled. She was only half-listening as she was trying to compose a letter to her mother detailing all the exciting things that had happened to her that week.

"There will be a lot of committees needing members now," Nancy thought aloud. She was sitting on a comfy wicker rocker sorting through the club luncheon invitations that had arrived in the morning's mail. "With Myra Meeks dethroned, this is the perfect time for Mother to make her re-entry into society," she schemed.

Rebecca Clue had made remarkable progress in the few days she had been home. Nancy had big plans; ones she hoped would make up for her mother's years of confinement. Nancy's lingering vestiges of guilt over killing her father had disappeared as Rebecca Clue related the events leading up to her incarceration in the River Depths Sanitarium. Nancy had wept when she heard her mother's tale of true love, a vengeful husband and his nefarious plan to do away with his wife, and the beloved girl child she had been forced to leave behind.

"Maybe River Depths society won't be such a snobby group with someone as nice as your mother at the helm," Velma said. She took up the magazine to once again admire the splendid full-color photo of Myra Meeks on the cover throwing up her hands in alarm. "What a lovely portrait, Uncle Nelly," Velma said. "You should be very proud."

"It's one of my best," Uncle Nelly blushed modestly. "I do believe I've really captured Myra's essence."

"Who wants a hot-cross sticky bun fresh from the oven and a cup of fresh-brewed coffee?" Willy cried as he came out to the porch.

Midge groaned. She was already stuffed from a delicious breakfast of blueberry waffles, sizzling sausage, cheese omelets and baking powder biscuits. "I may not be able to get up," Midge complained happily. "You're going to have to carry me onto that train tomorrow, swing and all." She selected a small bun, then licked the sweet stickiness from her fingers.

At the mention of their imminent departure, Velma bit her lower lip and blinked back tears. Jackie was downtown this very minute picking up four tickets for the *Western Express* leaving the next morning. It was going to be hard to break up the gay little group, but now that oil had been poured upon the turbulent waters of Nancy's family life, the good name of Hardly restored and the future of the Space Race assured, it looked like there was nothing left to do but go home.

Midge gave Velma's hand a little squeeze. "Honey, we'll be back," she promised. "And we'll get down to San Francisco as often as we can to see Cherry and Jackie."

At this, Cherry smiled. She never would have guessed, just one month before when she set out on a simple vacation, that she would end up having helped solve three baffling mysteries and find true love—twice! She couldn't wait to write to her chum, Nurse Penny Perkins, and tell her *all* the luscious details of her love affair, but right now she had a more important task at hand.

"I must finish this letter to Mother!" Cherry silently groaned. She got back to work.

5 August 1959

Dear Mother,

Please forgive my tardy reply to your gay letter as this has been a busier week than I had anticipated. I had an unexpected stint as a Sanitarium Nurse, which was brief but enlightening. I know what you're thinking. Wherever Cherry goes, sick people stick to her like glue! But I assure you my Midwestern vacation hasn't been all toil and trouble.

Mother, I've learned so many things this summer! I learned about the scientific applications in the fascinating world of criminal detection. Also, that manners and breeding are no substitute for good solid character. And mostly, I've learned the importance of choosing one's travel companion wisely. Some people have a different dress for every occasion. Other people, however, have a simple uniform that suits them no matter where they are.

It sounds like that particular resort is the right place for you and Father. As Aunt Gertrude always says, "Bloom where you're planted!" I now fully understand the meaning of those wise words. The Midwest has been fertile soil for a flower such as I. I've bloomed, too, Mother. I've really, really bloomed.

You know the darling pot-holders you offered to send me? Would you mind terribly mailing them to

San Francisco instead, as I've decided to become a Golden Gate Nurse. I'll send you an address as soon as I'm settled. Don't worry! I've made a close friend in the San Francisco Police Department, and I'll be in good hands.

> *Love,*
> *Your daughter,*
> *Cherry Aimless, R. N.*

A shiver went up Cherry's spine as she thought of *whose* hands she'd be in! She stuck the letter in a envelope and sealed it. "There," she said with a satisfied smile. "All my chores are finished. I've made my bed—*our* bed; washed out my panties and written out our travel itinerary. Now I can really relax!"

No sooner had Cherry stretched out on a chaise lounge than Fennel, Mrs. Hardly, Frank and Joe drove up in their sleek family sedan.

"Want to see my new suit?" Frank cried excitedly as he bounded onto the porch with a garment bag in his hand. He had a very special weekend engagement in Washington, DC, with a very special Secret Agent, and he wanted to look his very best!

"We went to Father's favorite men's shop and I got a whole new wardrobe," Frank enthused.

Joe rolled his eyes and reached for a sticky bun. He couldn't see what all the fuss over clothes was about when all a fellow really needed to look good was a trim-fitting uniform!

Frank slipped away to doff his chinos and cotton plaid shirt. When he returned, the collegiate lad with the well-scrubbed look was gone. In his place was a confident young man ready to step full-force into manhood, knowing he was dressed for it.

"*Nice* suit!" Midge jumped up to get a closer look at the Continental-cut double-breasted lightweight worsted-wool jacket with matching cuffless trousers. Frank and Fennel shared a secret grin. Little did Midge realize that an identical suit in a wider cut was awaiting her at Stan's Suit Shop.

"Oh, Francis," Mrs. Hardly exclaimed. "You're as handsome as your father."

Frank flushed happily. That was high praise, indeed!

Mr. Hardly took a starched white handkerchief of the finest linen from the breast pocket of his own suit and tucked it in Frank's pocket. With the back of his hand, he brushed the shoulders of the suit and gauged the drape of the jacket.

"This suit is the right choice, isn't it?" Frank asked earnestly.

"It's fine, son," Mr. Hardly replied softly. His eyes shone with love for his eldest son.

"After all my many adventures and death-defying feats, you wouldn't think I'd be nervous about going to the Spy Guy's Ball," Frank admitted, a little flustered. "Isn't that funny?"

Fennel gave Frank's shoulder a manful squeeze.

"I was worried about making a good impression in front of all those real-life Secret Agents, but suddenly when I slipped into this suit, I gained a new confidence. It's like donning a coat of armor. Is that silly, Father?" Frank blushed.

Fennel smiled tenderly. "Not at all, son," he reassured Frank. "After all, you know what I always say," he said with a sly wink.

"Clothes make the man!"

The End

About the Author

 Mabel Maney spent her formative years travelling the Midwest in a green wood-paneled station wagon with her parents, Mr. and Mrs. Maney, and three prize-winning black-and-white cocker spaniels, Taffy, Lady and Sadie, in search of blue ribbons and shiny trophies.

After her parents were lost at sea, Mabel and her dog chums settled with their maternal grandmother, Olive Krumpke, in Clear Lake, Wisconsin. Mabel received a strict Catholic education at Our Lady of the Lake School for Girls, where she devoted herself to clean living, community service and Catholic scholarship.

Her first full-length novel, *Pets of the Saints* (now out-of-print), won her accolades from around the state, and her macaroni model of the last days of Joan of Arc made apparent to all her artistic bent. After an unfortunate misstep prevented her from taking the veil, Mabel moved west, eventually settling in San Francisco where she lives happily with her beloved Miss Lily Bee.

Mabel Maney is the author of *The Case of the Not-So-Nice Nurse* (Cleis, 1993) and *The Case of the Good-For-Nothing Girlfriend* (Cleis, 1994). Her installation art and handmade books, self-published under the World O' Girls imprint, have earned her fellowships from The San Francisco Foundation and San Francisco State University, where she received her MFA in 1991. She is currently working on a musical based on the characters from *A Ghost in the Closet*.